THROUGH THE EYE
of the
Glacier

Michael R. Pollen

THROUGH THE EYE of the Glacier

A 12,000-Year Old Mystery is Revealed Inside an Alaska Glacier

Michael R. Pollen

Publication Consultants

PO Box 221974 Anchorage, Alaska 99522-1974

ISBN 1-888125-58-6

Library of Congress Catalog Card Number: 99-067479

Copyright 1999 by Michael R. Pollen
—First Edition 1999—
—Second Edition 2000—

Manufactured in the United States of America.

For Peggy, the soul of my inspiration.

Table of Contents

Introduction

L iving on the edge of the vast Alaska wilderness has been a source of strength and great pleasure in my life. Having built our home and raised our family here, having hunted, fished and gathered our sustenance from the land, and having spent countless hours awed by the power and beauty of the Aurora has given me considerable admiration for those who have lived in this valley for millennia. One becomes connected to the extreme changes of the seasons in Alaska. Spring is not just a transition from winter to summer here. It is a brief, dramatic reenactment of the end of the last ice age, with the warm earth and verdant forests emerging from the receding snow and ice under the radiant energy of nearly constant sunlight. It is an awakening, a rebirth.

This story is sculpted from the experiences of my family and this place. The humor of my two sons, the uncanny prescience of my amazingly tolerant wife, and the science, history, and character of Interior Alaska are all woven into this strange tale. The characters in the story are fictional. But like the fun TV series Northern Exposure, you can find someone in Alaska that is very much like each one of those characters. The fatal flaw is finding that many lucid characters in one town in Alaska.

Every attempt was made to be technically, geographically, and historically accurate, although science fiction is just that, fiction. It is amazing, though, that so much of what is imagined becomes reality some day. What is clearly real, though, is the strength, love, and spirit of the people who are so intimately connected to this beautiful land. Alaska is very real. Her spirit is very much alive.

Chapter I

The Mammoth Hunters
Late Fall, 10,000 B.C.

Kanak established his bravery as a hunter ten daylight seasons ago by single-handedly killing a large moose with a short spear. The spear, no longer than the hunter's arm, was sharpened with fire and an abrasive rock. Kanak wisely selected tight-grained diamond willow, which possessed an effective hand grip in the multicolored, contoured ovals of the wood. He waited silently for many hours in the dim morning light of early fall, watching the giant ungulate as it moved ever closer across the muskeg.

The moose thrashed brush and small trees with its antlers, loudly crashing about in sequences of three scrapes, responding to a similar challenge by another, perhaps smaller bull in an adjacent muskeg who was interested in the larger beast's harem. Kanak felt both great excitement and fear as he watched the antlers, which were as long as the teenage hunter was tall. They glistened in the mist as the moose turned to listen for a response to its challenge. The smaller bull thrashed again, and the larger moose rushed forward, momentarily stopping directly under Kanak's tree. Kanak remembered his father's advice: "Be like a falcon, act quickly and decisively when you know what your objective is."

Taking care to avoid dropping directly on the deadly antlers, Kanak landed straddling the moose's back, swung his left arm around the massive neck and stabbed the startled beast in the throat with the spear. The moose bucked violently to one side throwing Kanak off into the muskeg where he landed on his back, ice-cold water instantly soaking him and stealing his breath. The mortally wounded moose charged toward a small stand of scraggly black spruce trees, tossing his head wildly to dislodge the spear. Bright red blood spurted from his neck, spraying the yellow brush as he snorted and thrashed. Kanak gathered his wits and scurried back to the tamarack tree, both to climb out of danger and to see where the moose would go. He knew the injured moose could run a great distance before lying down to die.

Kanak's wet buckskin made climbing difficult. From the first large branch two body lengths off the ground, Kanak saw the bull turn, standing with its front legs slightly apart, antlers held high over its head. Red with blood, the spear remained in the moose's throat, as more blood pumped from the wound. The moose started toward Kanak, but suddenly slumped to its knees, front legs first, then slowly its hind legs. In slow motion, the moose lay down on its side, the spear pointing toward the sky, with weakening spurts of blood reaching a short distance up the crimson shaft.

Kanak watched the moose die. Morning sun was now above the horizon and a warm blanket of light began to burn off the mist. The moose exhaled one final time in a long, slow breath as the sunlight reached through the willows. Kanak, still clinging tightly to the tree, his fourteen-year-old body shivering, felt adrenaline rushing from him.

His mother would have a fine new moose hide, and his younger brother and two baby sisters a winter's supply of meat. His father would have been proud, watching his son share the liver, heart and tongue with the small band of Salchaket Athabaskans at the first fire after the kill. The elders would welcome the new hunter into their tribe as an equal, not just as a child who would gather berries, roots, and firewood, and help clean salmon. This was important, because Kanak's father had been a good hunter and provider for both his family and many others in their band before losing his life to a bear while defending the family's supply of drying salmon. The skull of the bear marked his father's shallow grave at the summer fish camp near the shores of the Tanana River.

But this had not been Kanak's first thought as he climbed down from the tree and walked to the moose. He felt the spirit of the moose as he gently stroked the dark brown hair on its side. He cupped his hand and filled it with blood from the moose's neck, then drank the hot, salty liquid as he thanked the moose for giving its life for him and his family. A large raven flew over, clucking loudly. Kanak looked up, then thanked his father for his advice and wisdom. The raven circled, clucking again, then called loudly as its strong wings swished through the air, lifting the large black bird over the trees and off to some distant place.

Kanak's younger brother, Tanak, arrived to see Kanak kneeling by the giant moose with its fresh blood on his hands and his spear in its neck. Tanak would tell of this moment many times around the fires as he proudly explained he had heard Kanak talk to the raven, and the raven had replied with the voice of their father.

Today, Kanak and Tanak led a small band of hunters up a rocky valley near the headwaters of a tributary of the Tanana. At twenty-four years of age, Kanak, now a senior hunter of the tribe, often talked with Tanak and the elders about possibly hunting a mammoth. Only twice in their family history had a mammoth been taken, each time beginning a time of plenty for their tribe. Many children, including his father and mother, had been born after mammoths were killed. Kanak believed it must be the sheer size of the mammoth's spirit that caused so many new lives to appear. Kanak wanted more than anything to share some mammoth's heart with Sheenak, his mate, who was a source of great joy for him, always laughing and playful. Sheenak had given him two strong daughters, both possessing their mother's fine dark hair and bright amber eyes. Their laughter filled the log and sod home with warm sounds. But Kanak wanted a son, and he believed a mammoth heart would bring Sheenak the spirit of a great hunter.

Kanak and Tanak traveled ahead of the other hunters, who were setting up shelters made of poles and skins near a clearwater creek overlooking the valley. Kanak's eyes traced the lines of rock up the mountain slopes, looking for spotting locations. The gray sky began to brighten, revealing a fresh snow cover that would be perfect to help trace animal movement. Kanak and Tanak selected a rocky outcrop overlooking the confluence of three streams. They decided to scale the ledge and spot briefly before returning to camp. Thin air made the trip seem long, and a cold, late afternoon breeze began to stir.

They moved steadily up the mountain, paralleling a silty stream, which Kanak knew must be from a glacier. Sharply chiseled, snow-capped peaks and rubble piles on the valley floor attested to recent glacial activity. Kanak and Tanak studied the high mountains, hoping these and a glacier at the head of the valley would be barriers to a mammoth's escape. Warm from the energy exerted by climbing, and from their soft moose-hide clothes and beaver fur caps, they paused near the base of the rock ledge. In the low afternoon sunlight, Kanak noticed some odd shadows in the snow by the nearest creek. He pointed at it and signaled to Tanak, who acknowledged his sighting.

Descending toward the creek, both hunters felt a heightened alertness. The snow was soft, dry and knee-deep where wind had begun to sculpt snowdrifts leeward of the rubble piles. Elsewhere, a steady wind had blown most of the snow off the rocky ground, revealing isolated patches of tall grass. Near the creek, Kanak and Tanak discovered that the shadows were actually footprints of a very large animal with round, hairy feet. Separated in distance more than a man's length, the giant footprints paralleled the silty stream. There were at least five sets of prints, one small, three somewhat larger, and one set clearly from a very large creature. A chill of excitement rushed through both Kanak and Tanak as they looked at each other with wide eyes and broad grins. It was very rare to see a mammoth, and even more unusual to find a small herd.

Kanak studied the prints carefully again. The rate of snow drifting and the rounding of the prints' outlines suggested they were probably less than a day old. Tanak watched his brother study the prints, noting his skilled interpretation of these signs. Tanak started toward the creek a short distance away, then stopped suddenly. Kanak saw his brother stop, and quickly stood up, alert. Without turning, Tanak waved his arm forward to signal him to come ahead. Kanak walked quickly toward Tanak, who was staring down at the silt near the creek.

Two sets of large bear prints, as wide as a man's foot was

long, crossed the creek following the mammoth tracks upstream. Both men had great respect for the short-faced bears, which were efficient and dangerous hunters. It was one of their smaller cousins, a 1,200-pound grizzly which their father had fought to his death to save their family's food supply. The elders had warned them to beware of the short-faced bears, which were known to be far more successful mammoth hunters than were the Athabaskans.

Kanak and Tanak estimated there was still enough time to climb the ledge and spot for a while before returning to camp to share their findings with the hunting party. No more prints were visible as they climbed toward the outcropping. From a vantage point twice as high above the valley floor as the tallest Tanana Valley spruce trees, the hunters could see nearly to the head of one of three valleys, and some distance up the other two, including the middle one with the mammoth tracks. No bears or mammoths, which were several times as tall as a man, could be seen. The valley with the mammoth tracks leveled off in a broad pass, which they judged would be a full day's hike. Several smaller glaciated valleys converged on the larger one, which they could now see might be low enough to allow passage through the mountains. Kanak and Tanak began to feel a sense of urgency, realizing the bears would probably not let the mammoths get that far.

Scanning the late afternoon sky again, Kanak saw high clouds arriving from the southwest, which could bring snow, but not a major storm. There was still time to return to camp and discuss relocating further up the valley tonight so they could be positioned better for a morning hunt. Tanak knew what Kanak was thinking, but cautioned his brother that they should go back and build their strength with food and sleep. They could cover the ground back to the outcropping very quickly in the morning, and advance up the valley by daylight.

As they returned to camp, Kanak smelled salmon cooking. Now realizing the magnitude of his hunger, he savored the aroma, and was glad the breeze was moving downhill, away from the outcropping and tracks. He nodded to Tanak who patted his stomach and grinned.

Kanak and Tanak were accompanied by five strong hunters, three from their band and two cousins from a band some distance down the Tanana River. They were all younger than Kanak, except for their cousin, Tomak, who was four years older. Tomak, who had been to this valley before, had even seen a mammoth during one of his journeys up here, and was an enthusiastic instigator of this expedition. Tomak was very happy to hunt with his brave cousin, Kanak, and had talked to him often about this moment. Looking up from the fire at the approaching hunters, Tomak could see in Kanak's eyes they had seen something. Intense excitement enveloped the seven men in the firelight as they created a crude map of the valley with sticks and rocks.

As elders of the hunting party, Tomak and Kanak determined a plan. They would arise early, break camp and move to the outcropping before sunrise. By dawn, they would already be spotting. Tomak used the map to show where another outcropping was located further up the valley, from which they could see the glacier. They decided to follow the tracks in that direction, working toward the upper spotting location as Tomak suggested. The final approach to the glacier would be decided then.

Night cooled off quickly now, falling below freezing. The dinner of warm fish and fresh berries provided a welcome inner fire to the men. As night descended, clouds moved up the valley, and a light, dry snow began to fall. In preparation for an early morning departure, the hunters packed all their gear except their shelters and weapons. They had both spears and longbows. Tomak, whose family was known for their skilled craftsmanship, tipped his arrows with bone or sharpened stone. At close to moderate range they were quite effective for moose or bear. Tomak's specialty was fitting his arrows with falcon feathers to give them a true flight, and to carry the spirit of the falcon toward their target.

The journey up the mountain pass from the river had taken nearly a full day, and the late afternoon hike up the valley had used up the rest of his energy. Kanak thought of Sheenak and his daughters' laughter as he drifted off to sleep. That night, he dreamed of a spear in flight, drifting in a long slow arc until it stuck solidly in the ground. Kanak's dream image followed the spear's flight path back to its source, a strong young boy with a bright grin who seemed pleased with his throw. The boy turned slowly and looked up at a raven which clucked loudly in approval of his accomplishment. Then the boy smiled at the raven, and the dream image changed to the raven's perspective, as he circled slowly overhead. From above, the boy looked just like Kanak, but he had Sheenak's eyes.

Tanak was the first to awake followed immediately by Kanak, who woke up when he heard his brother stir. They rolled up their caribou skin sleeping blankets and stepped out of their small shelter into the brisk morning air. The night's snowfall had only lightly dusted the previous day's accumulation, but would provide sufficient fresh cover to aid tracking. Within minutes they were all up and packing, taking only a few moments to chew on some dried moose jerky.

Within an hour, Kanak and Tomak had scaled the outcropping while Tanak led the other hunters to the mammoth and bear tracks. Early twilight began to reveal freshly snow-dusted mountain peaks, allowing Tomak to identify the ridge line ahead where he told Kanak the next spotting location would be.

The hunting party moved forward, paralleling the silty creek with the mammoth and bear tracks. Low subarctic morning sun angles lit the expansive Tanana valley behind them. By midmorning they reached the second outcropping, while bright sunlight reflected off brilliant white peaks with blinding intensity. The hunters each donned a caribou hide face mask with thin horizontal eye slits to protect their skin from the cold wind, and to dim the blinding light so they could see. The hunters climbed up the ledge, breathing heavily in the thin air.

From the outcropping, the valley opened up in magnificent splendor. White snowfields on steep mountain ridges angled downward to the valley floor. In the bowls of these sharply sculpted cirques, the deep aqua blue color of glacier ice was clearly visible in the intense light. Thin silty ribbons of water seeped out from under each of the sidewall glaciers, converging on the valley floor where the mammoth and bear tracks were. As awesome as the sidewall glaciers appeared, all seven men were simultaneously transfixed by the sight at the head of the valley. Arcing over the top of the mountains was a giant ice field, as deep as the mountains were tall. The front of the huge glacier spanned the entire width of the valley, which was several hours' march across for a man.

Fresh snow coated the glacier, but tall spires of intensely blue ice could be seen in crevices far up the reach of the ice field. The front wall of ice was gigantic, reaching more than ten times higher than the tallest spruce trees they had ever seen. Tomak recalled the only other time he had seen this glacier many years before, and thought the ice had been further up the valley. The front of the glacier was sharp and clean, which Tomak's father had explained years before, meant the glacier was advancing. A giant rubble pile at the toe of the glacier confirmed that the ice sheet was indeed moving relentlessly down the valley. For the other hunters, this was their first encounter with a truly giant glacier, and they stood in complete awe of its sheer mass and beauty.

A cold, steady wind rolled off the glacier's face, swirling dry snow into drifts in the valley. The hunters loosened their outer garments to let the moisture evaporate from their bodies, while retaining heat. As they started to spread out across the ledge to begin spotting, Kanak suddenly froze in mid-stride. The other hunters all stopped and watched as Kanak slowly knelt behind a rock and peered over the ledge onto the valley floor below. Kanak signaled for Tomak to come forward, motioning down with his hand to indicate that Tomak should stay low as he did. Peering over the rock, they saw that the snow below them was red with blood, and a black, hairy carcass lay in a snowdrift at the end of a trail of blood. Single file, the hunters moved forward to observe.

Leaving two men on the ledge as observers, Kanak, Tomak and the other hunters moved down to the valley floor. Weapons in hand, they moved quietly around the scene of what had obviously been a great battle between mammoths and short-faced bears. Kanak reached the carcass first. It was a bear dead from a gaping wound through its abdomen and from what appeared to be a crushed skull. Kanak placed his hand near the wound under the torn hide and found the huge bear's body still warm. Tomak immediately knew what Kanak had discovered when Kanak signaled a sign for warmth to the other hunters. A wide area of snow had been disturbed, and a trail of blood and tracks headed in a direction over another rock outcropping a short distance away.

Moving forward, they followed the sharp, fresh tracks in the new snow. Crawling on their stomachs to the edge, they stopped suddenly as a trumpeting call followed by a loud roar pierced the cold air. Peering down they saw the surviving bear locked in a death struggle with a very large mammoth. The body of a small, juvenile mammoth lay steaming in the snow by a small stream, breathing heavily and bleeding from the neck. The bear lunged at the large mammoth, then backed quickly away as the giant mammoth swung his huge tusks back and forth at the bear. The mammoth stood between the dying young mammoth and the bear, who did not appear to be wounded.

Some distance from the battle scene, the other mammoths gathered together bellowing and trumpeting as the giant mammoth confronted the bear. Suddenly, the mammoth ran forward at the bear, which turned and bounded up on a rock ledge. Now eye to eye with his adversary, the bear pawed the air in the mammoth's direction. Furious, the mammoth raised his trunk and bellowed so loudly at the bear that the air shook like thunder. As the sound reverberated in the narrow rocky gorge, an overhanging mass of snow gave way and began surging down the steep slopes toward both animals.

Tomak and Kanak looked up. Realizing they were in danger, they quickly began scrambling backward to avoid the onrushing avalanche. Falling snow, ice, and rock hit the bottom of the narrow gorge with a tremendous roar, and exploded over the ridge line at the retreating hunters who were now in a full run. Heavy snow blasted forward surrounding them, sweeping them off their feet and pushing them forward in a wave. They ran, swam, and fought furiously forward, clutching their weapons with all their might, trying to outrace the avalanche. Tomak yelled to the others to climb out of the gorge, and quickly did so himself. Several others followed, and stopped safely above the slowing river of snow and ice.

As the snow finally rumbled to a stop, Tomak, Kanak and three other hunters safely huddled together on the ledge. Tanak and another hunter were gone and an eerie silence filled the valley. The battleground of the short-faced bear and mammoth was buried under a sea of snow and ice. The yearling mammoth was also buried, and the three remaining mammoths began pacing back and forth anxiously at the foot of the snow slide, trumpeting to the others buried in the snow.

Kanak moved higher on the ledge and began scanning for signs of the two lost hunters. Then he saw a point of a spear poking out of the snow below them, and immediately scrambled down over the rocks into the snow toward the spear. The snow was agonizingly soft and difficult to move through, having been churned through the rocky gorge. Kanak half ran and half swam to the spear, and began to dig furiously. Others joined in now, digging a crater with their hands around the spear. As Kanak dug down, he reached a hand tightly grasping the spear's shaft. Digging steadily, the hunters watched as Kanak grasped the hand on the spear. The fingers moved, first slowly, then more rapidly, repeatedly grasping the spear and releasing it. The hunters dug furiously now, widening the crater even as the soft snow rushed in nearly as fast as they could scoop it out.

Suddenly a loud gasp and a cry burst forth as Tanak's head popped out of the hole near Tomak's knee. A small rivulet of blood trickled out of the corner of Tanak's face mask, but he was alive. Quickly they pulled the young hunter out and moved him to the top of the snow pile where he lay panting, still clutching his spear. His other arm was twisted badly, but his legs were fine. One of the two spotters who had remained on the first outcropping suddenly appeared, signaling that he had seen where the other man went down.

Leaving one of the younger hunters with Tanak, they scrambled and swam through the snow slide toward the ridge line where they had seen the bear and mammoth. Peering over, they saw their cousin crouching near the edge of a snow pile, apparently unhurt. They started to shout to him for joy that he was alive, but he quickly turned and silenced them. At that moment, Tomak and Kanak realized the other mammoths were pacing nervously back and forth at the face of the snow slide. One, a small male, began to venture forward, stomping in the snow and trumpeting to the fallen members of his small herd. Both females remained behind, but the mammoths had now seen the humans.

As the small male stomped forward, he raised his trunk through his curved ivory tusks and bellowed loudly at the men. A small ledge of snow remaining on the mountain broke loose and began to tumble down the gorge in a repeat avalanche. Looking up, the small mammoth quickly stepped back several paces. Seeing this avalanche was only a small relic of the first, the hunters retreated only a short distance out of the gorge. Then, as the new snow slide surged down into the residue of the first avalanche and began plowing forward, a great mound of snow exploded upward in front of the hunters. It was the giant mammoth, awakened from the shock of the first avalanche and now violently shaking off the snow and ice from his huge body.

The great beast was so close the hunters could feel the heat of its breath as it bellowed loudly in defiance of the snow, the bear, and now the humans. Tomak and Kanak stood forward of the other hunters facing the mammoth. Both men still had their longbows in hand and knew what they must do. The great beast raised his trunk and trumpeted again at the men. Falcon-feathered arrows silently sprung forward from the willow longbows, and found their mark. Kanak's arrow went directly into the mammoth's mouth, hitting him in the back of the throat. Tomak had fired exactly into the beast's eye, penetrating the eye cavity and terminating in the mammoth's skull. Gulping loudly, the mammoth rolled backward and down the snow slide, twisting in agony and confusion.

The other hunters watched in awe as Tomak and Kanak walked forward along the ridge line with quick but determined steps. At the edge of the snow pile, they stopped and drew two more arrows. The mammoth rolled over, rose and stumbled forward drunkenly, shaking his head and attempting to bellow, but he could only grunt with the arrow in his throat. The beast stopped at the edge of the snow pile where the two hunters stood, bows ready again. Together, Tomak and Kanak again fired their falcon-feathered arrows, which penetrated deeply into the mammoth's neck. Bright red blood immediately began to race down the shafts of the two arrows which had struck within a hand's width of each other. When the story of the mammoth kill would be told around the campfires in the future, Tomak and Kanak would be described as a single hunting spirit. They aimed together, fired together, and found their mark together.

Mortally wounded, the mammoth stumbled forward out onto the valley floor toward the stream. Tomak and Kanak walked forward with a confident intensity, drawing two more arrows simultaneously. Again the arrows found their mark within a hand's width of the other two. The mammoth fell to his knees only a short distance ahead of them, breathing heavily and bleeding steadily now. They walked up onto a ledge from where they could see the smaller male and two female mammoths, who were backing away from the battle scene while trumpeting to the wounded mammoth, urging him forward. Both females began to lope downstream in a steady gait, while the small male turned, bellowed again and started back toward the old bull, who was trying to stand.

In a final burst of strength, the mammoth stood up and began to stagger after his herd. The small male turned to follow the females, with the injured bull swaggering behind. Tomak and Kanak watched, knowing that the wounded mammoth was theirs. Slowly, the mammoth stopped and lay down beside the silty stream. Cold glacial wind swirled snow around its great hairy head, which rocked gently back and forth, swaying his huge curled tusks in the air. Then his head lay down one last time, and a long slow final exhale could be heard as the great animal's spirit left his body. The other mammoths had stopped and returned to their fallen comrade. Tomak and Kanak knew that the mammoth herd would need time to say good-bye to the old bull, so they turned and headed back to the other hunters.

Tanak's arm was broken, but was skillfully reset by Tomak, albeit to some ear-shattering screams. The hunting party moved their gear to a campsite in the lee of a small hill, safely away from potential avalanches and the glacier's constant cold wind. The hill provided a spotting location to watch for bears which might be interested in their kill. It also afforded a majestic view of the glacier. A clear-water stream was nearby as was a sizable stand of willow, dwarf birch, and small black spruce trees which would provide firewood, poles for shelter, and for transporting and hanging meat.

After camp was set up and Tanak was resting peacefully in his sleeping blanket, the hunters returned to the mammoth kill. The bull mammoth now lay alone by the stream. Tracks of the other three mammoths led off downstream, away from the kill and from their new campsite. In the late afternoon light, Kanak, Tomak and the other hunters shared the mammoth's blood. A small gourd of blood was drawn for Tanak, and brought back to him with the first segments of liver for that night's dinner.

Several days later, two hunters left with Tanak back down the valley. The journey to their home along the oxbows of the Tanana River would take at least five days, but they would carry home some mammoth meat. The four hunters who remained behind would continue the harvest, later to be joined by a large entourage from their two bands who would help transport the meat, hide, tusks, and useful pieces of bone back to their villages. This task would need to be completed quickly, lest the onset of winter force them to leave some of the valuable kill.

The four hunters worked hard, cutting and carrying meat, and building curing racks. Pausing only to eat and sleep, they completed the meat harvest and had all perishable components of the kill safely stored near the camp before the first of their band arrived. Only tusks and bones remained to be transported. Tomak and Kanak decided it would be best to set up a new camp one day's journey down the valley, and to move all the meat there before moving on. That way, they could move safely to a location that might be another week ahead of winter. Repeating this cycle with one or two other temporary camps until they arrived at the Tanana, they could make a final journey downriver by raft and canoe to their homes.

Sheenak arrived with the first twelve helpers from Kanak's band, having left their daughters safely with their grandmother in their home by the Tanana. Kanak was very happy to see Sheenak, and she was both proud and pleased with her strong husband. That night, Kanak prepared her a meal from the heart of the mammoth. As the setting sun cast its last light on the peaks of the mountains, Kanak and Sheenak watched from the hilltop near the camp. They huddled together under a black short-faced-bear hide, sharing warmth and closeness, and they watched as a great green arc filled the clear night sky.

The Auroral light was a pleasant and beautiful mystery to the Athabaskans. Soft, green light began to quiver and pulse, and long, thin streaks of even brighter green light began to dance across the sky like falling spears. As the intensity of the movement increased, the colors began to change, first to brighter green, then to red. At first only a dim pink hue, the red intensified, soon covering the bottom of what had become bright curtains of green light shimmering from horizon to horizon. The light was so intense that it was reflected in the glacier ice.

From the top of the hill, Kanak and Sheenak could see the white ribs of the mammoth kill near the silty stream, and could hear the happy murmur of their family and friends in the camp below. The light of the aurora blazed across the sky like a forest fire, only smokeless and strangely silent. After a particularly brilliant display, the energetic red light faded, but the long green arc reaching across the entire sky over the top of the ice field remained. The green glow appeared to fill the glacier, and some red light still seemed to radiate from within the ice. Kanak observed the red light inside the glacier with curiosity. It continued to glow even though only a green arc remained overhead. He pointed it out to Sheenak, who whispered to her brave husband that it must be the mammoth's spirit, alive and cradled deeply within the massive ice sheet.

That night Kanak and Sheenak both dreamed they were visited by a tall, fair-haired man. Their dream seemed very real, and the man spoke in a strange and quite voice. His skins appeared smooth, supple, and strangely cut. The man smiled and showed them bright objects with tiny fires which he held in his hand. They talked to him around the campfire for some time, telling him of their hunt. Although they could not understand his words, he seemed to understand theirs. He seemed friendly and patient, listening to them speak for a long time as the fire glowed in the night.

Later Kanak and Sheenak would both remember this strangely clear and lifelike dream. Although they had shared dreams before, this was new, but within what they perceived as their spiritual awareness of each other. They later remembered that the tall, fair-skinned man with the interesting sparkling objects in his hand had finally spoken to them in their own language. He had not spoken many words, but clearly had offered them kind greetings and had wished them well moving the bounty of the mammoth down the valley. They felt strangely at peace with the tall man. As he bid them farewell and rose to leave, he turned and looked deeply into their eyes and said in their own language, "Your son will be a great hunter, too." As Kanak and Sheenak looked at each other in surprise, the man had simply vanished.

When the dream was over, they slept soundly. The morning was filled with promise of a new day when hunters and their families would begin to move the camp and mammoth meat to the first new camp site. Kanak and Sheenak stood by the morning fire, each with one arm around the other, and with a soft skin draped over their shoulders and backs against the steady cold wind.

Kanak held a small round object in his hand which he had found by their sleeping blanket. No larger than a man's fist, it was hard and smooth like ivory, but clear like glacier ice. Inside, the object glowed with a dim reddish light, similar to the red light they had seen in the glacier the night before. Kanak and Sheenak did not know what it was or where it had come from, nor did any of the other members of the party when they were shown the object. Kanak held it up to the sky as if that would somehow reveal its meaning. He could see through it like air, as it appeared almost invisible against the light blue sky in the background except for the red interior glow. The object's perfect smoothness reminded them of the clean, smooth lines of the clothing of the fair-haired man from their dream.

Kanak handed the small sphere to Sheenak, who cupped it in her hands. The color inside changed from red to green, then to a deep blue like the sky. She told Kanak that she believed it must be from the mammoth's spirit, something mystical and of great portent to them and their people. Kanak had long learned to respect and admire Sheenak's spiritual awareness of their world. Her apparent understanding of unusual events in their lives and her simple but beautiful explanations of those events were a source of wonder not only to Kanak, but to their friends and family as well. Kanak told Sheenak to keep the object. She smiled at him and placed it in her leather pack.

Light snow, which had begun to fall the previous day, was now building in intensity, as was a cold wind descending from the giant ice field. As Kanak and Tomak had planned, they were in the final stages of transferring the camp to a site further down the valley. When the final loads were ready and some had already begun the slow trek downhill, Kanak and Sheenak walked back to the mammoth kill site one last time.

Sheenak stood inside the great beast's ribs. She ran her hand over the smooth bone of a massive rib arch rising into the gray sky, and tried to imagine what it was like to have been a mammoth. As she closed her eyes she began to feel the animal's strength, and could almost see the earth from the height of its eyes as it moved slowly down the broad mountain valley with its small herd. She knew a time was approaching when mammoths would no longer walk the long, fertile valleys. The mammoths' world had changed as the nearly arid grasslands had slowly become forested taiga, and animal predators and men had come to the valley in greater numbers. Once protected in the isolated valleys by ice fields and tall mountains, mammoth herds had flourished. As the end of the ice age approached, a new world unfolded before them, one in which their kind would not last much longer. Sheenak felt this deep in the spirit heart of the mammoth as she walked within the great beast in her mind's eye.

Kanak observed his wife's dreamlike state as she stood inside the mammoth's ribs with her head tilted back slightly and swaying, eyes closed. Then Sheenak reached into her pack, removed the round object and held it in her hand. It glowed with a deeper blue than glacier ice on a clear day. Inside the object, a single bright point of red light formed and began to pulse slowly. Sheenak held the object up and looked into it, then she began to sing softly to it and to the mammoth. Her song was a gentle lullaby she often sang to their daughters as they fell asleep. It was a song of resting after a long day of activity, and of giving thanks for being alive that day.

As she sang, now with her eyes open, the object began to pulse more rapidly, and felt light in her hand, almost like air. Sheenak had a clear and lovely voice, with nearly perfect pitch. As she neared the end of her lullaby, her voice dropping and rising through a series of harmonic octaves, the object suddenly rose up from her hand and began to spin. Pulsing even more rapidly, it emitted a tonal echo to her song, in perfect pitch to her singing, but transcending first several, then many octaves like the voice of a strong singer in a cave. Kanak was awed but startled by the sound, now realizing that it was not his wife's voice any longer, but something great and mysterious responding to her voice. At first he feared for what might happen, then stopped when he saw her smiling face watching the glowing, humming object, spinning in the air above her outstretched hand.

Tones from the sphere seemed to emanate from not only within it, but now from the wind around them. Finally, a long deep tone with harmonics so low that it could be felt as much as heard emanated from within the glacier. A point of deep blue and red light rose and pulsed within the glacier ice in time to the harmonic tone. The valley was filled with strange and beautiful tones now. No longer singing herself, she reached up and touched, then gently grasped the spinning sphere. The tone from the object faded quickly, as did the pulsing light. The sphere stopped spinning and settled into her hand as the last tonal echoes ceased.

Suddenly, the ground began to tremble, slowly at first, then in a steady rocking motion with greater intensity. The quaking of the earth seemed to echo the tones and pulsing of the light of the sphere. Up in the steep cirques of the mountains, snow slides and larger avalanches began cascading down the valley, triggered by the tremor. As the shaking subsided, the mammoth's white ribs swayed slowly several more times, echoing the final tremors. Sheenak still held the spherical object tightly in her hand. Kanak and Sheenak looked at each other in surprise and wondered what had just happened.

Looking first into Kanak's eyes, then kneeling inside the ribs of the mammoth, she took the object and wrapped it in a soft piece of moose-hide leather. Then she placed the small parcel in a pocket of bone where the mammoth's ribs joined the vertebrae. Stepping back from the mammoth now and into Kanak's arms, she turned to look at the small wrapped object nestled inside the rib cage. Sheenak told Kanak she believed the object was the heart of the mammoth's spirit, which was alive inside the glacier. She told Kanak of her vision of a walking mammoth, and the sense of time and change she felt from the mammoth's mind. That the mammoth's heart had responded to her lullaby of sleep and rest, and that the spirit had called to its heart and to her was all perfectly understandable. All that remained was for Sheenak to leave the great beast's spirit heart inside the open cavity of its chest, cradled in the arch of ribs bending into the sky. Nestled in her strong husband's arms with her back to him, she placed her hands on her belly and felt the stirring of a new life. Together they departed the valley.

The Athabaskans again entered a time of plenty as they shared stories of the mammoth hunt around their fires in the white spruce and birch forests of the Tanana valley. Many strong children were born the next spring.

Chapter 2
Black Rapids Glacier
Summer, A.D. 1974

Kenny was a graduate student at University of Alaska, Fairbanks, during construction of the Trans-Alaska Pipeline System (TAPS). His chosen field was archaeology, but with a strong biological sciences background he was more specifically training to be a paleobiologist. Actually, Kenny, and the few students who remained full time in the graduate programs at the University of Alaska, could choose just about anything they wanted. Every department on the campus was quite eager to offer whatever they could since the field of students had become so depleted over the past three years. It was hard to compete with the construction and engineering firms building TAPS which could offer $100,000 per year in gross wages to a laborer willing to work a schedule of nine weeks on, two weeks off, twelve hours per day, seven days per week. All the graduate programs could offer was something only slightly less grueling in terms of working hours, but at a pay scale barely above minimum wage.

But Kenny was different from the 30,000-plus workers in the eighteen main pipeline and nine pump station construction camps stretched along the 800-mile length of the project from Prudhoe Bay to Valdez, where the giant Valdez Marine Terminal was under construction. He was training to be a scientist, and the capital he was amassing was intellectual rather than fiscal. Kenny was no fool, however, and respected the fact that wealth was what facilitated the arts and sciences. He did not wish to live in poverty, and clearly did not intend to do so. In a sense, however, he was a futurist. Even at twenty-four, he knew that knowledge was the source of both spiritual and fiscal wealth, but that fiscal rewards would be somewhere much further down the road. To an alert mind, however, Kenny knew the stimulation of discovery was an immediate and almost daily reward in the sciences. The legions of tradesmen and women who labored to build the largest privately financed construction project in history in his backyard were focused on much different and more immediate objectives.

Kenny had visited both Valdez and Prudhoe Bay as an archaeological scientist, assisting the teams from UAF and other universities who participated in the environmental impact assessment which preceded pipeline construction. The environmental assessment had a significant sociological and archaeological component, particularly in light of the rich history of the prehistoric settlement of Alaska, and Kenny was fortunate to be able to participate in the field research. When Kenny had first come to Prince William Sound, as part of the assessment team, the marine terminal project was only in the blueprint stage. The inner harbor was as he remembered it as a boy when his father, a mining geologist with a Scandinavian heritage, had brought the family on fishing trips. The tall peaks of the Chugach Mountains plunged steeply into the deep harbor, providing one of the farthest north ice-free ports in the world. When the sun would finally appear from behind the agonizingly persistent clouds, the harbor was a jewel of aqua and green, trimmed along the top of the mountain ridges in brilliant white against the blue background of sky. A paradise of aquatic life, the Sound had provided his family a harvest of halibut, salmon, and shellfish for many years.

The Valdez Marine Terminal was, in some early sense of the futurists' phrase, a terraforming project. The giant tank farm and petroleum loading berths were to be constructed on the south side of the harbor. To do this, a mountain had to be trimmed back in steps to create horizontal surfaces for tanks and support facilities which would handle the warm Prudhoe Bay crude oil at a rate of more than 2,000,000 barrels per day. Kenny and the rest of the archeological team had investigated the site where rock would be drilled, blasted, and remolded into tiers of hard, granite work pads.

No significant archaeological discoveries were encountered at the VMT project site. For the members of the project team who had precariously clung to the steep slopes in the rain and wind, it was not a particularly stunning conclusion to recognize that only some sort of a prehistoric masochist would ever have wanted to settle there. Even when the sun did come out, the site was in the shadow of the mountains to the south which separated the inner harbor from the rest of Prince William Sound and the turbulent Gulf of Alaska. Not exactly a great building site, particularly when the Robe River and other glacial streams had deposited at the head of the harbor several square miles of level terrain with abundant stands of cottonwood and spruce trees. There had been prehistoric settlements in this area, but not hanging off a steep, windy, cold, shaded cliff.

They had to look, however. It was part of the environmental impact assessment mandated by Congress when the U.S. Senate finally passed the law which allowed pipeline construction to proceed. The Senate vote had been fifty-one to fifty, with U.S. Vice President Spiro Agnew casting the deciding vote in his capacity as Senate President. With the level of scrutiny which follows such a controversial megaproject, everything would have to be done just right. So Kenny, other archeologists, and the rest of the barely compensated field assistants had scoured the site in weather that only a duck or a Valdez fisherman could love. Besides, the extent of active glaciation which had repeatedly scoured this part of the world over time was extraordinary. The incessant rain which fell during summer turned to snow in winter. Up to five hundred inches of wet, heavy, glacier-producing snow. The giant ice fields which resulted had carved the harbors and molded the coastline of Southcentral Alaska. The Kayak and other natives who settled this area were in many respects isolated from the vast, dry interior of Alaska. The record of their existence was not as well preserved as a consequence of the glaciology and often brutal weather.

Prudhoe Bay proved to be another world entirely. The supergiant 20-billion-barrel field, largest of an enormous cluster of 100-million-barrel or larger fields in the area, was discovered on the edge of the Arctic Coastal Plain in the late 1960s. This physiographic region of Alaska was in reality an arctic desert, with only about five inches of precipitation per year. Relatively flat with only a few low hills, the plain was underlain with permafrost ranging from 1,000 to 2,000 feet in depth. The permafrost was in fact a glacier of ice and soil left solidly frozen from the end of the last ice age. That Alaska's glaciers were in the south rather than the north of the state was a fact of some surprise to many tourists. To the Inupiat who had inhabited the arctic coast for at least 13,000 years, glaciers were not even part of their folklore. The sea ice, however, was.

Only the top several feet of marshy tundra thawed in the 24-hour daylight of the relatively short summer. Kenny's first impression after landing at Deadhorse airport was that this might well be the soggiest desert on the planet. It was also, he soon discovered, home to arguably the world's largest and feistiest collection of mosquitoes. He supposed that being frozen in the tundra for more than nine months of the year would embitter each generation of mosquitoes sufficiently to maintain an aggressive heritage.

Kenny's second impression of Prudhoe was that the facilities being developed by the oil companies were more like some sort of a moon base than something terrestrial. Constructed on insulated gravel pads, the modules of the Prudhoe Bay field were scenes from a science fiction novel. One Base Operations Center was a series of multistoried metal-and-glass ovals mounted on steel pilings anchored solidly into the permafrost. The nearly constant northeasterly wind circulated without obstruction under the massive structures which were connected by enclosed, elevated walkways. Engineers learned the hard way that to build in the Arctic, one had to freeze the foundation of the structure and never let it thaw. The frozen ground had the tensile strength of super-hardened steel. Thawed, it was a lake of mud with zero load-bearing capacity. Several badly twisted prefabricated warehouse units built directly on uninsulated gravel pads in the early years of the exploration of Prudhoe Bay attested to this. Kenny's impression was that the development of Prudhoe had graduated from pioneering to engineering.

The archaeological field teams associated with the pipeline project were primarily concerned with the immediate area around Pump Station No. 1, which was the starting point for the 48-inch-diameter pipeline. The remainder of the field, including support modules and actual well sites had been examined by other teams. The pump station site was inland about ten miles from the coast. The terrain was typical for the area with several shallow, elongated, nearly rectangular lakes nearby. Like more than one million more nearly rectangular tundra lakes in Alaska which are oriented to the prevailing wind, these lakes had no names. The area immediately around the lakes was patterned in polygons, frozen ground features of geometric patterns created by repeated freezing and thawing of the ground. Being near the lakes, these polygons were low-centered, which meant that the edges had been pushed up into small piles of soil and tundra, and the centers, perhaps 20 feet across were sunken in a small marsh. Kenny found these sunken areas to be something of an Eden for mosquitoes and other teeming insect life. The mounded edges of the polygons provided abundant nesting habitat for birds, and the insects provided sustenance only a short distance away. Dwarf willows, grass, and wildflowers rooted into the upturned edges of the polygons provided scant relief from the nearly constant wind blowing across the treeless plain.

Kenny's team found few artifacts at the site, mostly wood and bone implements which appeared to have been broken and abandoned by wandering hunters. In the shallow excavations carefully dug at the site, they found no sign of dwellings or campfires. This was not surprising since the actual number of habitable sites on the Arctic Coastal Plain, were indeed few. It was also known that the Inupiat and their ancestors had shared the campsites, either in the fertile river basins where good water and fish were abundant, or on the coast. It was there, where driftwood platforms could be constructed to watch for whales when leads opened out beyond the shore fast ice in the spring, and when the ice pack was blown offshore for six to eight weeks in the fall, that the Inupiat had built fire pits carbon-14-dated to 11,000 B.C. The inland lakes such as at Pump Station No. 1 were only places where caribou had been hunted as the herds calved and grazed in summer.

Even though it was apparently not a significant archaeological site, Kenny felt a sense of mystery and wonder as they excavated the grid of shallow pits. He covered his face with a green mosquito net dangling from the brim of his hat and tied close around his neck so he could work with both hands instead of using one to uselessly sweep bugs away while he dug. Kenny discovered a short, ivory-tipped spear, perhaps as long as his arm. The driftwood handle appeared to be made of hard willow, similar to the diamond willow which grew in the Tanana valley near his family's home, but likely from Canada to the east, where the Mackenzie River disgorged a constant supply of wood which circulated west along the north coast of Alaska.

Kenny had slowly exposed the spear with a bristle brush, taking several hours to let the ground thaw, then brushing away the soil. The implement had finally come free from the organic muck and was extensively photographed and admired by the entire project team. Kenny lifted the spear from its resting place and held it in his hand as the other team members watched. The smooth wood was twisted in the common fashion of willows, and a natural hand grip resulted at a point perhaps a third of the way up the shaft. The ivory blade was still quite sharp, and could easily penetrate the hide of a caribou. Kenny wondered whether this was the weapon of a man, or of a youth. Deciding it was most likely the latter, he imagined an Inupiat father crouching inside the shallow edge of the polygon with his pre-teenage son, both watching a herd of caribou grazing on lichens along the shore of the lake. Kenny held the spear and closed his eyes, his face turned toward the low evening sun moving along the horizon. Still kneeling in the polygon where the spear had been unearthed, he could almost sense the excitement of the young boy on his first hunt. He shuddered briefly when he seemed to feel the hand of the boy's father touch his shoulder, then point to a lone caribou, a small male slowly ambling nearer to them.

Kenny's Athabaskan mother had shown him the ways of his heritage, and with her stories of their people had given his brothers and sisters a sense of life on the Tanana. Kenny had gained a sense of awareness of the continuity of life from his mother's traditional ways. He felt connected to the valley of his home, and to all the native peoples of Alaska, both living and past. At this moment, the spear in his hand was alive with the memory of another young man, discovering the world with his father, and learning the skills of survival for his family.

Kenny opened his eyes to see the team of his peers and his

project leader observing him. He suddenly felt embarrassed with them watching him crouched on the ground, spear in hand and eyes closed. He looked down at the spear as several who were facing him smiled, and turned it slowly in his hand. A dark streak of color, long since dried on the shaft of the spear near the tip was visible underneath. Fragments of hair were lodged under the ivory tip where it joined the wood, which had been carefully carved to receive and hold the ivory blade. The spear was cold when Kenny had first lifted it from the ground. It had likely been frozen since the day it was lost, perhaps fallen from a pack as the Inupiat father and son had returned to their umiak boat on the coast with the son's first kill.

Kenny departed on a combination cargo and passenger Boeing 737 jet which lifted off the gravel runway from the Prudhoe Bay airport and circled west toward Barrow for a stop on the way home to Fairbanks. The new oilfield spanned more than fifty miles to the southwest from the airport. The modern, expensive infrastructure only touched a tiny footprint of the tundra, with the drill sites being spaced miles apart, and multiple wells drilled directionally off each insulated pad. The gathering pipelines connecting the various modules were supported by vertical steel beams frozen into the ground. Kenny could visually trace the main connecting lines under construction heading toward the Pump Station No. 1 site where he had made his discovery.

As the small, powerful jet climbed into the clear sky, Kenny wondered what the Inupiat hunter and his young son would have thought if they had looked up over the rise of the polygon, and had seen the huge gray-green tanks of the pump station and the metal-jacketed pipeline standing on steel supports snaking south toward the foothills of the Brooks Range. He could clearly see the polygons now, some high-centered on drier ground away from the rivers and lakes which stretched off into the distance like silver rectangles embedded in a blanket of green and yellow tundra. As the jet rose over the ice pack, Kenny observed the geometry of the fractured sea ice, receding from the shore in the summer thaw. The same polygonal pattern in the tundra seemed to be repeated in the ice. He felt the excitement of another moment of discovery as he speculated that in naturally chaotic systems, certain patterns of organization seemed to repeat themselves in completely different structures.

The jet now reached its cruising altitude, then quieted down as the pilot throttled back the engines for the flight to Barrow. Tired from several weeks of field work in the long sunlit days and nights, he drifted off to sleep. In his dream, Kenny became the young hunter, this time arriving at the shore of the Sagavanirktok River where his family awaited him and his father. He saw a small, dark-haired woman smiling at him and his father. She laughed with joy at the sight of her son struggling to carry a piece of caribou nearly as large as he was. Kenny dropped the meat on the ground and ran to his mother who hugged him tightly as his small sister and brother excitedly ran first to Kenny, then to their father. Around the fire in the family's summer fish camp that evening his Inupiat father shared the story of how a new hunter had joined the family. The joy of this moment was saddened only slightly by the loss of his favorite spear.

Kenny had established his credentials as a thoughtful scientist through his summer field work. The short spear he had discovered at the Pump Station No. 1 site was on display at the University of Alaska Museum in the Eielson building in the center of the campus. The spear had been placed in one of the drawers below the glass-cased exhibits which could be opened and examined by visitors who wished to see more examples of a particular item. The museum staff had placed it in a display of weapons of the Inupiat after some discussion of whether or not it should be considered a plaything. The dried blood on the shaft of the spear had been the final determinant.

On the day that his spear went on display at the museum, Kenny invited his family to be the first to see it. The museum staff had been kind enough to waive the usual admission fee for this special occasion, so Kenny brought his entire family. Kenny's younger brother Tim had been the first to tell their friends about the discovery of the spear. Tim was so excited about seeing it in real life for the first time that he raced ahead into the arctic coast display area of the museum and immediately began searching every display case for his brother's discovery. Kenny's mother gripped his two little sisters' hands to keep them from wiggling excitedly away to chase after Tim.

Finally, with his family gathered about the display case, Kenny opened the drawer and with a nod from the museum director, lifted the spear from the blue felt and handed it to his father. His father took the spear with care and turned it over gently in his hands, only one of which still had a full range of motion. His father's left hand was gnarled with scar tissue from a fight with a grizzly bear during one of his field geology trips in the Circle mining district north of Fairbanks. The attacking bear's skull had been mounted on one of the corner stakes of the placer gold claim, appropriately named Grizzly 1. His father had dispatched the bear with six point-blank shots from a 44-magnum handgun, but only after the bear had left its mark on his arm and hand.

For a Norwegian, Carl Swanson was not a tall man, but was of a stocky build with green eyes and short, curly brown hair typical of his Lapp heritage. Carl could not have been more proud of his son. "It is a fine implement, Ken, and the blade is still incredibly sharp. What was the final outcome of the C-14 dating?"

"We estimate between 5,500 and 5,700 B.C.," the museum director acknowledged. "It is among the oldest finds from this region, and certainly one of the most intact. We are all very proud of Kenny for his discovery." Kenny's mom noticed her son blush slightly under his smile.

By this time, Tim and the girls were trapped somewhere between awe and a serious case of the fidgets. Dad held the spear and let each of the children touch the wood shaft which they all did at the same time. Then Tim reached for the spear point, which his father let him touch gently with his index finger while holding the spear firmly in his hands. Kenny loved that about his father. With only a look from his father's watchful eyes, Tim knew it was okay to touch the spear point, but to do so very carefully. Tim's "Wow!" was followed by "Me, too. Me, too!" from his sisters. Their father knelt down and let each one of his bright-eyed daughters touch the spear point with one finger. "It's smooth," said four-year old Carla. "Smoove," echoed two-year old Missy.

"Betty?" Carl said as he raised the spear to his wife. Kenny's mom took the spear in both hands, then ever so naturally found the hand grip in the wood. Holding it like a hunter, right hand in the grip and left up the shaft, she made a slow jabbing motion in the air, away from the kids. Kenny had seen his mother dance at the Potlatch ceremonies during winter fur festival in Fairbanks, and her graceful motion with the spear reminded him of that. He watched as his mother lowered her hands still holding the spear. Looking down, she closed her eyes for a moment, then looked up at Kenny, deeply into his eyes. "It tells a wonderful story to us," she said. "It has great memories."

Kenny remembered his dream in the airplane, and somehow knew his mother knew, even though he hadn't told anyone. Handing the spear back to Kenny, then holding his hands as he held the spear, she said, "I think this spear has made a hunter of two young men."

By now, Tim had taken both of his sisters by the hand to see the mammoth display in the center of the museum. "It's a hairy elephant," said Carla. "Tarry ephant," echoed Missy. Ignoring his sisters, Tim was lost in the diorama of the mammoth hunters of the Pleistocene. "Wow, look at those teeth!" he exclaimed, pointing at the saber-toothed tiger in the background. Tim nearly jumped out of his skin when his father walked up quietly behind him, suddenly put both hands on Tim's shoulders and growled like a tiger. "Ach! Don't do that," he yelled, this admonition falling uselessly on his family who were practically falling over themselves with laughter.

Kenny handed the spear back to the museum director, a scientist of some stature of her own in the field of carbon dating. Dr. Wescott took the spear and wiped the entire object carefully with a lint-free cloth to remove any oils from the hands of those that had admiringly held it during this special showing. She placed it carefully in the drawer, replacing the elastic bands which held it firmly in place near its label. "Spear of Young Inupiat Caribou Hunter, Sagavanirktok River, ca. 5,600 B.C., K. Swanson, 1977," it proclaimed.

"Thank you, Dr. Wescott. I know that it is against the rules to handle these, but this was very special for my family."

"I'm quite happy to make an exception for your extraordinary discovery, Kenny."

Sitting peacefully on a south-facing hill, the West Ridge of the University of Alaska campus gathered the sun in all its subarctic glory, even in the low angles of the brief winter daylight. In summer and early fall, Kenny and his colleagues would often take their lunch on the well-manicured lawn in front of the West Ridge, where they could see the full northern arc of the Alaska Range to the south and the expanse of the Tanana Valley below. It was here that Kenny and his cousin Tom began to formulate the idea of a multidisciplinary research project. Tom, who had been born and raised in Nenana, was a graduate geology student with a specific interest in glaciology.

"At the headwaters of the Tanana and Delta Rivers, the glaciers are receding at a sufficient rate to uncover area that has never been explored before," Tom offered. "Dr. Wescott says that mammoth skeletons have been found there years ago, in excellent condition, some with the hide and flesh still intact." Lifting his head off the neatly trimmed grass, he looked over at Kenny like a fisherman dangling a lure in front of rainbow trout in a clear stream.

"Yes, I know. I saw some of the stomach content specimens in the biology lab last semester," Kenny noted. He was lying flat on his back with the sun warming the outside of his eyelids. Slowly, he opened his eyes, squinting at Tom. "You want to go camping this weekend? Maybe hike up to one of the glaciers and poke around a bit?"

"Gee, I thought you'd never ask." Tom sat up and stretched, gazing out at a low, off-white mound in the distance to the southwest. "We could climb Denali and check out the glaciers there," Tom said grinning and nodding at the peak which appeared taller than it actually was due to the lens effect of the late afternoon atmosphere. "If we found mammoth remains at 20,000 feet altitude, wouldn't that make a splash?"

"Call me when you get to the top and I'll notify the press of our discovery," Kenny said slowly, again closing his eyes at his cousin's nonsense.

"Oh, come on! You're wasting your time trying to tan anything but the Norwegian half of your hide anyway. Let's take Friday off and do a three-day hike up the Black Rapids Glacier," Tom said, poking Kenny in the ribs.

Kenny laughed and sat upright, pushing Tom away but accepting his offer. "Since it's your idea, you're the expedition leader and you get to bring the beer."

The early Friday morning two-hour trip to Delta Junction in Tom's Ford pickup provided a magnificent view of the northern slopes of the Alaska Range. Mt. Hayes, Mt. Deborah, and Mt. Hess rose starkly against a clear blue sky to the southeast as they paralleled the silty oxbows of the Tanana River. Kenny and Tom both enjoyed the clear light of Interior Alaska's early morning, so rising at 4 A.M. to head out on a journey into the wilderness was hardly a chore.

Parts of the Richardson Highway pavement were underlain with permafrost which had partially melted and settled unevenly. Being skilled Alaskan drivers, both young men knew how to pour coffee and maintain a cup unspilled as the truck heaved and bounced through the occasional collection of dips and bumps.

"You about ready for some breakfast?" Tom queried as they passed by the Quartz Lake cutoff road a few miles outside Delta Junction.

"Works for me. Let's pull in at the Evergreen Lodge and do a couple stacks of blueberry pancakes."

"Done!" Tom agreed.

The pickup suddenly bounced upward out of a dip which straddled the full width of the road. "Ice lens!" they called out simultaneously, a lowbrow comedy routine which they both believed impressed coeds (particularly freshmen). "Good one. Check the load." Kenny twisted around in the seat and noted that the heavy military surplus canvas cover was still roped down snugly in the bed of the truck.

"Looks good, although we just passed a 30-H.P. Evinrude outboard with a jet unit that looks exactly like yours lying by the side of the road back there. It's amazing what people will throw away with all the pipeline money flowing around these days."

Tom grinned at his cousin while deftly maneuvering the Ford around another series of dips and heaves in the mangled asphalt. "Could you imagine traveling the full 360 miles of this highway from Fairbanks to Valdez over two mountain passes in the winter in a horse-drawn sledge?"

"Actually, I could, although it would've admittedly been quite a challenge. I think the best part would have been the roadhouses along the way."

"I'll bet those intrepid souls never dreamed that a 48-inch

diameter hot oil pipeline would be winding its way down the same path three quarters of a century later," Tom added as the truck rumbled down a hill approaching the Tanana River bridge. The concrete footings for a second, modern, river-spanning structure were being poured by pipeline work crews on each shore of the river. Tom slowed the truck to watch. Kenny sat upright in the bench seat of the pickup truck as they passed over the river. He was observing the river level as much as the work crews.

"These guys are really going full bore, aren't they?" Kenny said as the truck continued to head southeast, now following the weaving channels of the silty Delta River.

"You bet. Serious dinero at stake here. Rock bottom minimum: about one-quarter of a trillion dollars, and probably twice that if the price of a barrel stays above $20 and other fields are proven in the area around the main Prudhoe Bay reservoir."

Kenny slumped back down into the seat, sliding his right foot up on the dashboard to get comfortable. "Serious dinero, indeed," he confirmed, staring off into the clear azure sky above the looming mountains. He thought again of the archeological site at Pump Station No. 1 where he had discovered the spear, and then of the graceful way in which his mother had held the implement at the museum. He remembered her words, and today, felt the thrill of a hunter. He slid upright again in the seat with a fresh charge of mental energy rushing through him as they approached the neat wooden Welcome to Delta Junction sign on the outskirts of town.

"Bean time!" they shouted in unison.

An hour later, the truck was topped off with fuel, and the explorers were topped off with blueberry pancakes and bacon. The Richardson Highway out of Delta veered in a more southerly direction. The road smoothed out now they were on higher ground heading up into the northern foothills of the Alaska Range, still paralleling the turbulent Delta River. A few miles south of Delta they passed Fort Greeley, the U.S. Army's Cold Regions Test Center. The road eased over a small rise forested with dwarf aspen and spruce trees, and a five-mile straight stretch opened across a valley, and disappeared over a distant ridge. On the west side of the road in the distance, the smooth round hump of Donnelly Dome rose nearly 2,000 feet above the glacial plain.

Lying in the valley on the east side of the road were several white geodesic domes housing a radar installation for the Army base. Sharply offsetting the broad, green expanse of the valley, the geodesics appeared as artifacts of some giant ethereal golf course, teed up and awaiting some godlike thundering voice to call out "Fore!" while a 1,000-yard-long golf club arced out of the sky to meet the radar-equipped golf balls. "Nice weather. Looks like the Jolly Green Giant might be out to shoot a few holes today." Tom smiled and shook his head at Kenny.

Past Donnelly Dome the road again met the Delta River with its milk-chocolate-colored water churning over the rocky rubble of the wide valley. They passed Black Rapids Lodge, and turned off on a small access road to the river which ended on a boulder-strewn shore. Tom parked the truck on a level spot and the two young men hopped out into the cool breeze of the morning.

Black Rapids Glacier was visible across the Delta River, which was nearly an eighth of a mile across at this point. A creek extended several kilometers up toward the receding ice mass nestled into a U-shaped valley rimmed by tall, snow-capped peaks of the Alaska Range. The nearly 14,000-foot summit of Mt. Hayes was just visible to the west over the top of the peaks immediately surrounding the glacier.

Kenny and Tom stood quietly taking in the vista, and letting the steady rushing noise of the river and breeze replace the whining of the tires. The sky was crystal clear, and the sun shone broadly on the brilliant white of the mountain peaks. Alaska embraced the two young men in all her glory, seductively presenting the timeless palette of ancient and new wilderness, while simultaneously overwhelming every human sense with pure sound, smells, and light. A cool breeze descending from the glacier through the valley only heightened the experience by sharpening nerve endings. Finally, when the sheer beauty and awe of the scene were the dominant element of their consciousness, a hawk streaked silently downward into their field of view and disappeared into the forest further downstream.

"This is awesome," Tom sighed.

"Indeed. Let's go exploring."

Within half an hour, a twelve-foot inflatable Zodiac raft stood ready on the shore of the river, and the two young men muscled the Evinrude onto the wood motor mount on the back of the craft. Kenny strapped in the dry bags with their camping gear and supplies. Meanwhile, Tom penciled a note that they were crossing the river and heading toward the glacier, folded it and stuffed it into a plastic bag which he wedged into the window of the truck. The canvas tarp was left in the back of the truck covering two spare five-gallon gas cans, but otherwise the vehicle was locked up and secure. Tom handed Kenny the spare truck key before they slipped into their rainproof windbreakers and strapped into lifejackets. Both men were wearing hip waders with the straps cut off so they could remove them quickly in an accident with the raft.

Kenny and Tom eased the back of the Zodiac into an eddy of the river, just submerging the jet unit. The Evinrude came alive in a steady drone on Tom's second pull of the starter cord. A waft of blue smoke curled away from the engine dissipating in the steady breeze following the rushing river downstream. "Ready?" Tom queried. "Let's do it," Kenny replied, and they slid the Zodiac into the cold turbid river. Tom switched the motor into forward and throttled up, turning the bow out from the shore, then quickly downstream into an open channel. The Zodiac jumped up on step instantly with a twist of the throttle, as Kenny leaned forward in the front of the boat to weight down the bow.

Tom banked the agile craft to the left, and began weaving through boulders in the river toward the opposite shore and the mouth of the stream channel leading up to the glacier. A blast of gritty, wind-scattered spray blew over the bow as Tom turned the Zodiac directly into the swift current, throttling down enough to hold the boat in a nearly steady position while remaining on step. A three-foot standing wave curled menacingly near the bow. He mentally traced the last few moves through the silty channels of the river to reach the far shore, while slowly crabbing the gray boat to the right across the river channel. Finally, a hundred feet out from the mouth of the glacier creek, he banked the Zodiac hard to the right with more throttle and aimed straight into the mouth of the creek. Within seconds the inflatable boat safely entered the much calmer mouth of the creek and touched bottom. Tom revved the engine hard and the boat leapt over the small gravel bar at the confluence of the creek and river, and the water deepened again.

The Zodiac skimmed easily up the smaller stream, which was perhaps thirty yards across and several feet deep for most of a half mile. The boat slipped over the rounded rocks and gravel bars of the creek with ease for the first quarter mile, then began to fall off step. Tom revved the engine as the craft settled further into the water, finally touching bottom as he nosed it toward the north shore of the creek. Tom killed the engine as Kenny jumped out with a rope and waded the last few yards toward the shore in shallow water. Kenny held the rope steady while his cousin propped up the motor and produced an over-sized screw driver from the plastic pail which functioned as a tool kit. While Tom pried out the gravel stuck in the jet unit, Kenny looked back across the Delta River. The truck sat serenely on the far shore waiting for their return.

Being a skilled jet unit field surgeon, Dr. Tom had extracted the gravel within a minute and was ready to restart the engine. "How's the creek look from up there?"

"Looks like an okay channel for maybe an eighth of a mile or so, then it gets pretty rocky. We might want to walk it from there."

"Okay, let's do it." Tom restarted the venerable Evinrude with a single pull of the starter cord. Kenny moved way up into the bow as a counterweight to the motor and Tom in the back as the engine revved. The Zodiac jumped up on step and the next several hundred yards of creek slipped under the boat in less than a minute. Again the Zodiac scraped bottom, but this time Tom quickly tilted the motor forward slightly, preventing gravel from being sucked into the jet unit.

The creek was getting steeper and the craft had to work ever harder for each gain in upstream position. The next hundred yards took nearly five minutes of running, pulling up the motor and revving back up on step again. Finally Tom nosed the bow toward the shore and revved the engine one last time. The boat quickly came to a stop and Kenny jumped out with the bow line. "Enough fun for me," Tom said as he tilted the motor forward and locked it into upright position.

Kenny nodded in agreement and together they slid the boat

completely out of the water using the side handles for leverage. With the gear removed from the boat, they slid it even further up on shore, now some twenty-five feet from the water, above the highest visible recent high-water mark for the creek. Kenny fastened the bowline around a large boulder as a final safety anchor. "If the creek rises enough to move that boulder, it can have the boat, because I, for one, don't want to be on the water at that time. I'll just hook up a ride with Noah instead."

Tom grinned at his cousin's effort, and began unfastening his life jacket. With all the boat-related gear secured in dry bags or stuffed under the bow cover, the remaining camping and field equipment was reduced to just two comfortable pack frames. They paused for a water and apple break before continuing up the reach of the creek. The mouth of the glacier valley loomed ahead now. A steady breeze rolled directly down at them on the final mile and a half of the rubble-strewn glacial valley as they started hiking up the creek.

The afternoon sun was far to the west now, painting a warm pattern of amber colors on the peaks of the mountains rising steeply above Kenny and Tom. The breeze rolling down the long narrow glacial valley had quieted as the sun settled lower in the sky. Tom scanned the ridge line opposite a small hill they climbed to get a better view of the valley and the face of the glacier. He was sitting on the ground resting his elbows on his knees to steady the Bushnell binoculars. "Sheep! Eight total, one serious ram, at least a full curl and a half."

"Where?" Kenny asked, looking up from the map he was seriously studying.

"Opposite ridge, three o'clock, up twenty degrees." Tom handed Kenny the black binoculars. He sat next to Tom, and peered through the ten-power lenses. The gray and brown rocks of the distant ridge came sharply into focus. The snow-white hides of the sheep stood out clearly in the sun.

"Yup. There he is. Grand Master of the ridge. A right handsome fellow. Looks like a whole flock of ewes madly in love with him, too," Kenny lowered the binoculars. With a fix on the location he could see the Dall sheep without binoculars. He handed them back to Tom, who was leaning back on his elbows now with a long, thoughtful look in his eyes.

"I hear the gears clanking, cousin Tom. Those sheep are at

least three miles away and 2,000 feet up, and there is a glacier between us and them. Furthermore it is a week until hunting season and we have a job to do."

"I know, I know. Just daydreaming. Nice just to see them and know they're making more."

Kenny had returned to his map while Tom was admiring the large ram and his extended family sunning themselves on the narrow grassy ledge above the glacier in the distance. Kenny noted that the glacier had receded at least another half mile since the U.S.G.S. map was last drawn in 1967. "I know why they call her the Galloping Glacier," he said. "Look at this!" Tom set the binoculars carefully down on his pack and looked over at the map, then up at the glacier. "Caramba. That feller's crawled back up into the valley a fair bit in the last decade. Look at the creek line on the map, and where it is now."

Kenny checked the map and then the valley floor beneath them, nodding in confirmation. "Shifted from north side to south side, almost completely across the valley floor, didn't it?"

"Plan suggestion. We walk transects between here and the river north to south, then south to north at 100-yard intervals, side by side. We should be able to cover most of the ground between here and the big rubble pile off the face of the glacier." Tom pointed to the west at the receding glacier.

"Campsite?" Kenny asked.

"Let's see what we find, but knock off in time to head back to the Zodiac if we decide. It's only an hour or so away, and there was a sheltered area with some spruce and aspen nearby."

"Good plan. Let's do it."

Pioneering vegetation was reclaiming the valley floor. Grasses, fireweed, willows, and several clusters of small spruce and birch were bedding into the silty soil between boulders strewn about by the glacier. Tom and Kenny paced ahead steadily down toward the creek, viewing from side to side. They arrived at the creek within fifteen minutes, and stopped to admire the chocolate-brown silty water swirling noisily down the valley toward where they had landed the Zodiac. Then they turned upstream and hiked about 100 yards, turned back to the north and began working across the valley to the north again. On the third north-to-south transect, about halfway to the creek, Kenny stopped and called out to Tom. "Tracks. Grizzly. Small but less than one week old." Tom nodded and motioned to continue.

Kenny followed the tracks down to the river where they turned toward the glacial rubble pile. Tom walked up to Kenny's location and inspected the tracks, which were partially eroded by the creek just ahead. "Young one. Probably having sheep-hunting daydreams," Tom chuckled. "No other tracks about, so it looks like he passed through, climbed up over the rubble pile at the face of the glacier and continued south, maybe up through the pass. Keep your eyes open cousin Kenny, just in case he's hanging in the rocks waiting for some sheep to come down off the ridge onto the valley floor to lunch on some fresh grass here."

The next transect was within 200 yards of the final rubble pile in front of the glacier. The cold of the ice was driving the early-evening temperature downward rapidly now. Kenny's path was intersected by the face of a ledge of silt and gravel, taller than he was. Tom had already gone up the same rise, which was a more gentle slope along his path. At about 100 more yards up the line Tom stopped, noting that Kenny had not come up over the ledge yet. He turned and waited for Kenny to catch up, admiring the face of the glacier over the top of the rubble pile. The Black Rapids Glacier was streaked with grit, rock and sand, particularly at this time of the year when the first snow was still at least a month away. Under the gritty, broken upper crust of ice and melting snow, slivers of deep crystalline blue peered out like sapphires. The hard, pure ice of the interior of the glacier mirrored the deepening blue of the Alaska sky. Tom shivered as the cool of the evening and the proximity to the face of the glacier began to suggest it was getting close to time to set up camp. Still no Kenny.

Tom walked back to the edge of the rise toward Kenny's location. Kenny was crouching down at the face of the silt ledge. His pack was off, leaning against a boulder behind him. Tom called to him, "Find something?"

Kenny looked up with a huge smile and nodded at Tom. Even at fifty yards away, Tom could see Kenny's eyes sparkle. He quickly covered the short distance and saw what had captured his cousin's fascination. A set of six giant rib bones was just visible in the face of the ledge, spaced perhaps one foot apart. About three to four feet of each rib was visible in the center, and less toward the edges where the natural arc of the rib cage disappeared into the silt and sand of the vertical ledge. "Mammoth!" Kenny exclaimed. "We found one. And if these ribs are any indication, the rest is right here in the ledge."

"All right!" Tom exclaimed in approval. Kenny stood and the two young men clasped hands in a congratulatory pause. "Photos first," Kenny said, going to work. "Then we plan an excavation." Tom looked up at the deepening blue of the sky and shivered again. "Photos and planning tonight," he agreed, "then we go make camp."

Kenny was ready to work all night. In his eagerness he was ignoring his own shivering. Tom grinned at him. "Those aren't the goose bumps of discovery, Kenny. We need to get away from the face of this glacier, build a fire and have something hot to eat. Then we need a good night's sleep so we can work a full day on this fella. He's been here for 10,000 years. He'll be here tomorrow. If we don't do as I suggest, Mr. Archaeologist, our hypothermic bodies just might join our ancient friend in his eternal reverie."

Kenny shivered again, now becoming aware of the evening chill. The windbreakers they had on for hiking were fine for walking while generating body heat, but were thin cover for standing near the face of a glacier at the onset of an Alaska night.

"Okay, Tom. You're right. But we need at least some discovery photos." Tom snapped several careful shots of the area, of the rib cage as they had found it, of Kenny by the rib cage, and finally of them both at the find, using the timer on the 35-mm Pentax. The fact they were using a flash for the photos was the final nudge they needed to get the last hour of hiking out of the way back to the Zodiac where dinner, a tent, and goosedown sleeping bags awaited them. It was a spirited walk back.

One of the great joys of living in Alaska was being able to savor a clear, starlit night in the depth of the wilderness beside a campfire. Shadows of the two young men flickered on the face of the tent perched in a clearing behind them. The soft volatile spruce ignited the fire quickly, but the long slow burn was from the hard, fine-grained birch. The fire had mellowed over the last hour, darkening the campsite as the last embers of twilight faded in the northwest sky.

The glacial creek murmured in the background just out of the field of view, and the bow of the Zodiac was still visible in the darkening night nearly a hundred yards from the campfire. Kenny and Tom were not surprised when a long green arc began to trace across the sky from northwest to southeast. The dance of aurora had begun. Their camp site was blanketed with moss and grasses, providing a fine surface to lie back upon and watch the energy of the northern lights build, luminesce, and entertain.

Ionized particles blown out from solar eruptions perhaps four days ago had been captured in earth's magnetosphere only 93 million miles into their journey. Trapped in magnetic lines of force, the leading edge of the wave of particles descended quickly down an invisible funnel terminating at the magnetic north pole in northern Canada. But some 500 miles up, some of the particles began to collide with the upper atmosphere. Electrons quickly shifted to higher, then back to lower orbital shells in each of the colliding particles, and the excess energy dissipated as light. As the leading edge of the solar wave descended to about 100 miles above the surface of the planet, the funnel sliced precisely over the top of the Tanana Valley. Electronic monitoring equipment at the Geophysical Institute of the University of Alaska and at its privately owned rocket launching facility at Poker Flats twenty-five miles to the northeast began to download a flood of incoming data. This was going to be a big one.

"Good lord! Look at that!" Tom exclaimed as the bottom edge of the green arc sharpened in contrast, twisted into a ribbon and began to glow with a reddish hue. The intensity grew even more, as the ribbon began to pulse in waves across the entire north-to-south length. Then streaks of green began to shoot across the sky in another arc further to the northeast, and within seconds, a mirror image of the first auroral band was gyrating silently in the starlit sky. "Shadows," Kenny whispered as if to not disturb the silence of the auroral show. "It's so bright it's casting shadows." Tom turned to look at the ground and saw what Kenny had noticed.

"Listen," Tom whispered. Kenny sat up and could hear a faint hiss in the background, which did not match the murmur of the creek or the gentle brushing sound of the aspen leaves twisting slowly in the breeze. The hiss was more like radio static now, growing in intensity as a third arc erupted in the night sky even further to the northeast. Three giant auroral arcs now pulsed with growing energy, twisting and curling in sharp-edged ribbons with waves shooting through their entire 200- to 300-mile visible length. "I think it's generating static electricity," Tom said. Kenny stood up now, head tilted back and cupping his ears away from the creek. "Yup. Loud and clear. Got a light bulb we can screw into the ground to check it out?"

"Not on me," Tom chuckled. Man, I've seen a lot of auroras, but this one is hot!"

Both young men were now standing with their backs to the fire, watching the brilliant display as two of the three arcs sliced through the familiar star pattern of the Big Dipper. Kenny turned slightly to the southeast, then reached over and tugged at Tom's sleeve.

"Check that out. Tom turned to witness the beginning of the next light show. The moon, in three-quarter phase, had risen quietly in the background of the noisy auroral show, and was now passing between two mountain peaks. The aurora was casting shadows on the snow of the mountains, hissing with energy and streaking furiously across the sky. Meanwhile, the cool, mellow light of the moon had begun to enter the scene, backlighting the valley in a celestial encore to the aurora.

"If it gets any better than this, I think I will likely forget to breathe," Kenny said. Tom nodded in agreement as he watched the third auroral arc begin to fade. Kenny turned to walk away from the campfire, toward the glacier. "Nature calls," he told Tom as he headed out of the edge of the wooded area to a place where he could mark their territory.

"Good call," Tom observed, and joined him. Both young men selected a willow bush and watered away. They had established the convention years ago that if one was to recycle nutrients in the wilderness, one might as well feed a willow bush that would someday feed a moose, that might someday feed your family so you could go back out and water another willow bush and so forth.

Upon completion of the recycling mission, Tom turned back toward camp and observed the auroral display and the moon again. The second arc had now faded, and the first arc was dividing into regions of green and red spears, still with a high energy level, but long and thin now, rather than in broad curtains. "Tom! Look at the glacier!" Kenny exclaimed. "It's glowing!"

Tom turned and gasped. "What in blazes is that!" he asked as he saw the reddish glow emanating from beneath the mottled snow layer on top of the ice.

"It's got to be a reflection of the aurora," Kenny offered. "But it's incredibly bright."

Tom glanced back and saw that the aurora was indeed bright red now, but not as bright or focused as the light which seemed to be emanating from within the mass of glacial ice. "This is eerie," Kenny said, noting the red of the aurora, too. "Just too weird." They watched for perhaps five minutes more as the internal red glow inside the ice slowly changed to a green hue, then faded out. Overhead, the aurora had begun the same color change, ramping down to a lower energy level. The fire of the northern lights seemed to have been quenched by the cooler yellow light of the moon. The glow inside the glacier was gone now.

"I have never seen anything like that before, and I am having a hard time believing that was just a reflection from the aurora. It was just too bright and focused. More like a point source, like a floodlight inside the glacier," Kenny said.

"I agree." Tom shrugged. "But unless we hack our way into the ice, we probably will not be able to confirm it. I think the show is over now, and we need to get some sleep. We have a mammoth to wake up in the morning."

"We should have tried to get a photo of the glow in the glacier. No one is going to believe us when we tell them what we saw. Something is going on inside that block of ice, Tom. Something that needs to be figured out."

"Probably. I am fairly certain, though, that when we tell the folks at the Gee Whiz Institute on campus that we saw a floodlight inside a 10,000-year-old glacier while we were listening to the aurora that they will be all over themselves to come right out and start digging into the ice."

Kenny looked at Tom and laughed. "Cynics. They're all nothing but a bunch of cynics. Too many hours in front of CRTs and behind the lenses of 3 million A.S.A. cameras. They just don't have a sense of adventure. Cynics, all. To bed, comrade. On the morrow we shall bring the cynics bones of a great beast and humble them before our archeological skills and tales of daring." Tom laughed as they headed off to the tent and the soft goosedown of warm sleeping bags.

Kenny watched his mother's hands sway gently over her head as she danced to the murmur of the stream and the rhythmic thump of a skin drum. The glacier glowed deep red behind her, pulsing to the rhythm of the drum. Braids of her long black hair brushed the back of her ornately beaded caribou skin dress, as she turned slowly around toward the drummer. Her eyes were closed, her head rocking gently back and forth, then she opened her eyes and smiled serenely at the drummer, Kenny's father. The intensity of the drumming increased as his father's eyes smiled back at his wife and her lovely dance. She spun around now, lowering her hands, slowly crouching to the ground, and then settled into a position kneeling on one knee.

The drumming stopped, and only the murmur of the stream continued. Kenny saw that she was inside the upraised bleached rib bones of a mammoth. She reached down and picked up a glowing red orb from a crevasse in the vertebrae. Its smooth, glass-like surface changed color to a deep blue where her fingers touched it. The crystalline orb filled her hands and pulsed with color. The light in the glacier changed to the same deep blue, and began to pulse with the same rhythm. She turned and rose, arms extended, and presented the glowing orb to Kenny. He reached out, hands upturned and accepted the object. It was smooth and warm to the touch. In his hands, its color began to change to green. Holding the object, he felt a static tingle as it began to hum faintly.

At first the tone was a single note, then it increased in volume until a second harmonic above, and then another below the first note became distinct. The object began slowly rotating in his hand, changing color in various shades of green, blue, and red as the volume of the harmonic chord increased. The orb became warmer as the rotational rate increased. Then the object levitated upward out of his upturned palms, spinning even more rapidly, and the volume of the tone grew. Kenny's hair began to stand up on his head, charged with static electricity from the object. At least five octaves of the single chord could now clearly be heard, two above and two below the first.

Suddenly, the light inside the orb burst out in a spiral, filling the air around Kenny. Static was so intense he felt himself become lighter, almost rising off of the ground where he stood. Expanding light was followed by more octaves of the tonal chord above and below the first five, with the lowest tones increasing in volume below the range of hearing. The sound from the spinning, translucent orb echoed from within the glacier now, with ever-deepening tones. The upper octaves began to fade even as the lower ones strengthened. Then the earth began to resonate to the harmonics. Kenny could see the ground began to move, but could not feel it, as he began to realize that he and the spinning orb were hovering in the air.

In a final wave, the tone deepened, intensified, and fell completely below the range of hearing. Kenny could see the face of the glacier heaving in tectonic waves until a huge frontal slab calved off and thundered to the ground in slow motion. A bright area of red light now was plainly visible low in the front of the ice mass. It was circular and rotating like the orb above his hands. The two spheres spun in perfect precision of motion and light as the ground swayed hard. In the mountains above the glacier, high in the steep cirques, avalanches began to cascade down into the valley, dislodged by the intense movement of the ground. Kenny dreamed now that he could hear a voice calling to him ….

"Wake up Kenny! Earthquake! Wake up!" Tom shouted, tugging at Kenny's sleeping bag. "It's a big one!" Kenny sat up quickly, feeling nauseated from the swaying of the ground and from the intensity of the dream. The tent shook violently as the ground heaved up and down. Tom had a flashlight on now, and Kenny finally was fully awake. "Holy cow!" Kenny muttered halfheartedly as the two frantically fought the zippers on their sleeping bags. Finally out of the bags and with unlaced boots slipped on, they unzipped the front of the tent and scurried out.

The tremors subsided, but the distant roar of avalanches echoed off the walls of the valley behind the glacier for several more seconds. Predawn twilight was rising in the northeast, just enough so they could see the outline of the mountain rising above them, and confirm that there was no danger of avalanches or rock slides in their immediate vicinity. "Whoa. That was incredible. You okay, Kenny?" Tom asked as he arced the flashlight around to find the Zodiac still safely perched where they had beached it the previous day.

"I think so," Kenny replied. "I was having an incredible dream about the mammoth skeleton, the glacier and, I think, this earthquake." He paused for a moment looking up at the faint green of the rising twilight. "There was something else, though," he said hesitantly. "A round object about the size of a softball. It was self-levitating, full of colors, sound, and static electricity. I mean it was so real that I could feel it. It was smooth and warm, and came from inside the mammoth. Mom was dancing in my dream, inside the rib cage of the mammoth, and she handed it to me. The tone from the spinning orb seemed to resonate in the glacier, then built up to a volume that started this earthquake. Tom, this was just too real. There is something inside that glacier. It is large, spherical, it spins and changes color, and has musical tones."

Tom looked long and hard at his cousin. "You had a vision, my half-Athabaskan friend, didn't you?" Kenny just looked up at Tom and nodded.

"Something is there, Tom. Something important. I know it and I felt it."

Tom put his hand on Kenny's shoulder, and turned his head toward the glacier. The outline of the ice mass was faintly visible in the emerging twilight. "I think you may be right, Kenny. That light last night from inside the glacier was not anything explainable by our current understanding of how things work. It's early, but I think I'm ready to boil up a pot of coffee and go look at the skeleton and the glacier again." Kenny nodded again and bent down to tie his shoelaces.

The silt around the mammoth's ribs had been partly washed away by the surging stream during the earthquake. A huge part of the front of the glacier had calved away and fallen into a pool of water, which had washed up the bank of the stream and reached the mammoth skeleton. "It's a damn good thing we weren't camped on the edge of the stream," Tom observed when he saw the bleached bones of the mammoth arcing gracefully out of the eroded hillside. The flood line was clearly visible down the creek, and their footprints from the previous day were gone.

Kenny scrambled down the hillside and began digging in the center of the rib cage near the vertebrae. Still keeping an eye on his cousin, Tom climbed up on a rubble pile above the find and examined the glacier. The front of the ice mass was now perhaps a hundred yards further back, with the residue of the first hundred yards piled up like a giant bag of spilled ice cubes. Tom could see that the pile would melt away quickly, perhaps not by this winter, but certainly by midsummer next year. Whatever might be in that glacial mass would be a whole lot more accessible then. He turned to look down at Kenny, and gasped at what he saw.

Kenny stood upright in the center of the rib cage, hands outstretched with palms up. A round, glass-like, silt-coated sphere was in his hands. Kenny gently brushed away the silt, and the sphere glowed slightly where it had been touched. It was a gentle green color, like the earlier twilight which was resolving itself into the warmth of morning. Kenny looked up at Tom, still holding the orb in his outstretched hands. The orb glowed faintly. "Let's take our little friend home," Kenny finally said. "Let's see what it has to say." Tom nodded slowly in agreement, glancing back at the rubble pile of glacial ice. They would be back.

CHAPTER 3

The Beacon
Spring, A.D. 1975

Kenny first noticed her very bright red hair, then her intensely green eyes. It was almost enough to make a student consider mathematics as a course of study. "Hi. I'm Kenny Swanson. You must be Shanna."

"So you're the one," she said in a very lovely voice. "You created quite a stir with your little crystal. Thanks for coming over. I think you'll be interested in what we've found."

The early morning light of April was visible outside the window of the small office in the Geophysical Institute. On the distant horizon, sharp lines of Mt. Hess, Mt. Deborah, and Mt. Hayes stood like teeth of a giant chainsaw. The sun, rising in a low arc east of the peaks, cast a reddish tint to the sky accenting her hair like a halo. Kenny was completely transfixed by the color of the sky and her hair as he started to sit down.

Looking straight ahead, he completely missed the chair and crashed loudly to the floor beside her desk. "Ow. Damn it. Sorry, I ... uh ...." He looked sheepishly up from his sitting position on the floor.

"Have a seat, Kenny," she laughed.

"Fine, thank you, but I am already quite comfortable. Old Athabaskan tradition. We usually just sit on the floor. Cultural sort of thing." He smiled. Kenny was quick. Clumsy, perhaps, but quick.

Still giggling, she brushed her hair to one side over her shoulder. "No really, go ahead and use a chair. Being from New England, I find some of the local customs entertaining but not critical to my scientific pursuits." Kenny nodded an okay, then jumped up smartly and settled into the squeaky-wheeled chair.

"Actually, I rarely fall down when I meet people for the first time. You were saying about your findings."

Shanna smiled again and reached for a stack of papers held together with a binder clip. "Your little orb is almost perfectly spherical, Kenny, with an extraordinary degree of precision." Kenny sat back and got a bit more serious. "How so?"

She turned and picked up a small hard plastic case from the corner of the desk and handed it to him. He examined the contents through the clear plastic window, since the case was completely sealed and apparently could not be opened without some sort of special tool. "Those are precision titanium ball bearings. They were centrifugally cast from molten metal in the Skylab space station in 1973. They are very precisely round, with a variance of less than a ten millionth of their diameter. If these bearings were used in a standard automobile with a V-8 engine that usually gets, let's say, fifteen miles per gallon, that vehicle would probably get closer to 150 miles per gallon with these."

"Whew," Kenny whistled looking at the three tiny marbleized ball bearings in the case. "Pretty expensive, I bet."

"Yes. About ten thousand dollars each at current prices, including launch cost, partial amortization of the Apollo vehicle, and the launch facility. But—" she paused. "These are stone age compared to your find. The roundness of the orb, which we still do not know the composition of yet by the way, is at least one hundred trillion times more precisely spherical. That is as far as we can presently measure, and that is a bit of an educated guess. In other words, your automobile would get something in the magnitude of about the distance between here and the center of the galaxy per gallon. We're talking pretty round."

Kenny knew that when the physicists at the University of Alaska had started to examine the object, they had soon decided to bring in help. Shanna McLane was a Ph.D. student in theoretical mathematics from Harvard, and was one of a team of eight physics and math specialists studying the orb in a special project on the UAF campus. But up to now he had only been aware that they were running various tests and measurements on it, trying to decipher its still plentiful mysteries.

"There's more. The math and physics team would like to interview you if that's okay. We are interested in its light and tonal qualities. The problem is, its characteristics seem to vary with each person who comes in contact with it. We want to measure what it does when you are near."

Kenny sat back in his chair and felt a tingle go straight up his spine to the top of his head. "Okay. But if that's what you're interested in, I may have another twist for you."

Shanna became very alert. At twenty-one years old, her intuitive, mathematically advanced brain had moved her quickly through an accelerated high school and undergraduate career. She had a knack for finding the unusual in a pattern of numbers (she had discovered one new prime number already during a master's project) and had an ability to spot the extraordinary in natural patterns. Her specialty was chaos theory. Kenny's light blue eyes churned with chaos right now, and Shanna could sense that. "Okay, she said. What would that be?"

"My mother," he said directly.

Shanna leaned back in her chair and studied Kenny's black, curly hair, wondering where in his genetic history those misty blue eyes came from. She now felt a tingling in her spine, which she knew would herald a discovery. "Your mother?"

"Yes, my mother."

The physics lab had been set up like a recording studio, with microphones, tape recorders, and video cameras. Oscilloscopes and other instruments with CRT's were alive and pulsing, ready to accept electronic information through a number of sensors which could be taped to the skin, or attached to a grid of support stands around an open area in the center of the lab. The room was filled with a collection of scientists and graduate students, plus a few administrator types trying to understand why the National Science Foundation had been so willing to dispatch a $5 million grant for this project with so little encouragement.

Shanna worked with Kenny in the center of the lab, taping several electronic sensors to his temples, arms, and the back of his hands. He stood in the center of an area with a red circle about one and one-half meters in diameter drawn on the floor with a magic marker. The surface of the circle was covered with a plate of glass, and underneath the glass was an additional array of sensors which could read static electric voltage, magnetic fields, and a host of other parameters. Kenny wore a UAF Nanooks basketball team T-shirt, so his arms were bare. He had removed his shoes and socks, and now stood barefoot on the glass circle. He was glad they had not asked him to take off his Levi's. He had started to get worried when they began asking him to shed various layers of clothing.

Shanna finished attaching the last of the taped sensors to the back of his hand, and stepped back looking him over. She studied the position of the array of probes and sensors which nearly completely surrounded Kenny like a cage. "Okay. Extend your arms and turn in a full circle slowly clockwise, then back counterclockwise." She leaned toward him with twinkling eyes, and added in a whisper, "Try not to fall down this time." Kenny rolled his eyes and began turning as requested.

Betty Swanson watched the pretty red-haired young woman lean forward to whisper something to her son. She smiled. She was very proud of Kenny and was fascinated with the "experiment" as he had referred to it. Kenny had related the story of his and Tom's discovery to his Mom and Dad, and to his brother and sisters. Tim, Carla, and Missy had been particularly fascinated with their older brother's story of the earthquake, and their discovery of the bear tracks by the creek. The science part of the discovery was lost to them somewhere behind the adventure part. Carl Swanson had absorbed it all, though. He knew Kenny had discovered something important, and was fascinated with the growing magnitude of scientific investigation. Carl stood quietly beside his wife, and also noticed the bright red hair of the pretty young scientist as she worked with his son. He smiled, too.

Kenny had presented the orb to Dr. Wescott in the museum when he and Tom returned from the Black Rapids Glacier the previous fall. Winter arrived suddenly after that, quickly eliminating any possibility of returning to the site for further investigation until the following spring. The plan to return to the site was being mobilized now, with Kenny as a principal investigator. Tom was also involved, leading the organization of the field equipment and logistics. Dr. Wescott had examined the orb, and immediately pulled together a team of the top scientists from every department in the University.

A research plan was originally designed using only nondestructive testing. The object was not to be dissected, drilled or otherwise damaged, according to the plan. Those early precautions had proven to be needless when they discovered that the sphere was virtually indestructible. In fact, no one had so much as a clue how they could get it apart even if they wanted to. The mechanical engineering department had damaged or ruined several tension meters, vises, and finally drill bits before they determined that, short of explosives, this thing was going to stay intact. And no one was even sure about explosives, conventional or otherwise. That was the first week. By the end of the second week, the NSF grant had been solicited, and a national team assembled. Kenny had only seen the orb through the wall of a glass case twice since it had been handed off to the physics and math team. Now, for the first time since he removed it from his back pack and handed it to Dr. Wescott, he would again touch the sphere.

Dr. George Tamura from UCLA was the physics team leader. When Shanna finished attaching the skin sensors to Kenny, she retired to a set of monitors at a lab table a few meters away. Dr. Tamura walked to the center of the room and approached Kenny. "Thank you for your cooperation, Mr. Swanson. We greatly appreciate your help."

Kenny nodded and smiled. "Sure, Dr. Tamura. Anything I can do to help figure out what this is all about is fine with me." Dr. Tamura then opened a stainless steel case on a mobile lab cart near the experimental platform. In the case the orb rested in a padded insert molded to the diameter of the sphere. He removed the top half of the case and set it on the cart. Dr. Tamura paused to look around the room at the array of researchers and observers to make sure everyone was ready, then picked up the bottom half of the case.

Kenny looked at the orb. Translucent and lifeless, it reflected the dark velvet color of the padding in the case, but otherwise looked simply like a small glass ball. Dr. Tamura nodded to Kenny to take the orb. "Pick it up and hold it, please. Handle it however it seems natural to you, but please turn around several times as you do so the full field of the sensors is exposed to whatever might occur. Okay, everybody. Stay alert."

Kenny picked up the orb with his right hand, and lifted it just high enough to raise it out of the dimple in the case, then slid his left hand under it. Dr. Tamura lowered the case away, set it on the lab cart and walked back to his lab table to observe. Kenny held his arms out in front of him with palms up. Tom was standing beside his aunt and uncle across the room. "That is how Kenny held it when he recovered it from the mammoth skeleton," Tom explained quietly. Betty and Carl nodded in confirmation and all three watched Kenny intently.

Kenny began to turn clockwise slowly, still holding the orb in his extended hands. As he turned he saw Shanna studying him carefully. Her green eyes sparkled in the late afternoon light filtering in through the windows which were partially shielded with venetian blinds. He paused in his circular path when he saw her and smiled. She smiled back and his hands suddenLy began to feel warm. The orb glowed faintly as several of the researchers suddenly came to attention.

Dr. Tamura nodded and observed silently. Kenny continued until he had turned a full circle facing away from Shanna. The glow in the orb faded slightly. He then began a slow turn back around, and as he turned toward Shanna, the object glowed green and felt warm to the touch again. He sensed a small static tingle this time, and again paused facing her. The orb was pulsing very gently now. Kenny felt the rhythm and suddenly became aware it was synchronized to his cardiac pulse. He then continued to turn counterclockwise completing the full circle back. The orb was pulsing faintly, but grew dimmer.

Dr. Tamura signaled to him to turn again. Kenny's arms were now beginning to tire a bit, so he pulled the sphere closer to his chest, bending his elbows slightly. As he turned toward Shanna, the light grew again and pulsed with slightly more intensity this time, then faded as he completed the circle. Dr. Tamura signaled again for Kenny to reverse rotation. This time, he noticed his mother and father standing near the back of the room with Tom. He smiled at them and they beamed back. The orb pulsed a slightly different color, more of an aqua hue, then faded back to green when he rotated slowly back to Shanna. Dr. Tamura raised his hand in a signal for Kenny to stop, and then motioned for Shanna to walk forward. She acknowledged and stepped forward to within a meter of the sensor area, directly in front of Kenny. The orb continued to pulse gently at first, then with greater intensity. Dr. Tamura signaled again to Kenny to continue his counterclockwise rotation. As Kenny turned away from Shanna, the light faded slightly, but not as much as previously.

He turned back toward Shanna, still holding the sphere close to his chest. When he was facing her, he extended his arms holding the orb directly below his line of sight to her eyes. The orb began to pulse more rapidly now, and the variety of green hues expanded. He felt the static tingle in his arms and now on his head. The orb began to rotate slowly in his hands and began emitting the melodic tone he had heard in his dream just before the earthquake at the glacier. Within a few seconds, three octaves could be heard distinctly. The volume of the tone grew slightly then leveled off when five octaves became distinct.

The colors were pulsing through several shades of green and the spring rate was constant. The object felt light in Kenny's hands. He slid his right hand under the spinning sphere, and removed his left hand, which he held out through the sensor array toward Shanna. She blushed, then reached up and touched his fingers very slightly with her left hand. At that instant, a second pulsing pattern started, then faded quickly when she suddenly drew her hand away. Dr. Tamura nodded to her, and she reached back up and gently grasped Kenny's outstretched hand.

The second pulsing pattern quickly began again, but was a different color, this time with a more blue tinge. The tonal pattern also changed, no longer simple harmonics of the same note, but rather as a third, creating a warm and beautiful chord. One of the technicians monitoring the sound system gasped and looked up suddenly. The intensity of the light and the sound was growing as the spinning rate of the orb increased. Then, the orb began to slowly levitate above Kenny's outstretched hand. Shanna's mouth opened in amazement, and immediately the second pulsing pattern quickened. It was now beating to her heart rate as well as his. This was the first time the science team had observed levitation of the object, and they were completely awed. Kenny just smiled then looked over at his mother.

Dr. Tamura nodded to Kenny and signaled to Betty Swanson to come down to the center of the room. Her walk down the steps toward the center of the room was graceful. Betty now stood beside Shanna, whom she had only been introduced to an hour before. The two women smiled at each other and then at Kenny. The orb rotated slowly, levitating above his right hand as Betty reached out to also touch Kenny's fingers. She cupped her hand under Kenny's while Shanna's fingers were on top of his hand. When all three were touching, a new tone began to emanate from the spinning orb, this time a fifth harmonic from the first tone. The chord evolved to a deep, melodious drone of perhaps fifty decibels, a bit like an electronic organ.

A third pulsing pattern formed, but with a deep blue light pattern. Betty closed her eyes listening to the music of the spinning sphere. Her other hand began to sway, sweeping the air softly like a feather. She seemed lost in a trance-like state. Her hand then formed a cup facing upward as she brushed the air between her and Kenny in a dance like motion. Suddenly, the orb slipped away from Kenny's upturned hand and moved directly over the top of his mother's upturned palm. She opened her eyes and looked deeply into the dark blue pulsing light of the spinning sphere and slowly raised her other hand under the sphere. Shanna stepped back, and Kenny let his hands settle slowly to his sides.

Betty Swanson held her arms above her head, slightly in front of her. The orb continued to levitate above her cupped hands, spinning and pulsing now in deep blue colors. The tones deepened further, dropping to lower octaves, quickly falling out of the range of hearing. Just as the sound fell below the range of hearing, the room began to vibrate in a harmonic frequency several octaves below the last audible range. The field of light around the orb was now several meters in diameter, and Betty glowed with the light from the sphere. The room began to sway and equipment began to shake. Betty felt the tremor in the room, and reached up and clasped the sphere in her hands. Her silky black hair stood straight out from her head in every direction as the static energy field around the object grounded out.

She looked up at Kenny and Shanna, smiling now, holding the sphere tightly in her hands. It still glowed softly, but was no longer rotating. The sound was gone and the tremors had ceased. Betty walked over and set the orb in the bottom half of the padded storage case, then turned to Dr. Tamura. He was standing completely still, mouth agape at the incredible scene he had just witnessed. She calmly said, "Dr. Tamura, the orb is a beacon. It wants to go back to where Kenny found it. It has something to show you there." She smiled at him, turned and walked over to Kenny and touched his hand gently. Then she turned and smiled at Shanna. "You have beautiful hair, Shanna. It reminds me of the brightest auroras." Betty turned and left the room with Carl, who nodded and waved to Kenny as they departed.

The entire research team sat in stunned silence. They looked as if they had just seen God.

A red and white Alaska Helicopters Bell 206 Jet Ranger moved swiftly up the Delta River valley. The morning sun was rising in the southeast. Kenny watched the shadow of the sleek craft racing along with them like a magic carpet slipping over the wind-drifted snow below the helicopter. Dr. Tamura twisted around from the front passenger's seat and looked back at Kenny and Tom in the back and smiled.

The helicopter passed Donnelly Dome and headed up the valley. Kenny could see the sharp outline of Mt. Hess in the clear, late winter light. Heavy snowfall had left the entire vista buried in a deep blanket of white. The moon, waning in its final crescent stage, hung low in the northwest like a silvery Christmas ornament. Kenny had flown in helicopters only a few times before, and was thrilled to have the opportunity to do so again. This was the way to see Alaska, flying along above the frozen terrain in a warm, transparent bubble, which could stop and hover at will, or land almost anywhere. Even the noisy rotor was muffled to a steady thumping noise inside the machine.

The pilot nosed the chopper down slightly as they passed Black Rapids Lodge, then slowed the Jet Ranger to a hover, turning to the left. Dr. Tamura turned back toward Tom and pointed down at the edge of the River near the Richardson Highway. Tom nodded back, motioning straight down with his index finger through the floor of the hovering helicopter. Dr. Tamura motioned to the pilot who backed the Jet Ranger up and descended to within a hundred feet of the ground. Tom pointed again at the shore, showing where they had parked the truck the previous fall and where they had crossed the Delta River in the Zodiac. He pointed out the path of the stream leading to Black Rapids Glacier. The stream bed was buried in snow.

The pilot skillfully twisted the collective control and the helicopter moved neatly to the right, and down slightly, precisely tracing the path the Zodiac had followed. Tom tapped Dr. Tamura on the shoulder when they reached the point where they had beached the raft and made camp. Dr. Tamura spoke to the pilot through the headset and the pilot deftly lowered the chopper near to the ground. The snow beneath them erupted into a whirlwind, rising, spinning, then flowing away in the wind. The chopper hovered in place about ten meters above the ground effectively clearing a landing spot of loose snow.

Then, with a landing spot opened, Dr. Tamura spoke again to the pilot, who nodded, and eased the collective up. The agile helicopter rose thirty meters like an elevator and began advancing forward toward the face of the glacier. The entire valley of cirque and mountain peaks was bathed in glaring white light.

But for the presence of a rotary-winged aircraft with turbine engines, it could have been a scene from 10,000 B.C. Dr. Tamura sat back in awed delight at the sheer magnificence of the scene. Tom and Kenny both watched him and smiled.

The chopper edged forward, now only a few hundred meters from the face of the glacier, and settled into a hover again. The pilot glanced warily up each of the steep mountainsides. Tom pointed straight down at the location where he thought the mammoth find was, and looked over at Kenny, who was also scanning the area through the window. Kenny looked out the left side of the chopper and nodded his agreement. Dr. Tamura spoke to the pilot again who was still looking up out of the bubble at the mountains. The pilot spoke back briefly, and very slowly lowered the chopper down to the area where the mammoth find lay. Again, the powerful downwash of the rotor blades whipped up the snow beneath them, but this time the fine powder completely enveloped the helicopter, blocking out all visibility.

The pilot quickly lifted the collective and the chopper darted straight up nearly fifty meters, just above the snowstorm they had created. The pilot was shaking his head, and Dr. Tamura was nodding in agreement. They moved back down the creek and slowly settled into the cleared area where the campsite had been. When the ski-shaped runners of the chopper were solidly on the ground, the pilot eased back on the throttle, and the rotor wound down to a steady thump, thump, thump as he let the engine cool off a bit before shutting down. Finally, when the engine was silent, the pilot turned and spoke to all three men. "Max, thirty minutes till I'm going to have to restart before the engine cools too much. Unless we all want to walk back."

"Okay'" Dr. Tamura said. "Let's go have a look."

Even through heavy parkas and snow pants the steady, cold wind let its presence be known. The light was blinding to unprotected eyes, so each man wore ski goggles. Surplus military "bunny boots" provided both excellent traction and protection from the cold. Spring was beginning in the Tanana Valley, but winter was loathe to relax its grip at the face of a glacier on the north side of the Alaska Range. Kenny and Tom spent about ten minutes recalling as precisely as possible the events of their last night and day here the previous fall. Dr. Tamura listened intently, then checked his watch. He glanced back at the pilot who held up ten fingers twice, signaling twenty minutes to go.

Dr. Tamura was busy taking photos, while he and Kenny walked some distance up the creek toward the glacier. The mammoth would be at least a two-hour walk in this snow, which really required snowshoes. They stopped a few hundred meters from the helicopter on a small rise where the face of the glacier could be seen in the distance. The massive rubble pile which had formed in the earthquake was just visible under a deep blanket of snow. Tom, meanwhile, had been busy marking several trees with ribbons of fluorescent surveyor's flagging. He joined the other two. "The heavy snow this year is going to delay this whole operation quite a bit. The glacier has been fed and may even grow some. We'll have to see what the spring thaw looks like before we can make a judgment call on burrowing into the ice."

"It appears as such," Dr. Tamura agreed. "This is a good location to set up a forward research station, though. I think we should proceed as planned with getting some shelter and equipment up here."

"Can do," Tom replied. "The chopper sure is a nice way of getting in here. It beats the Zodiac hands down."

"Yeah, but you miss out on all the fun navigating a three-foot standing wave in fast, silty, freezing water," Kenny added. Dr. Tamura just smiled and motioned that it was time to leave.

After leaving the camp area, they approached the face of the glacier in the chopper one more time. Dr. Tamura continued taking photographs, and studying the scene below. Kenny looked out the side window of the helicopter, straight down over the mammoth find, and studied the site intensely. He closed his eyes and recalled the moment when he had discovered, then lifted the sphere from the cradle of bones below the hovering chopper. Then the Jet Ranger rose, turned and nosed forward, back down the stream toward the Delta River. The gentle, steady rhythm of rotor and the drone of the turbine engine vibrated through the helicopter. The pilot had turned up the cabin heat as the three men removed their heavy parkas. Kenny leaned his head against the side window of the helicopter and felt the sun on his hair.

Kenny watched with curiosity as the tall blond man with silvery blue eyes seated himself by the campfire. He pulled the heavy fur around him and Shanna as the night breeze swirled through the fire, whipping up a small spiral of glowing embers that dissipated in the dark night air as quickly as they formed and rose. The warm fragrance of birch smoke wafted around the three of them. The blond man smiled, and reached forward with a small hand-held device with tiny flashing lights. He nodded to Kenny and Shanna, as if asking them to speak. Shanna spoke first, welcoming the gentle stranger to their fire. Kenny only watched, ever more curious about what was happening.

Shanna spoke slowly and clearly, telling the man about their expedition, and about how proud she was of Kenny and Tom for having killed the mammoth. She told him of the long journey ahead in which they would carry the meat and ivory tusks down the valley to the great river, where they would build rafts upon which to travel home. Kenny felt oddly at peace with Shanna nestled under his arm. He could feel her voice in his chest as she spoke. Her voice was soft and musical, and her bright red hair glowed in the light of the fire.

Shanna paused and the blond man smiled, then settled back. He pulled the small sparkling device toward him from where he had held it between him and Shanna as she had spoken. He placed the object in his lap and studied it for a moment, then looked up at them. He spoke very slowly, but clearly. The words sounded foreign, like a Germanic language, but still seemed to have a slight familiarity to them. Kenny looked inquisitive and said, "I don't understand."

The blond man repeated himself again. This time the words were clear and more familiar. Kenny believed he was saying thank you for their kindness in sharing their fire with him. Then he said that Shanna and Kenny would have a son who would become a great hunter.

Suddenly the ground jolted hard and something hit Kenny on the side of the head. He opened his eyes and winced as his head bounced against the Plexiglass of the helicopter window as the chopper bumped up and down in a brief spell of turbulence. The chopper was passing by Delta Junction and had turned west down the Tanana valley. Kenny sat up, rubbed his head with his hand, stretched, and looked over at Tom who was sound asleep. Tom had wisely used his parka as a pillow, and had stayed asleep through the brief turbulence. Then Kenny remembered the dream. Very curious, almost like a deja vu experience. He glanced at Tom and wondered how in blazes they could kill a mammoth without a gun. Then he thought of Shanna and a son who would be a hunter. He remembered the intense feeling of confidence and of peace. A curious dream. Her hair would indeed be lovely by firelight.

"Good morning everyone. Thank you for coming, particularly for those of you who have interrupted other important research work to join the project. As you know, this meeting will serve both as an update on our first field trip to the site and as a project planning meeting for the next phase of this effort. First, the update."

As Dr. Tamura spoke, the group of more than fifty participants in the conference room of the Duckering Building sat in silent attentiveness. Several members of the now expanded research team had arrived only the night before, having flown from the Lower 48 farther north than they had ever been. Alaska had put on a show outside the window of the Alaska Airlines Boeing 727 jet, with a moderately active aurora streaming in a celestial dance across the night sky. For at least one scientist whose specialty area was laser physics, the auroral display was more than entertaining, it was an expansion of his consciousness. The standard paradigm of the east-west vastness of the continent had already been shattered when the jet took nearly as long flying straight north to get to Fairbanks from Seattle as his first flight did to get from Michigan to the west coast. Charles Singer, Ph.D., had become physically aware of the true dimensional vastness of his home planet.

"On April 3 I traveled by helicopter to the site with Kenny Swanson, UAF graduate student in paleontology, who discovered the mammoth skeleton and the sphere, and Tom Peters, UAF graduate student in glaciology, the codiscoverer of this amazing find." Dr. Tamura switched on the slide projector with the remote control from the podium, and the lights dimmed in the room. A scene looking up the Delta River valley out of the window of the Jet Ranger chopper filled the screen. The morning sun was casting rays of reddish light through the sharply chiseled peaks of the Alaska Range in the background, and the full breadth of the valley was blanketed in brilliant white snow. The round mass of Donnelly Dome was on the left side of the scene. Charles Singer and the other new researchers were transfixed by the intense, primeval beauty of the scene. Dr. Tamura observed the reaction from the audience, particularly the newcomers, and added, "Those of you who have spent your professional lives inside a laboratory, you are in for quite an experience."

The next slide was of the US Army Black Rapids Training Site. "This facility is on the east side of the Delta River within fifteen miles of the site. It will serve as a logistics base for a team of military support personnel who will provide security for the operation, emergency evacuation capability if needed, and other extraordinary logistical capability as required. Colonel Wells is the principal representative of the Army's support role, and is with us today. I know that working with the military is unusual for some of you, but, as most people who live here have discovered, I believe you will find the armed services in Alaska quite a good neighbor with some extraordinary capabilities. Fort Greeley is, after all, the US Army's Cold Regions Test Center."

The third slide was of Black Rapids Lodge, and the fourth the location where Tom and Kenny had parked the truck to cross the Delta River in the Zodiac. "Our intrepid young explorers ventured forth from this location in an inflatable craft last fall. Just for the record, the Delta River has a mean annual temperature of about one degree Celsius, is very turbid with glacial silt, and at this location, is about a class three white water, to use the term somewhat loosely. This degree of logistical complexity is, oddly enough, considered by the residents of Alaska to be some form of recreation." The audience was enjoying Dr. Tamura's presentation. Kenny and Tom were sitting in the front row, and were both humbled a bit by the magnitude of the brain trust assembled around them, and by the apparent affection for them both that Dr. Tamura seemed to have adopted.

"This is the point of crossing, which looks fairly benign in this late winter scene. Note the mouth of the stream from the glacier which enters here." Dr. Tamura walked toward the screen with a pointer. "The landing spot was here." He indicated a point halfway to the glacier, which was in the background. "We cleared the snow from a level area here, near the discovery camp site, using downwash from the rotor. We landed at this location after approaching the glacier in the helicopter."

"This is Black Rapids Glacier." The next slide was a close-up of the face of the glacier with the collapsed face and ice rubble pile. The sun was now bright yellow on the south side of the cirque forming the imposing valley that spawned the glacier. "It is known as the 'Galloping Glacier' because it is known to advance or recede rather rapidly depending on the snowfall accumulation over the previous several winters. By rapidly, I mean this mass of ice can slide forward or backward at the rate of up to one-half meter per day. You can outwalk it, but watch where you pitch your tent." A murmur of laughter rippled through the audience. "And here"—the pointer centered on the screen as the next slide appeared showing a nondescript, snow-blanketed stream bed—"is where the mammoth was discovered. You have all read the briefing report prepared by Kenny and Tom, so you should be familiar with the specifics of the find, and

71

extraordinary events of their observations that night. The as yet invalidated observation of greatest interest is their description of the light from within the glacier itself.

"This event, clearly observed by both Kenny and Tom, was followed by Kenny's dream—he describes it as a vision—of the discovery of the sphere within the exposed skeleton of the mammoth. That was followed the next morning by the discovery of the sphere in the mammoth skeleton exposed by sluicing action from water released during a major calving event on the face of the glacier, precipitated by an earthquake. Kenny's dream terminated in an earthquake which he describes as originating from harmonic resonation from the sphere as it was emitting light and sound, and levitating from his mother's hands in the dream.

"For the record, each of the properties of the sphere described in Kenny's dream were validated in a laboratory in the Geophysical Institute on this campus ten days ago. This includes levitation and harmonic tonal emissions sufficient to generate a local tremor, which was recorded by the seismic monitoring station, also on the West Ridge of this campus. The epicenter, confirmed by two other seismic stations in Alaska, was the West Ridge of the UAF campus. The report of that experiment is being handed out to you now."

The audience was starting to murmur now as two graduate students moved up and down the aisles distributing copies of the report abstract and executive summary. Dr. Tamura advanced the next slide, and the scene of the snow-covered valley disappeared, and was replaced by one of the physics lab. Kenny was in the center of the slide along with Shanna and his mother. All three were touching hands and the sphere was levitating above them, emitting an intense blue light which radiated off their faces.

"The full text of the report with all the original data is on file in a library set up in the Elvey building for this project. The executive summary you have now contains a key to the data. We have assigned a custodian to archive and manage all the project files."

"Now I would like to show you why you are all here." The slide faded, and was replaced by a video of the experiment. The audience was transfixed by the fifteen-minute video. Shanna was sitting next to Kenny in the front row, and blushed slightly when she saw herself enter the scene and the sphere respond to her. More specifically, when the sphere seemed to echo Kenny's response to her. Kenny blushed a bit too. He glanced at her now and saw her green eyes reflecting the light of the video, and she smiled at him. He smiled back and turned to watch as his mother entered the scene. The extraordinary events that occurred when Betty Swanson joined the experiment caused several gasps in the audience, not all from newcomers. Colonel Wells had been sitting attentively, listening and observing with clinical interest until now. "My god," he exclaimed out loud.

The video ended. Dr. Tamura asked for the lights to come back on and addressed the audience again. "We still do not know the composition of the sphere. We do not know its origin, its age, or its energy source. We do know that it is more perfectly spherical than any object that has ever been created by the most technologically advanced experiments of modern science including titanium ball bearings manufactured in microgravity experiments in the Skylab space station. We know that it is so far indestructible by mechanical means, but we have ceased any further attempts to dissect it chemically or mechanically. We know it responds to human touch as you can see from the video, and the level of response is different for different people."

"Our statistical group suggests that the response is stronger in certain family lineage, specifically in Kenny's family. You should know that his mother is, we believe, full-blooded Athabaskan. Her ancestors have inhabited this valley for more than ten thousand years. It is altogether possible that Betty and Kenny Swanson's ancestors hunted and killed that mammoth, and, based on the age of the find, may have seen the sphere themselves. Indeed, they may have placed the sphere in the mammoth skeleton where Kenny discovered it. Admittedly, that may appear to be a lot of speculation based on what would, under any other circumstances, be considered to be closer to religious mysticism than to sound science. But let me tell you what I think we do know, which may explain why I am on this track." Dr. Tamura paused and looked over the entire audience, which was now completely at attention. "Betty Swanson told me what the object is, and my gut feeling is that she is right. She believes ... no, it is stronger than that. She knows that the sphere is a beacon. She said that it wants to go back to where Kenny found it and that it has something to show us there."

The audience was silent. Dr. Tamura paused again to let the last statement sink in. Then, he continued, "I have a standing policy in my research. Any time I find an indestructible, perfectly spherical object that predates all known scientific and technological developments in human civilization, that demonstrates antigravity properties while generating earth tremors from harmonic emissions with no apparent energy source, all the while pulsing with light that appears to be selectively linked to a certain DNA subgroup, I check it out. Just a quirk of mine." The audience responded with another murmur of nervous laughter. "Now we will explain the logistics of the field station. Tom Peters is the logistics supervisor for this project, and he has been very busy making arrangements for you all."

CHAPTER 4
The Tunnel
Summer, A.D. 1975

Tom had arranged the walled tents which served as sleeping quarters, kitchen, and washrooms in a semicircle in the wooded area where he and Kenny had camped before. The military-style canvas structures were set on wood platforms, and were equipped with oil stoves. A field lab had been set up in an ATCO unit, a prefabricated sheet metal and wood frame structure that was the office equivalent of a mobile home. Finding one of these available had been no easy task since they had become the basic building blocks for the camps and office facilities used by the contractors building the Trans-Alaska Pipeline. Unfortunately, a lot of other field supplies had proven hard to come by, were unusually expensive, or both, for the same reason.

But in his considerable mix of talent, Tom was, above all else, resourceful. Lumber shortages? No problem. He had simply made arrangements with a small lumber milling operation in Delta Junction which had access to several square miles of tall white spruce trees common throughout the Tanana Valley. They routinely harvested selected trees during winter, using the frozen river as access. Hauling was done in part by draft horses, very much as it had been during the gold rush in the early part of the century. The small mill, set up at a hay farm just outside of town, was powered by a diesel engine appropriated from a D-7 Cat which had been acquired in an auction of Federal surplus equipment. The lumber was milled to Tom's specifications and delivered by truck to the job site where it was queued up with other supplies on the east shore of the Delta River.

The military provided several Nodwell tracked vehicles which used an ice bridge across the river to move the heavy supplies to the job site. The Army had lived up to Dr. Tamura's billing as a most capable and welcome Alaskan neighbor. Much of the tent camp hardware had been provided by them. Similarly, nearly all the heavy hauling and much of the assembly work had been accomplished by the young and curious soldiers who seemed quite happy to be working on this project while their less fortunate peers were still out on a "Jack Frost" arctic survival exercise somewhere in the Brooks Range. Overall, Tom was pleased with the progress, and had taken considerable care to transfer as much of the heavy inventory as possible across the river before the onset of spring isolated the camp.

Spring thaw had indeed been an event, particularly for the researchers who were visiting Alaska for the first time. They discovered that Alaska played out a live reenactment of the end of the last ice age each spring. Spring had been preceded by the return of nearly constant light. By the end of April, the sun extended its daily path above the horizon to the far northeast and northwest, and began casting its warmth on the north side of the Alaska Range. The high valleys in the northern foothills of the range thawed during June, in what had proven to be a particularly long winter. When it finally began, a torrent of melting snow and ice surged down the rivers, carrying glacial flour ground from the bedrock under the glaciers. The clear waters of the Tanana that had been flowing from spring water under the ice cover returned to various shades of brown and gray as the silt flooded into the valley seeking quiet spots to settle and change the course of the river.

Tom completed the camp setup just in time to watch the Delta River disgorge its ice in a massive surge. The ice bridge, which they had reinforced by drilling holes in the ice and pumping water onto the surface like clear pavement, vanished in less than thirty minutes from the time the first shoreline cracks appeared. About a dozen members of the research team gathered on the shore when Tom first saw the cracks appear and the ice shift downriver slightly. Suddenly, in a low groan the ice began to move, lifted by the rising river level. The dull thud of ice chunks ramming together, lifting up and then re-settling into the now churning, silty water presented an eerie scene. Only one day before, the last of the loads of fuel had been carried by the Nodwells across the ice bridge. Now the bridge was gone and the research camp was cut off from the road system. Spring had arrived.

Shanna was fascinated with the braided appearance of the Tanana Valley as the large Alaska Helicopters Bell 205 cruised up river toward the project site. Birch trees were beginning to turn lime green with new leaves, particularly on the south-facing hillsides. She was amazed at how quickly green had arrived. Within a few days bright red of new twigs had begun to transform into a mosaic of green and red patches, and shortly after, the hillsides were a carpet of fresh green color.

She saw several moose grazing in a shallow lake formed by one of many old oxbows off the main river channel. One moose's head disappeared completely beneath the water, then popped back up when the giant ungulate had a tasty mouthful of weeds. Some of the vegetation was hanging off of the young bull's newly forming antlers. He paid little attention to the sound of the civilian Huey churning its way up the valley only a few hundred meters overhead.

Shanna was accompanied by eight other members of the research team, with their personal gear and additional equipment. This group would round out the field team to a population of about twenty, seven of which were support staff who cooked the meals, maintained camp, the generators, water and wastewater treatment equipment, and managed the inventory of supplies. This group included the geology and glaciology team, tasked with determining how best to open up access to the glacier once it had been determined where to dig, blast or melt, as the case might be. Her job, and that of several other members of the math and physics team, was to decide where to dig.

She looked forward with great anticipation to working with Kenny. Some of her anticipation was pure science, an opportunity to repeat the experiment with the orb near the face of the glacier. Yet some of her anticipation was something else, perhaps something to do with Kenny's misty blue eyes and sense of humor. Until now, Shanna had been all books and brains as a gifted student, and had always found her studies so fulfilling that nothing else mattered. Recently, she'd found herself thinking of him as often as she thought of the project.

Kenny watched from the edge of the helipad as the 205 thudded up the valley toward the camp. Tom checked the wind sock which the Army set up. A steady breeze was funneling down the Delta River valley indicating fine conditions for landing. The pilot set the large chopper down on the circular pad and slowed the engines to an idle for several minutes before shutting down. Kenny saw Shanna's red hair through the side window and his heart skipped a beat. She was smiling at him and waved.

"Looks like you have a friend," Tom said to Kenny as they waited for the rotor to stop.

"Yeah, and she can balance a checkbook without a calculator, too."

"Well, cousin, that is certainly quite an asset, but I don't think she's interested in your checkbook. Last time I saw it, Mr. Ed could have balanced what you had in it by tapping his hoof three times."

"At least she's not after my money."

Tom chuckled. "I think not."

This was the first time that most of the eight passengers in the chopper had been to the site. The newcomers were doing "the dance," Kenny and Tom observed. The moves were: stop, tilt back the head, drop the jaw and turn slowly 360 degrees at least twice while mouthing something along the lines of, "This is awesome!" The first three who stepped out onto the pad were already performing. Kenny and Tom looked at each other and said in unison, "The dance."

Shanna was the fourth person to exit the helicopter, and she made it nearly across the landing pad to Kenny before she got caught. He walked up to her and smiled as she completed her first rotation. Her head tilted down and she saw him coming. She had the greatest urge to throw her arms around his neck and hug him, but instead reached out in a timid handshake. Kenny took her hand and gave it a professional grip, plus a slight extra squeeze which she did not miss. "Welcome to Black Rapids. It's very nice to have you here."

"Thanks, Kenny. That was a beautiful ride up the valley. This place is incredible. It is," she paused, searching for a proper adjective, "primeval."

"Yup," he smiled. "Alaska puts on quite a show. Just about the time you start to take it for granted, she trots a grizzly bear across your path or something to remind you where you are. Come on. Let's get you settled in." He picked up her duffel bag and she grabbed her day pack and a small instrument case and they headed to the tent camp.

On a low rise just ahead of the camp area, Kenny paused and pointed to the glacier. "This is where Tom and I were standing when we saw the light in the glacier. It was on the left and looked like a spotlight shining from inside." Snow off the glacier's face, had begun to melt, exposing the rubble pile and the mottled surface.

"Where is the mammoth skeleton?"

"Straight up ahead and to the right on the edge of the stream. We cleared the snow away and it's thawing out now. A tour is planned for later this afternoon."

"Great, I'm really looking forward to it."

"Here are the women's quarters." Kenny pointed out two of the wall tents. "Men's quarters are over there." He nodded to three other walled tents across the semicircular area. "These will sleep eight to ten GI's, or four to five civilians. Should be plenty of room to stow your gear," he said flipping back the tent flap. She ducked in and saw the array of cots and mattresses, each with a foot locker and a small folding chair nearby.

"Wow, this is camping! Is there room service, too?"

Kenny just smiled and seized the opportunity, "Sure. Depends on what you want and who you want to have serve it."

She stopped and looked at him squarely, "Cute, Mr. Swanson. I'll let you know if I need anything." She was supposed to have been blushing according to how he understood these things to work. Somehow the script got reversed, and he was blushing while she was smiling.

Then he executed one of his famous quick recoveries, "For the lady, I recommend the accommodations adjacent to the central heating system. It is more comfortable when the night chill is upon us and it does have the advantage of a modest view." He flipped down a canvas flap to reveal a small, mosquito net-covered window. The mountainside above the glacier filled the small window. A high rock outcropping was visible in the near distance above the camp site, and on the rocks was a Dall sheep, standing and stretching.

Shanna gasped. "Is that a sheep?" Kenny and Tom had been spotting the small flock for several days and knew that they liked to frequent that ledge which apparently had some dried grass left over from last fall and was in the direct path of the morning sun. At that moment, the ram turned and watched as a ewe walked up to him nudging along a lamb. The tiny sheep wobbled a bit and walked right under the ram. His curl of horns glistened as he lowered his handsome head and nudged the lamb with his nose. The lamb rubbed against Daddy's legs as mom watched. Shanna was totally amazed.

"Aye, m'Lady. 'Tis a family of Dall sheep. Newborn of the spring accompanying. Just another crummy day in Alaska." He smiled again, bowed slightly and started to exit. "Perhaps a bit of lunch after you have settled in? Dinning facilities are located in the modest canvas structure over yonder. Twelvish, per-chance?" He bowed again, cocking his head slightly to the side in a querying look.

"That is a truly gracious proposal, sir. I would be so inclined to engage the local cuisine at noon." She curtsied ever so mod-estly and smiled.

"Until, then, I depart." Kenny disappeared and the front flap of the tent closed behind him. Shanna turned and watched the sheep again. The lamb ambled off after its mother, now appar-ently ready for a meal. Dad turned and held his head high in the sun, looking altogether magnificent and proud. Shanna just shook her head slowly and muttered, "This is awesome."

Lunch was soup and sandwiches, served cafeteria style in the mess tent just large enough to seat the full research team and most of the support staff. Dr. Tamura spoke to the assembled group of researchers after lunch was more or less complete. "Good afternoon, everybody. First, Tom Peters will explain about the camp. Then I will provide a brief outline of the next several days of activity which we have planned. The results of that effort will determine what we do next. Tom."

"Thank you Dr. Tamura. Greetings everybody. Since most of

you have already been here for a while you know where every-thing is so I'll make my comments brief and trust the Sour-doughs of the camp to assist the Cheechakos with their orienta-tion. Meals are served on a regular schedule, with breakfast from 6:30 to 8:00 AM, lunch from 11:30 to 1:00 PM and dinner from 6:00 to 7:30 in the evening. A snack bar is available if you get hungry out of sync with the others' biorhythms. Coffee and hot water are always available.

"We ask that you be responsible for keeping your own sleep-ing quarters clean and organized. The maintenance crew will check the oil stoves every day, so you shouldn't have to worry about that. They are quite helpful with other mechanical prob-lems as well. Shower and restroom facilities are behind the main circle of tents. We have a good water supply from an infiltration gallery tapped into a spring above camp. Please take care if you are hiking not to contaminate the water source although it is filtered and disinfected. Water is plentiful and we have a septic tank with a disposal field in well-drained gravel downstream from camp.

"Electricity is supplied by three diesel electric generators on the far side of the washrooms. Power is relatively stable for most 120V equipment, but if you need 208V or more stable power for instruments, let the electrician know and they'll fix you up. The lab is small, so we have to ration space a bit. We're framing in an addition next to the ATCO trailer unit which houses the lab. That should be available in a few days for additional offices and workbenches."

"Tom." Chuck Singer spoke up in the back of the room. "How stable is the foundation in the ATCO unit?"

"Good question, Dr. Singer. I think it is fairly strong. We built up the foundation with 12x12 timbers, but let me know if you need something more stable."

"Thanks. We've got some pretty sensitive vibration sensors we need to calibrate.

"Okay, moving on to communications. We've set up a sys-tem with field radios and radio phones for calling to town. The military has a small guard unit posted down the creek where they set up a communications center staffed around the clock. Dr. Tamura will assign the portable radio sets. As a general rule, you should always have a radio with you when you are out of camp. Radio phones are available for personal use as needed, but please limit your calls as a courtesy to others since we have only a few outgoing channels."

"Let's see, what else." Tom thumbed through a few pages in a small note pad. "Oh yeah. If you decide to take a hike, let somebody know where you're going so we know where to locate your remains when the bears are finished with you." The audience emitted a nervous laugh. "Actually, we haven't seen a bear in the camp since just before breakfast this morning, so don't worry about it." More nervous laughter. "Bears don't particularly like to be around people, so if you make some noise, they won't bother you. My cousin Kenny has some bear whistles with him which you can borrow to make extra noise. See him if you want one. Just blow it a bit when you go around a blind corner or are moving through high brush. You get the idea. The military guards have weapons in case bears get particularly obnoxious or if the physics team starts hogging too much of the lab space." More laughter. Tom was clearly on a roll.

"Finally, do not, under any circumstances, attempt to use the ice bridge. It is having a small mechanical problem which will not be repaired until," Tom glanced at his watch, then looked up, "November." The researchers were enjoying this as was Dr. Tamura. Tom smiled at him and said, "That's pretty much it. Any questions?"

Dr. Singer, spoke up again. "Tom, will you be coordinating the flight schedule for the choppers and for supplies and personnel in and out of the research station?"

"Yes. Just call me on the radio, or see me in the office to the right of the ATCO unit. We plan to have at least one flight per day out of Fairbanks, and extra runs if needed. The Army has emergency helicopter capability on standby at Fort Greeley."

"Thank you."

"Any other questions?" Tom asked. Seeing none, he said, "Before I hand back the floor to Dr. Tamura I wanted to add one point to the rules on hiking. It is helpful to identify the species of animals you may encounter on the trail. Let's see ..." Tom paused, looking around the room.

Shanna noticed Kenny smiling, shaking his head and muttering, "No, no, no, please, no, don't do it." Tom found his target, a young woman in the back of the room with the biology team.

"Dr. Randall, would you be so kind as to explain to the group the different characteristics of black bear versus brown bear feces so we can identify them on the trail." Dr. Tamura looked on with some curiosity and Shanna saw Kenny slump down in his chair still shaking his head. "No, no, no ..."

Dr. Leslie Randall, geneticist and exobiologist, mustered her best effort to recall her limited scope of wildlife biology and responded. "Well, Tom, I believe grizzly bear feces are larger and ..." she paused. "Actually, I don't have a clue," she finally conceded. "I could fingerprint the DNA patterns for you with gel electrophoresis, but I wouldn't know which is which if I stepped in it." She sat back resigned at her feeble attempt, and now a bit curious about this interesting young man and his odd question.

"Well," Tom picked up, "it's quite simple. The grizzly bear feces have these little whistles in them." The first round of laughter came and paused. Then the rest of the room shifted from analytical to common sense mode, and the room filled with more laughter, then applause. Tom bowed to the audience, and acknowledged Dr. Tamura.

Shanna was starting to see a common thread between Kenny, who was slumped almost out of his chair now and still shaking his head, and Tom. Humor, she rationalized, seems to be an opiate for sanity during the long winters here. These guys were a constant comedy act. She filed that for future reference as Dr. Tamura stood up again.

"Thank you Tom." He was already impressed by Tom's technical and managerial skills, and had a growing appreciation for Tom's talent to relax people and to help add an appropriate and refreshing dose of levity to this otherwise serious and somewhat Spartan undertaking. "I would encourage all of you to take this afternoon to tour the site. Kenny will lead the new arrivals on a tour of the mammoth skeleton, and then to the face of the glacier. Then later this afternoon, you are to assemble with your team leaders by discipline and organize your lab gear and identify any hardware requirements beyond those already arranged. The next two days will be dedicated to finishing the setup of lab and monitoring equipment. Then, on Friday, we will transfer the orb from the University by helicopter and perform the location experiment. That will occur in the afternoon when the sun angles are slightly below the mountains so we can monitor any light emissions from inside the glacier."

"Each day, we will use the lunch hour to gather as a group as we have done today to discuss matters of interest to the entire research team. These meetings are not mandatory for everyone, but each team should be represented. We will try to hold these to no more than about one half hour, between 12:30 and 1:00 P.M. Does anybody have any questions?" Everyone seemed more interested in going for a hike to the mammoth skeleton and the glacier, so the meeting ended with no further questions. "Kenny, where and when would you like to have the orientation tour begin?"

Kenny stood and addressed the group. "Let's meet in thirty minutes by the ATCO unit. Bring a day pack with some fluids and your hiking boots. The trail is cleared of snow, and we will not have to cross any streams, so waterproof boots are not necessary. It will be cool up the trail by the face of the glacier, so dress warm. Sunglasses are handy by the way."

By 1:30 P.M. the sun was well above the peaks south of the camp, and was providing some warmth. Snow was melting rapidly now, exposing rocky terrain and the first hardy patches of grass and sedges which were turning green at the prompting of the sun. A light breeze from the glacial valley greeted the scientists as they hiked up the trail on the north side of the creek. Kenny and Shanna walked at the front of the group. Her eyes and ears were alive with the sights and sounds of spring in Alaska. Birds flitted about in the willows and alders, squirrels chased after each other in the clumps of small spruce trees, and the first mosquitoes of the year were out droning around in search of a meal. The pace of the group and the breeze kept the pesky insects from landing and digging in. Besides, these were the big, slow, stupid ones that you could reach out and grab with one hand and crush, a procedure Kenny had been only too willing to demonstrate to Shanna, who was marginally impressed.

As they approached the mammoth find, Shanna noted that Kenny turned more serious. None of the research team, save Dr. Randall, who now wore a plastic toy bear whistle on a string necklace, had ever seen a skeleton of prehistoric origin in nature. The long ribs of the great beast which rose like inverted flying buttresses into the clear sky, were a sight to behold. Snow had been cleared away, and the skeleton was fully exposed in the sun. Shanna and Leslie Randall walked over to the skeleton, and stood near the ribs. Kenny turned to address the group. "Here he is. Please watch where you step, but it is okay to touch the bones. We've picked over the area pretty carefully, but if you see something that seems odd, leave it in place and let me know."

The breeze from the glacier was cooler and brisker now. The scientists barely noticed, having been caught in the spell of the mammoth. Kenny walked over to the neck area and knelt down. "We found something interesting here a few days ago." He knelt down near the neck and reached out with his left hand. "This is a series of four small indentations in the vertebrae of the neck. They are grouped in two pairs, within a few inches of each other, and appear to have been caused by sharp, high velocity objects which we think were most likely arrowheads. This big fella was apparently the victim of a hunting party some 10,000 years ago when the front of the glacier extended over the face of the mountain pass to the south. Black Rapids was nothing more than a tributary glacier to the big ice field at that time."

Shanna and Leslie looked closely at the marks in the neck vertebrae and could clearly see the points where the bone had been gouged by the arrowheads. "Why are they in pairs?" Leslie asked Kenny. "Well, Dr. Randall. ..." Kenny started.

"Please, just call me Leslie." Kenny smiled with a wide Athabaskan grin and Leslie Randall saw his eyes sparkle with friendliness. She could clearly see now what had caught Shanna McLane's fancy about this charming young man.

"Leslie," he went on, "our best guess is that the mammoth was hunted by a group of people. These arrowhead strike points may represent some fairly sophisticated level of coordinated marksmanship on the part of two hunters. Note that the gouges are slightly different, as if made by slightly different types of arrowheads. The pattern repeats itself here, and here." Kenny pointed out that each pair was a similar grouping of one each of the two types of marks.

Chuck Singer had noted this conversation with interest. "The two hunters who did this must have had nerves of steel. Could you imagine this towering, bellowing beast stomping about in a threatening way while two prehistoric Athabaskan hunters casually walked up and shot it in the neck with Olympic quality bowmanship, not once, but twice?"

Kenny stood up now, nodding. "Yeah, Tom and I had the same realization, Dr. Singer."

"Chuck," Dr. Singer said, casting a quick smile to Leslie Randall.

"You folks are working up to become honorary Alaskans," Kenny said cheerfully. "Okay, Chuck, add to your scenario the fact that it was probably a lot colder, and the hunting party had to walk to here from, most likely, the lower Tanana Valley where the prehistoric settlements have been found nearly 100 miles away." At that moment this group of nine Ph.D.s and Ph.D. candidates collectively realized how it was that young Kenny Swanson's ancestors had managed to successfully add their lineage to the human family tree. These were tough and resourceful people, who had adapted to a remarkably beautiful but severe environment. And they had survived. The fact that the two marksmen who downed this mammoth predated the Egyptian Pharaohs by at least 6 thousand years was not lost in this realization. And here, in 1975, Kenny Swanson was rediscovering his heritage before their eyes.

Shanna shuddered in the cool breeze as her mind's eye saw the glacier grow bright and large before them. She could faintly hear the echo of the mammoth's trumpeting call ricocheting off the steep cirques of the glacial valley. She could almost see Kenny as the hunter, drawing an arrow back in his bow, and looking hard into the eyes of the mammoth. She closed her eyes and could feel the arrow take flight. Now two arrows. Like falcons.

A high-pitched cry echoed overhead, and the group of hiker-scientist-explorers turned to look up. A gyrfalcon rose in the sky, circling on the updraft wind from the glacier, effortlessly gliding up and up. Then, the v-shaped wings folded in against its sleek frame and the falcon dove in a straight line into a clump of willow trees. The raptor struck silently, seizing a tiny field vole in its talons, then surged upward again, wings beating hard. In complete silence, the aerodynamic predator flew off into the wooded distance, and disappeared. "Gyrfalcon," Kenny said.

Friday was the fourth completely clear day in a row. The turquoise blue morning sky framed the mountain ridges to the east, south, and west. The broad expanse of the Delta River valley filled the view to the north, glowing in the soft light of the early morning sun in the northeast. Kenny and Shanna sat on a log near the edge of the helicopter pad, watching to the north and listening. He held her hand now, and she leaned slightly against him. They had taken walks together each evening for two days.

Last night, under a bright and active aurora, Kenny Swanson had kissed Shanna McLane very, very softly. She had stood, eyes closed, completely motionless after this gesture of affection was complete, savoring the cool breeze on her lips where Kenny had kissed her. "Hello," he said after a full minute had passed. "Anyone home?"

Her lips pursed into a smile and her green eyes opened slowly. "Nope, nobody home here. Countdown complete, booster lifted off. I'll report back in at orbital perigee," she said smiling. Her eyes closed again. He reached out and pulled her close to him, opening his summer parka and letting her snuggle against him as he closed it around her. There they had stood motionless for a long while.

A pair of large helicopters appeared on the horizon, and quickly became audible as they worked their way up the valley. The two Alaska Helicopter Bell 205s arced around slightly to the east, then began an approach to the camp site. In the distance, two smaller helicopters in military olive green livery trailed up behind the two civilian Hueys which carried the remainder of the research team. The Army choppers were barely visible from the front, but the sleek, ominous outlines of the Cobra gunships became clear as the two escorts banked wide in a circle away from the 205s.

A number of ground support staff had gathered as the first 205 landed on the helipad and began the cooldown cycle. The second red and white Huey hovered a half mile away waiting for the first chopper to shut down. Within five minutes, the second chopper deftly touched down on the pad. The two helicopters filled the pad. Overhead, the Cobras circled once then rolled hard to one side passing by the steep face of the nearest mountain with their right sides nearly parallel to the ground.

The pair leveled out and accelerated north, first dropping low toward the river only a few hundred feet above the tree line. Then the gunships vanished.

People and equipment were disgorged from the large choppers on the ground now. The research and support team on the ground became porters, transporting gear to the edge of the helipad and up to the lab in the ATCO unit and the wooden offices. Dr. Tamura greeted the new arrivals in the first chopper, then signaled to Kenny and Shanna to follow him to the second. As they approached the second chopper, Kenny could see his mother's smiling face peering through the side window. She waved at him and Shanna as they approached.

When Betty Swanson stepped out of the helicopter, she immediately gave Kenny a big hug. Then she turned to Shanna and gently put her hand on the side of Shanna's face. "It is good to see you again, Shanna. Kenny tells me you are becoming good friends."

Shanna reached forward and gave Betty Swanson a hug. "Welcome to Black Rapids, Mrs. Swanson. It is good to see you again, too." Shanna stepped back and stood close to Kenny.

Dr. Tamura now stepped forward and shook Betty Swanson's hand. "May I add my welcome, too? It is very kind of you to join us here today."

"Oh, thank you, Dr. Tamura. And thank you for the ride in the helicopter. That was my first, and it was very exciting!" Betty's eyes sparkled with delight. George Tamura had grown to admire Kenny and his family. His understanding of the depth of generosity and kindness of this gentle but resourceful culture in this magnificent valley was growing each day. He was becoming more fascinated with the project as the connection between these people and this strange and wonderful discovery became stronger. He was also quite aware of the growing affection between Kenny and Shanna. His analytical side observed with scientific curiosity how their interaction would guide the next phase of the investigation. His human side was just simply happy for these two young and energetic people who loved science very deeply, and now, perhaps each other.

Two members of the ground support team removed a rectangular case from the helicopter. They carried it carefully between them holding side handles on the case. Dr. Tamura excused himself and went with the two men and the case. The orb had returned to its place of discovery.

"Time: 16:00 hours," Dr. Tamura spoke into a microphone. The afternoon sun was descending in a long arc to the west, now just below the highest peaks of the mountains surrounding Black Rapids Glacier. Video cameras whirred and a plethora of scientific instruments began taking data.

"Okay, Kenny. Let's begin."

Kenny lifted the orb from the open case which had been positioned on a small platform near the mammoth skeleton. He held the orb in the palms of his hands and turned toward the mammoth skeleton. The orb was already glowing and attempting to levitate out of Kenny's hands. Dr. Tamura noted the significantly increased energy level it displayed at this location compared to when it was in the Geophysical Building on the UAF campus. Kenny was startled by the energetic behavior, too, and glanced furtively at Dr. Tamura. He slid one palm over the top of the orb to keep it from rising completely out of his hands and the object levitated perfectly between his two palms, one above and one below the orb. It had begun to spin and emit a green light and a low tone. Dr. Tamura looked back at Kenny and shrugged sort of oddly. "It's your show, Kenny. Do what seems natural to you."

Kenny turned toward his mother who was standing inside the ribs of the skeleton. The orb spun smoothly, but energetically between his outstretched palms. Betty Swanson reached up and placed her hands along the sides of the orb when Kenny approached her. Neither of them were touching the sphere, which was levitating and spinning even more rapidly now. As her palms approached the sides of the sphere, a blue color began to weave into the spinning green pattern, and a second harmonic tone became audible. Kenny and his mother were now standing inside the mammoth rib cage, facing each other with palms outstretched around the sides, top, and bottom of the spinning orb. The intensity of the spinning, color, and tone grew. Then the mammoth ribs began to vibrate.

At first it was just a gentle quiver. The white bones vibrated like aspen saplings in a steady breeze. Then they began quivering in waves along the length of the skeleton, and began emitting a low harmonic tone in perfect key to the orb. Tom Peters was standing on the rocky ridge above the experiment, alternately watching Kenny and his aunt, and then the glacier. The harmonic tones grew in intensity from the orb and the mammoth ribs which were vibrating in waves. Tom was the first to see the ice of the glacier began to pulse in a slow rolling wave. He signaled to Dr. Tamura, pointed at the glacier and glanced furtively up at the steep cirques behind the glacier.

Nearly fifty researchers and support staff were gathered around the site now, observing, checking instruments, recording and taking data. Not a soul was unmoved by the incredible scene. A blue halo of static electricity began to glow around Betty, and a similar but green halo around Kenny. The static charge field grew and encompassed the mammoth skeleton which continued to steadily vibrate in waves, emitting ever deeper harmonic tones. The static charge field expanded to the inner perimeter of the assembled research team. The light was so intense now that Kenny, Betty and the mammoth were almost invisible inside. A pulsing light began to appear inside the glacier.

"Time 16:15:10 hours," Dr. Tamura spoke into the microphone again. "Dr. Singer?"

"I have it," Charles Singer called back. "The range finder is marking a precise location at twenty meters radius inside the glacier. The radius is refining, now eighteen meters."

"Good," Dr. Tamura called back. He turned again to Kenny and Betty. They were lost in a blur in the pulsing light field. Inside, Kenny and Betty watched each other carefully. Betty's hair stood out vertically from her head in the static charge, as did Kenny's. They were both slightly amused by their odd appearance, but somewhat unsure of what to do next.

"Grasp the orb with me now," Betty told her son. "It is time." Kenny nodded in agreement, and their palms closed in slowly on the spinning sphere. The object felt cool to the touch even though it spun with great intensity as their hands rested lightly upon it. "Squeeze," she said. "Now."

They both pressed their hands firmly against the sphere, his on the top and bottom, hers on the side. The object suddenly stopped spinning. From deep inside the orb, a point of violet light began to glow intensely, then quickly expanded to the edge of the sphere, then burst outward in a brilliant, silent explosion passing right through Kenny and Betty, then through the mammoth ribs and out to the perimeter of the research team past Dr. Tamura. The tone had stopped with the cessation of the orb's spinning. Then, the violet light rapidly imploded back into the sphere and simultaneously a red point of light appeared inside the glacier.

"Laser range finder marks a four meter radius now," Dr. Singer shouted.

Tom Peters saw the light and recognized it immediately. "We're back," he muttered softly to the red spotlight inside the glacier. He noted a small avalanche slide off of a steep slope across the valley behind the glacier.

"Time 16:15:55 hours," Dr. Tamura spoke into the microphone. Shanna looked up suddenly from a monitoring panel just outside the area where the violet light had reached.

"No," she called out, "mark time as 16:18:50 hours." Dr. Tamura looked up and then back at a computer time clock open in front of him. He glanced at his watch, and called out to the research team. "Confirm the time now!"

"16:18:30 hours," Shanna called back.

"Confirmed at 16:18.:30 hours," Dr. Singer reported. Three other researchers called out the same time.

Dr. Tamura turned to look at Kenny and Betty, who were standing motionless with the orb between them. The orb was steady, but glowing green and blue where their hands held it firmly. Dr. Tamura looked up at the encircled group of researchers, and spoke quietly but evenly. "I mark the present time as 16:17 hours, now. Stop the experiment and download the time data. I believe we have anomalies in the time clocks near the experimental node. For the record, it has also affected my wristwatch. Kenny, please check your watch and note the time."

Without removing his hands from the orb, Kenny looked at his wristwatch, and gasped. "I … I mark the time as 16:12:15 hours," he said in surprise. Betty was not wearing a watch, but could see the surprise in Kenny's eyes and knew that something important had occurred. Betty removed her hands from the orb and Kenny returned it to the case. He closed the cover, snapped the latches shut and removed his watch from his wrist. He handed it to Dr. Tamura who had removed his wristwatch, and compared the time.

"What happened?" Kenny asked.

"I'm not sure," Dr. Tamura said. "But it appears that during the experiment, time may have been altered near the orb. How do you feel, Kenny?"

"Fine," Kenny responded. They looked over at Betty who shrugged and smiled. "I'm fine, too," she said. "Perhaps a bit younger, though." Betty grinned.

Dr. Tamura smiled back, shaking his head. He very much enjoyed these people and their delightful sense of humor.

The research team was all business now. Tom Peters and Chuck Singer were marking a series of lines with stakes and flagging toward the glacier, using the laser instruments as direction finders. Others were downloading files, backing up floppy disks and reloading cameras. The evening sun was settling lower behind the mountains to the west, and a cold wind was beginning to descend from the glacial valley. "We have data to collate, team," Dr. Tamura said. "And we have a location for the next phase of the project."

Shanna joined Kenny and Betty near the mammoth, and had hugged each of them. She had a look of concern on her face. "Don't worry, we're fine, Shanna," Betty said. "We're more than fine. We have heard a voice from the past here. Kenny knows."

Shanna looked into Kenny's blue eyes. "It was like an echo," he said. "Like an echo of a million voices calling out together. It was like they were calling to us to join them, peaceful, but energetic. Odd."

Dr. Tamura was listening with great interest. "You heard voices?" he asked Kenny and Betty.

"Yes," they answered in unison, startling each other and Dr. Tamura as well. Kenny waited as his mother explained first. "It was like being in a concert hall or a stadium. I heard many voices, but I couldn't understand what they were saying. But I agree with Kenny, they were warm, peaceful voices, filled with energy and life."

Dr. Tamura looked up to be certain that some of the video cameras were still running. "And you Kenny?" he queried.

"Yes, Dr. Tamura. Like a concert hall or a stadium when the crowd acknowledges a score in a soccer game. Shouting, but happy. I almost called back, because it was so clear ...." he searched carefully for his words, "… and compelling. It was like they wanted us to talk to them. I didn't know what to say."

Dr. Tamura looked squarely at Betty now. "Is this what you expected, Betty? What you felt would happen?"

She thought about that for a moment, and responded. "I think so. But it was more intense than I thought it might be. The violet color was very odd, and the voices were strange. But beautiful," she added in an afterthought. She looked up at him and smiled calmly. "It is home now, Dr. Tamura. The orb is where it is supposed to be. It has shown us where to go next and has announced our arrival." Shanna snuggled close to Kenny as he reached out to take his mother's hand. A tingle ran straight up Dr. Tamura's spine.

The diesel engine of the olive green D-7 snarled as it crawled backward with the blade down. Chunks of broken ice, wet gravel, and round boulders were being back-bladed into a rudimentary road by the D-7 operator, a skilled young corporal who truly enjoyed his work. A sergeant stood nearby directing his small team of soldiers as they carved a path up to the front of the glacier. The road crossed the stream in the front of the ice rubble pile, but the water was shallow and vehicles could ford the stream without difficulty. Later, the sergeant thought, they could install a culvert or two and build up the road. Piece of cake. He was focused on the task at hand and was only passively curious why these scientists were so eager to dig a tunnel into Black Rapids Glacier. Besides, when Colonel Wells said build a road and dig a tunnel, the only response was "where and how long." Sergeant Case was all business at that point.

Colonel Wells stood in the lee of a Weasel, a tracked all-terrain vehicle which was particularly well suited for Alaska's terrain. Dr. Tamura, Chuck Singer and Tom Peters huddled with him, appreciative of the relief from the steady cold breeze emanating from the glacier which was blocked by the boxy, armored ATV.

"Dr. Singer, I think we're almost ready to open the adit," Colonel Wells said. "The opening will be encased in a steel shroud to protect people and equipment entering the tunnel from small chunks of ice which might calve off the glacier. The face of the glacier is not particularly high here, perhaps fifteen meters, and it tapers back a bit, so a major calving event should not occur." He looked up at Tom Peters who had been intensively analyzing the physics of the glacier.

"I agree, Colonel," Tom confirmed. "My main concern is the possibility of this glacier starting to move quickly, as it has been known to do in the past. Bedrock here is smooth and the feeder valley is long, narrow, and collects snow well. A slight increase in precipitation and the valley fills with snow. The full weight of the snow load transfers to the front of the glacier, and there is no braking mechanism, just a smooth rock surface to slide on."

Dr. Tamura turned to look up at the steep cirques along the walls of the valley feeding the glacier. "What is your best prognosis, Tom, given what we know of the snowfall levels for the past several years?"

Tom, too, now stepped back and looked at the reach of the mountain ridges up the valley. "We took a heavy load last winter. The previous two or three years were more or less average, so it is difficult to predict. Under normal conditions, I would expect continued melting and receding, but last winter's snowfall may have temporarily shifted the balance. My best prognosis? Keep digging, but stay alert."

Chuck Singer spoke up now. "Tom and I have placed a laser range finder on the right and left sides of the face of the glacier to document any movement. Strain gauges will be placed strategically in the tunnel to monitor internal changes in the ice, and will be equipped with transmitters to alert us if something moves more than a few centimeters."

"Colonel?" Dr. Tamura queried.

"I'm comfortable going in," Colonel Wells responded. "But I want everyone inside wearing hard hats. We are going to build several emergency rooms with steel frames and heavy corrugated steel walls. Sort of a crash shelter for emergencies, if you will. Also, critical equipment can be placed there."

"Fine," Dr. Tamura said. "Then let's go in."

Colonel Well's aide, a young lieutenant had been standing by some distance away. The colonel looked up at him now and nodded. He spoke into a radiophone to Sergeant Case, who had signaled to the young corporal on the D-7 to stand by. The rough road was right up to the face of the ice, cut cleanly through the ice rubble pile strewn in front of the glacier. Sergeant Case put down the radiophone, and circled his hand over the top of his head twice. His D-7 operator acknowledged, and began backing the tractor away from the glacier, dropping the blade down to smooth the road a bit more as he pulled back. Sergeant Case noted this small extra effort on the part of his man and hoped the colonel was watching. He was.

A second tracked vehicle now approached, driven by another young soldier. The chassis was a Caterpillar D-6, but instead of a blade it had a hydraulic rock drill attached to the lifting arms. A power takeoff from the Cat diesel engine drove a hydraulic motor which spun the drill bit. The bit could be extended forward up to ten feet in front of the D-6, and could be raised or lowered by the lifting arms, or angled side to side nearly thirty degrees in either direction. The operator was shielded in a heavy armored housing that bridged over the top of the tractor. This was a serious tunneling machine, and the private who operated it was from a family of hard rock miners in Colorado. PFC Dan Kelsey was ready for this.

The diesel engine growled as he pushed in the throttle. The drill began to spin, and cut into the hard, blue ice like it was butter. Sergeant Case observed the first boring from behind the machine, then turned toward the lieutenant who was standing on a rock ridge nearly a quarter mile away. He waved once over his head, then held one thumb straight up for the lieutenant to see. Even without binoculars, the lieutenant could see Sergeant Case's acknowledgment that this was going to work just fine. Colonel Wells could see the sergeant, too. He had every right to be proud of his capable and dedicated troops. They were the best in the Army, and were good at what they were asked to do.

The first fifteen meters of the tunnel was shielded with steel arches and thick corrugated metal, like a heavy duty Quonset hut with no end walls. Tom led a small group into the tunnel, which was silent now, except for the dripping of water from melting ice. The scientists all wore Parkas, bunny boots and hard hats with insulated liners. Chuck Singer and Tom were in front. Dr. Tamura, Kenny and two other researchers followed behind. Beams from their flashlights lit up the inside of the rounded tunnel, revealing a deep aqua color. The ice, sparkling like sapphires, was breathtaking. The tunnel was now nearly 200 meters long, a distance the group walked in only a few minutes. One of the emergency shelters was in place, forming an alcove just off the right side of the tunnel about twenty meters from the end.

The drill had advanced quickly, boring the first 15 meters of the tunnel so the adit shield could be set in place. Then, the diesel engine tractor had been withdrawn, having gone as far as it reasonably could in the confined space of the tunnel. A generator outside the tunnel had been set up to run another hydraulic rock drill, this one mounted on a small tracked frame. This electrically powered unit had only taken three days to reach this point from where its D-6 counterpart had left off. Ice rubble had been scooped up by a small front end loader powered by a propane gas engine. Now the smaller drill stood silent at the end of the tunnel, the drill bit inserted into the wall straight ahead. Colonel Wells, Sergeant Case and three of his men waited patiently for the researchers to arrive.

Bright floodlights on the front of the drill machine were directed forward at the drill bit, which was stuck in the wall of ice. Tom arrived first, then the others gathered around as they could find room in the now crowded tunnel. Colonel Wells nodded to PFC Kelsey who had been operating the drill rig, then climbed carefully up the ice rubble pile under the drill bit. "I was drilling where you see the bit now," the young soldier said. "Then the bit just broke through and there was no resistance. It felt like there was nothing on the other side of the ice wall, so I stopped drilling and left the bit in place. Then I called Sergeant Case and he alerted Colonel Wells."

Colonel Wells nodded to Sergeant Case, who then continued. "After Private Kelsey called me, I came in to check it out." He climbed up on the ice pile now, and put his hand near the drill bit point of entry. "Turn off the lights, and I'll show you what we found." The flashlights had already been shut off since the floodlights from the drill machine were sufficient to illuminate the entire area. One of the soldiers clicked off the floodlights and the tunnel became dark. Light from the adit became visible as their eyes adjusted to the reduced light level. Then they all saw it. The hole in the ice where the drill bit had penetrated was ringed with a pulsing red halo of light. A very faint hum could be heard, fluctuating at the frequency of the pulsing red light. Tom climbed forward onto the rubble pile where he could get close to the drill bit and look in along the shaft. The pulsing red light was all he could see.

One by one, each member of the research team examined the boring closely, then Dr. Tamura stepped forward. He turned to one of the other researchers, who was holding a small instrument. "Any significant radiation, Dr. Smith?" he asked.

Ben Smith, Ph.D. was a senior researcher with the EPA radiation monitoring laboratory in Las Vegas, and was one of the best in the country in his field. "Nothing much more than background for this area," Dr. Smith reported. "A very slight alpha blip, but in the single digit picocuries magnitude. It could be nothing more than some ore body with an alpha emitter in the bedrock here. I think we're fine, but I'll keep monitoring."

"Okay, let's pull the drill bit out very slowly, and see what happens," Dr. Tamura said. "Keep the floodlights off for now, but use the flashlights if you need to." Colonel Wells nodded to Sergeant Case, who signaled to Private Kelsey. The electric motor on the hydraulic pump wound up, and the arm holding the bit began to pull back slowly. The shaft of the drill stayed precisely level as it backed slowly out of the bore hole. When the drill bit was visible, and nearly out of the hole, Dr. Tamura held up his hand. "Very slowly now, please."

PFC Kelsey slowed the backout rate to less than one inch per minute, keeping one hand just over the kill switch. Sergeant Case watched carefully as his young charge operated the heavy drill machine like a brain surgeon. The bit finally cleared the hole and the red pulsing light filled the chamber. Dr. Tamura signaled to Dr. Smith, who had stepped forward with his radiation monitor.

"No change," Ben Smith said.

"Okay," Dr. Tamura said, "retract the drill stem fully, but keep it targeted right at the hole so we can put it back in place quickly if necessary."

"Yes Sir," PFC Kelsey responded without hesitation. The shaft of the drill moved backward about five feet, staying perfectly level. The motor whirred smoothly, and both PFC Kelsey and Sergeant Case stood within ready reach of the controls.

Dr. Tamura had a pair of safety goggles on now, and climbed up on the rubble pile. He peered in through the four-inch diameter hole, then gasped audibly. He stepped back and turned toward the research team and soldiers, bracing himself against the side of the tunnel. "It's another orb," he whispered. "Only much larger."

Tom stepped up and looked in next. He could see part of a perfectly round chamber etched in the bedrock. Nearly filling the chamber was a large sphere, perhaps two meters in diameter spinning in place, not touching the rock, and pulsing with red light. The low hum was now clearly audible, like a generator, but with deeper harmonics.

This was what they had come to find, what the small orb had led them to like a beacon. But none of this world-class assemblage of scientists had the faintest clue what it was they had discovered. Kenny, who had been watching from the side of the tunnel, now seemed to be listening more intently to the hum. He pulled off his hard hat, and placed his ear close to the wall of ice. "Dr. Tamura," Kenny asked, "do you hear voices?"

CHAPTER 5

Greetings

Fall, A.D. 1975

Over the summer, the facilities at the Black Rapids site had been upgraded from side wall canvas tents to more permanent Quonset huts to provide better shelter in the coming winter. Tom Peters coordinated the layout of the facility with Colonel Wells, who transferred the military surplus shelters to the site by heavy lift helicopters and ordered their assembly by a company of soldiers. The soldiers quickly completed the construction work once the giant insect-like Sikorsky Sky Cranes deposited the huts on the wood platforms which served as floors.

Tom was grateful for being relieved of his logistical burden, because that freed him up to focus on monitoring the glacier. A few weeks earlier, the forward wall of ice had slid forward rapidly about ten meters, nearly severing the adit and collapsing the tunnel. The motion alarms had gone off, with flashing blue lights and wailing horns responding to the ice movement. Tom alerted Dr. Tamura by radiophone back at the University where he was designing an experiment for the newly discovered two-meter orb.

With great concern, Tom watched the late August monsoon, which traditionally produces half the annual rainfall in the Tanana Valley, drench the site. The rain and late summer sun had conspired to increase the snow melt in the glacial feeder valley, as attested by a greatly increased flow of water emanating from under the ice. The small stream grew into a steady torrent, nearly one meter deep at the center. The glacier had been lubricated by the sheet of water and began to slide along the smooth bedrock as he had predicted. The deep snowfall of the previous winter apparently provided sufficient additional mass to the glacier that the only missing element had been something to reduce the friction between the ice and the rock. Lots of water did the trick.

The research team, safely out of the tunnel, watched helplessly as millions of tons of ice and snow succumbed to the steady pull of gravity. Then, the temperature dropped suddenly in a pre-winter blast of cold, and the melt subsided. The glacier settled slowly onto the bedrock again as the creek flow diminished. The whole event lasted only ten days. The tunnel had to be rebuilt near the adit where the thick corrugated steel arches now sported an ominous bow on the uphill side. The tunnel itself was no longer straight. It gently arched back up to a cavern hollowed out of the ice around the orb. The roughly octagonal cavern had been distorted into a more rounded shape by the ice movement.

The orb, however, did not move. It continued to spin, pulse red light and hum in steady, low-frequency harmonics. The perfectly spherical hole it was in was half bedrock and half ice. Tom had been the first to reenter the tunnel after the ice movement ceased, and found the orb undisturbed. The uphill wall of ice had encroached, almost touching the orb. Where the ice had come within one meter of the orb, however, a large dimple existed, perfectly aligned with the semi-spherical depression in the rock. The orb appeared to be precisely fixed in its location, and any mass, be it ice, rock or whatever, seemed to vanish when it got within about a meter of the steadily spinning sphere.

Tom observed this phenomenon with amazement and wondered about continental drift and geological uplifting. It would take several years to prove that the orb would sculpt the rock as it had done to the advancing ice. He watched the orb spinning steadily in the faint light of the tunnel remaining after he had shut off his flashlight. Somehow he was certain it would not tolerate the rock encroaching on it any more than it would ice. This thing had chosen its location and was not going to move unless it wanted to. He thought about that for a moment in the silence of the tunnel punctuated by the steady dripping of water. "What it wanted to do ..." he thought out loud. He leaned close to the spinning orb, holding his face only a few centimeters from it and gazed hard into the translucent red glow and asked out loud, "What **do** you want to do?"

The orb continued to spin and pulse steadily, seemingly refusing to answer. It did not respond significantly to touch, sound or light in the first series of attempts by the research team to probe it. The only measurable change when the perfectly smooth, oddly warm surface was touched was a slight fluctuation in tone. Even Kenny's attempts had not elicited any more response than those of the other members of the research team. Uncertain about what to do next, Dr. Tamura had left a few members of the research team to monitor the orb, and to work with the Army as they upgraded the camp in preparation for winter. Tom remained to monitor the glacier, and now, from deep inside the twisted sapphire tunnel, he pondered what the ice mass would do next. And he pondered what the orb wanted.

Tom knelt near the orb, as if he was sitting at the knee of an elder as a child. He closed his eyes and listened to the gentle fluctuations in the harmonic tones and could feel the red light pulsing on the inside of his eyelids. Slowly, his mind wandered back to when he was a child in Nenana. His father and mother had taken him and his brother and sister to a potlatch to celebrate a successful harvest of late-summer king salmon.

Tom recalled the steady rhythm of the skin drums as his mother and Kenny's mother, who were sisters, smiled and swayed to the beat of the drums and chanting of the singers. Their arms undulated up and down like a salmon swimming upstream against the steady current until they found a back eddy in the river. The two smiling women spun slowly around letting their arms relax to their sides, then suddenly they hopped upward, threw their arms in the air and shouted, "Hey!" The drummers pounded one last triple thump, thump, thump in unison, and shouted back another "Hey" in response. The music stopped and the women laughed loudly and hugged each other as four male dancers encircled them with hands joined like a net. The salmon-ladies had been caught, and would be food for the lucky Athabaskans who had netted them. Tom's father was one of the lucky fishermen. He reached in and hugged his laughing wife and nibbled playfully on her ear. The room filled with laughter, as Tom looked up admiringly at his parents.

Subconsciously, half daydreaming, Tom's hands had tapped out the rhythm of the drum beat on the orb. He felt the warmth and smoothness of the sphere. His daydream returned to the present moment as his tapping stopped. He startled himself when he laughed out loud at the thought of his father "catching" then nibbling on his mother. He felt oddly embarrassed in the presence of the spinning orb having gotten lost in his memory for a few moments. Then the hair stood up on the back of his neck and he quickly stood up facing the orb.

The pulsing rhythm of the orb had changed. Almost imperceptibly, but distinctly different in frequency it had begun pulsing in a triad, then a pause, then a triad, another pause, and so on. Not the steady, even rhythm it had demonstrated since they discovered it. Tom stopped to listen and observe, comparing the triads of pulsing to the steady drip, drip, drip, drip of water back in the tunnel. The pulsing rhythm clearly was in groups of three now. It was beating with the rhythm of the potlatch drums which he had tapped out semiconsciously on its surface.

Tom was unsure what to do next. Alone in the tunnel, he had just elicited the first significantly measurable response from the orb since they discovered it. Why him, and why now? He watched the red pulses precisely matching the triads of harmonic tones, and turned to confirm that a video camera and other instruments were recording this. He felt almost drawn to the orb now, compelled to it like to the call of a friend to see something interesting he had not seen before. He slowly reached back and began tapping on the orb with his left hand in the triad rhythm of the drums, matching the orb's pulses as closely as possible. The intensity of the light field from within the orb grew, as did the level of tone. Another harmonic above, then below the original tone began, then increased in volume. Tom reached forward with his right hand and began tapping in earnest with both hands, lightly at first, then more firmly. The orb responded visually and audibly, reinforcing the pattern of three pulses followed by a pause.

He was getting excited now, and could feel static electricity tingling around him as the light began to shift slightly in color and the tone grew louder. The red color began shifting subtly toward violet. He began to chant like the drummers, "Hey ay ay … Hey ay ay …" while increasing the intensity of his drumming. The tunnel began to echo his chanting, reverberating back just slightly out of sync with his voice like reverb on an electric guitar amplifier. The orb's harmonic tones grew louder and deeper, now with another harmonic step lower than the previously lowest note.

Suddenly, he thought he felt the rock began to move. It felt like a tremor. He stopped and looked up at the ice overhead and saw it undulating slightly. A small slab of about one square foot in area and perhaps an inch thick broke loose and began to fall straight down on top of the orb. Tom jumped back as the slab dropped into the spherical space on top of the orb and vanished. It didn't shatter or melt. It simply disappeared. The ground was definitely shaking now, seemingly fed by the harmonics from the orb.

He looked about quickly, scanning in every direction and saw more pieces of ice break loose from the top of the tunnel's arch, and fall to the floor. Realizing that he could be in danger, he scurried to the emergency shelter where the video camera was positioned. The corrugated metal arch was holding solidly, but the video camera tripod was lurching up and down, almost tipping over. Tom reached out and righted the camera, keeping the lens focused on the orb at first. He watched two more pieces of ice fall onto the orb and disappear. He angled the camera up slightly at the ceiling of ice above the orb to be sure he captured this in detail. Soon, another ice chunk, this one nearly three times as large as the first, broke loose and plunged downward. Without using the viewfinder, Tom brought the camera lens down as evenly as possible to trace the ice slab falling onto the orb. The slab vanished.

Slowly, the orb began to quiet down and the tremor subsided. The harmonic tones decreased back to an octave less than what had triggered the tremor, and the volume declined. The pulsing pattern remained in the triad pattern, and the light had a distinctive violet tinge added to the original red color. Otherwise, the orb had settled into what appeared to be a new steady state. Tom turned to the sound of footsteps running up the tunnel. He saw Ben Smith, the radiologist, and

Sergeant Case, followed by several other soldiers with helmets and flashlights.

"Mr. Peters, are you all right?" Sergeant Case called out as he approached. Tom stepped out from the emergency shelter and acknowledged with a wave of his hand. The group slowed to a walk and gathered around him. Sergeant Case and his troops were scanning the inside of the cavern with their flashlights now, and he was looking very much like he wanted to get out of there soon.

"I'm fine. I've just been talking to the orb." Ben Smith looked at Tom first, then the orb.

"Yeah, I saw it, too," Ben acknowledged. "The whole thing is on tape back at the lab. We were watching you and saw the orb respond. What were you thinking about when you were kneeling by it, just before it changed rhythm?"

Tom glanced at the orb, which was still pulsing in the new triad-pause-triad-pause frequency, then turned to Ben. "I was daydreaming about catching some fish. King salmon, actually." Ben studied the Athabaskan geologist carefully, sensing there was more to the story and knowing that Tom would tell it all in good time. Ben checked his portable radiation monitor in a leather case slung over his shoulder to confirm that no new invisible danger was present. Satisfied with that, he noted Sergeant Case's concern and reached out to touch Tom's arm. Tom, seemingly lost in the aura of the spinning sphere, finally acknowledged.

"Okay, let's get out of here."

Tom turned to look at the orb one last time as the group headed down the tunnel. He tilted his head slightly listening to the tone. He swore he could hear voices. Thousands of voices.

Dr. Tamura watched the video closely for the third time, taking particular interest in Tom's demeanor at the time he began to "communicate" with the orb. He wondered what was going on in Tom's mind as he watched the handsome young Athabaskan close his eyes in a dreamlike state and begin to tap his hand rhythmically on the surface of the orb. His scientific mind wondered again why Tom's hand could enter the spherical region of the orb and not suffer the same fate as inanimate objects which were apparently dispatched out of existence when they approached it. The other side of his brain saw something else, though. Something distantly familiar. He watched Tom's half-dreamlike state and the look of peace which seemed to radiate from his face as his hand tapped the drum beat on the orb. Then he saw Tom smile, and precisely at that instant, the orb responded.

George Tamura had been raised in Southern California, the son of immigrant textile workers who had arrived from Okinawa a few years before the second World War. His parents and his two brothers and sister had been relocated away from the coast during the war, to a detention camp with many other people from Okinawa and Japan. He was only eight years old at that time, but he clearly remembered the efforts on the part of his parents and other elders in the temporary community to continue to teach the children, not only the requisite educational skills, but their traditions. From that stark experience, George Tamura had learned tradition, and understood its value in maintaining a historical thread in a community. As he watched the video, he wondered how far in time tradition could maintain such a thread.

Then Dr. Tamura's keen sense of observation awoke. He quickly clicked the pause button on the video control. The screen stopped, flickering slightly but holding steady on the scene where Tom, now awakened, had suddenly become aware of the change in the rhythm of the orb. He tapped a few keys on a computer key board and zoomed in on Tom's hand. The picture became increasingly grainy, but was still clear enough to see Tom's precisely calibrated watch. The time on the watch was 3:31:50 P.M. A time marker in the lower right hand corner of the video showed 15:31:55. Dr. Tamura played the tape forward slowly, watching again as Tom reentered the scene and began tapping on the surface of the orb with his left, then both hands.

Then, he saw another clear shot of Tom's left hand, now surrounded by increasingly intense red light, but with a violet aura. Dr. Tamura again paused the video and zoomed in to Tom's left wrist. The grainy scene was clear enough to show the Breitling Aviator Chronometer on Tom's wrist reading 3:33:45. A tingle of discovery and awareness ran the length of Dr. Tamura's spine as he wrote down the video time marker for that scene: 15:34:10. The video had lapsed two minutes and fifteen seconds, but Tom's watch had only logged one minute and fifty-five seconds.

This was the second time that he seen a temporal anomaly with the orb. After the first occurrence with Kenny and his mother and the small orb, the project team had set up a series of time-monitoring experiments using the small orb. No anomalies were noted when the orb was in its steady, or "idling state" as it was now referred to. Another series of precisely calibrated time monitors had been set up in a line approaching the large orb, but again failed to detect any temporal anomalies. Tom's wrist-watch was the first such observation with the larger orb.

Dr. Tamura accessed the project data base on a computer next to the video monitor. The time monitors had been left in place in a line extending from the video camera to the edge of the spherical region surrounding the orb. The team had originally placed one monitor inside the orb's spherical "protection zone" as they referred to it, and it was just fine until the researcher removed his hand. The time monitor was a precisely calibrated quartz clock mounted on a small, adjustable stand. The bottom of the stand, a tripod of adjustable legs, and approximately one-half meter of the riser were still present. The riser tube had a precise circular cut approximately one meter from the surface of the orb. The rest of the stand and the time piece were gone. It was an inanimate object, and was extending inside the protection zone. As long as a human hand touched it, the orb ignored it. Dr. Tamura thought about that for a minute and corrected himself. Maybe the orb "allowed" it into the protection zone to "observe" it, and was, by elimination, ignoring all other inanimate objects that entered the zone.

The remaining time monitors had been left in place, and continued to run. He accessed the time data series corresponding to Tom's interaction with the orb and confirmed the time anomaly. The time distortion event was proportional to the radius of the distance from the orb. The closer to the orb, the greater the distortion. The maximum difference was still only ten seconds on the time monitor closest to the orb, but was still at least one second different five meters away. All the monitors flashed in precise unison on the computer screen, but all those within five meters of the orb were now reading different values.

He dialed the phone number to the Black Rapids field station. Tom's event had only occurred one hour ago, but the data transmission to the Geophysical Institute was in real time, so the research team could continue to monitor events as they occurred. Other members of the research team began to arrive at the lab as Dr. Tamura reached the field communications center for the project. "I would like to speak to Tom Peters, please."

"Yes, sir. Please hold," the PFC on the phone said. He could hear the young soldier contact Tom by radio, then return to the phone.

"Would you like to hold, sir? Mr. Peters will be here in approximately five minutes."

"Thank you, I'll hold." He placed his hand over the speaker and nodded to Shanna McLane and Charles Singer who had both just arrived. He waved them over and showed them the computer screen with the time data. Then he replayed the video, pausing at the scenes where he had marked the time anomalies. Shanna and Chuck both caught the significance immediately.

"Wow," Shanna exclaimed. "Tom really connected, didn't he?"

Dr. Tamura watched Shanna observe the video, still holding his hand over the speaker on the phone. "Connected," he whispered, pulling the phone away from his ear and looking at it like he was seeing it for the first time. There had been a slight echo in the transmission between the field site and the lab on the UAF campus. Although only about 160 kilometers away in direct geographical distance, the com link was via satellite in a stable geosynchronous orbit twenty-seven thousand kilometers above the equator. The signal had traveled over fifty-four thousand kilometers round trip, adding some distance for the fact that UAF was near the 65th parallel, close to the Arctic Circle. The echo was a time delay for the signal, although traveling at the speed of light, to reach the satellite where it was received, retransmitted by a transponder, and forwarded to him.

"Connected," Dr. Tamura whispered again. Shanna turned and watched as Dr. Tamura stood up and pushed his chair back. "Connected!" he spoke out loud just as Tom Peters picked up the phone.

"Hello, Tom here, Dr. Tamura. Connected to what?" Tom said, and paused.

"That is precisely the question, Tom." Chuck Singer and

Shanna McLane looked at each other then at Dr. Tamura. They very rarely saw the even-tempered, mild-mannered Dr. George Tamura, UCLA physicist, and probable Nobel candidate for his work in antimatter theory, get really excited.

"Hello," Tom said again half in jest. "Is this Tommy's Elbow Room on Second Avenue? Sounds like a party going on. What's up?"

"Connected!" Dr. Tamura nearly shouted. "You were connected, communicating, plugged in." He paused. "Tom, what were you thinking when the orb began to change rhythm? And did you see your wristwatch?" he asked without letting Tom answer the first question. Shanna and Chuck leaned back in their chairs and watched Dr. Tamura pace with the phone in his ear and speaking excitedly to Tom Peters. The phone cord had now completely wrapped itself around Dr. Tamura who was completely oblivious to that.

"I was thinking about my parents in Nenana, and my mother and Betty Swanson dancing a traditional salmon dance. I think it was when I thought of my father catching my mother and nibbling on her ear that I noticed the orb responding. I think I laughed," Tom explained. Then he added, "My wristwatch? It seems fine." Tom paused to check the communications room clock, "but it's off about one minute from the clock here. One minute slow, actually. Why?"

"Tom, we documented a temporal shift again. Check the time monitor data and replay the video. Look closely at your watch at 15:31:55 and 15:34:10 in the video. Did you feel, hear or observe anything else?" Dr. Tamura looked up at Shanna and Chuck as he posed that question, now curious at their apparent amusement. He wrinkled his brow a bit, then noticed he had wrapped the phone cord around himself. They both smiled at him, and he grinned back as he turned slowly around counterclockwise to unravel the cord.

"Dr. Tamura," Tom said slowly, "I heard voices. Many voices, all in unison like they were singing. It was like a choir, more or less. Very pleasant, harmonic and … distant."

"Thank you, Tom. Look over the video carefully and document what you have just told me. We are going to redesign the experiment we had been planning. Good work and thank you." Dr. Tamura placed the phone receiver back on the cradle in the control panel, and turned to Shanna and Chuck who sat attentively. "I think the orb is a communications link to somewhere, and/or some time distant from here. And I think Tom has discovered that whatever is there likes music. I also think Betty Swanson figured this out some time ago, and she has been waiting patiently for us to catch up with her realization. Let's get busy people. We have a concert to prepare."

The area around the orb inside the glacier had been hollowed out to enlarge the work room to a diameter of some thirty-five meters. A geodesic dome of aluminum struts and plates now protected the research team and instruments from falling ice. The tunnel had also been shored up with more reinforcing metal arches, so that access to the domed experimental chamber was as safe as possible. All of this, Tom knew, would be moot if the Galloping Glacier decided to move, particularly as it had done in 1936 and 1937, when it had raced forward, nearly engulfing the Richardson Highway before it began to recede again.

Tom examined the superstructure of the geodesic closely, looking for any buckling or other signs of stress. The frame appeared to be solid and none of the plates showed any bulging. Several technicians bustled about hooking up wires and sensors, connecting cables to computer consoles and aligning instruments in an array around the orb. Every now and again, one of the technicians would stop to admire the glowing, slowly spinning object, which continued to pulse in the three-pulse pattern followed by a pause which Tom had somehow initiated. Within a few hours, everything would be ready.

The helicopters arrived with the remaining members of the chorus experiment team by mid-morning under slightly overcast skies and a steady wind funneling off the glacier. Within thirty minutes Dr. Tamura had assembled all of the choir, as he called them, into the now very crowded mess tent. Since the duration of the experiment was uncertain, he had arranged for sandwiches and drinks to be available as an early lunch. Nearly eighty people were gathered in the tent, munching on sandwiches, sipping hot coffee and sodas and listening intently as Dr. Tamura reviewed the experimental process one last time.

"Remember, be alert. We don't know exactly what is going to happen, but our hope is that we will be able to document another time anomaly, and, just perhaps, open up a broader band of communications with whoever is on the other end." He looked over the entire room, and paused when his gaze reached Betty and Kenny Swanson. "Betty, is there anything you would like to add before we go in?"

Betty Swanson had been thinking a lot about this moment, and had discussed it at length with Kenny, and with her husband Carl. She was a strong-willed woman, but one of great sensitivity to those about her. Her family knew this and deeply loved her for it. Others who had the good fortune of working closely with her had come to respect her for her simple, yet enlightening comments. Betty seemed thoughtful for a moment, then nodded to Dr. Tamura that she would indeed like to say something.

As she stepped forward, the room became quieter. People stopped eating and listened carefully, partly because they knew she had a quiet voice, but mostly because they were intent on what she had to say. "Thank you Dr. Tamura," Betty started out. "I would like you all to know what I am feeling, because I think it may be useful. I feel a sense of peace in the presence of the orb. I sense no hostility and no danger. Last night I dreamed we were on a threshold of awareness, but we are like children in its presence. We may be surprised by what the orb does, but my feeling is that we should not be afraid. Observe as if through the eyes of a child. Offer no presumptions about what the orb is trying to tell us. I believe it is a gift to us, and we should carefully open this gift with the wonder and surprise of a child unwrapping a present."

The entire room was still, not just silent, but motionless. Her words had filled the air with a new and wonderful anticipation beyond the clinical experimental protocols which had been carefully laid out by the science team. Betty looked carefully around the room, and added, "I also wanted to thank you for finding gainful employment for Kenny." She stopped and flashed her bright Athabaskan smile as the room began to reverberate in laughter.

Dr. Tamura grinned as Betty looked at him. Just about the time he thought he had reached the pinnacle of respect for this slight, but thoughtful Native woman, he found himself again amazed that in this very controlled and tense situation, she had captured the essence of easing the moment with humor. "Thank you Betty," he said. There was nothing else he could add.

The large orb spun silently in place, a luminescent green in color with the intensity pulsing steadily in the triad-pause rhythm which Tom had initiated ten days before. Kenny watched as two soldiers carefully set the case containing the smaller orb down on a stand near an elevated platform next to the larger orb. As they unlatched the case, he felt a tingling of anticipation. Shanna paused from her work at a console and looked up at Kenny. The reflected light from the interior of the aluminum geodesic dome accentuated the red color of her hair. Kenny looked up and saw her watching him. They smiled at each other as their eyes met.

The soldiers opened the case locks and slowly raised the cover on its hinges. "Look!" Kenny gasped out loud. The room quieted as Dr. Tamura approached the case and stood beside Kenny. The smaller orb was spinning silently in place in perfect emulation of the larger orb, glowing luminescent green and pulsing in the triad-pause rhythm of the two-meter orb. This was the first time the smaller orb had exhibited this pattern. "The smaller orb was motionless and colorless when it was last checked at the UAF campus," Dr. Tamura said. "This behavior ..." he paused at his own selection of words, "... is new. It is somehow communicating with the larger orb or is being influenced by it."

With an intensified sense of anticipation, the research team finished setting up the last of the equipment. In the center of the dome was the two-meter orb and the octagonal, elevated wood frame platform, about one-half meter high and twelve meters in diameter. The platform completely surrounded the orb where it pulsed inside a three-meter circular hole in the center of the platform. The top half of the orb extended above the platform's surface.

The array of equipment around the edge of the platform included a quadraphonic sound system and a ruby laser controlled by a computer which could be programmed with any number of frequencies and patterns. Dr. Tamura did not know if the orb would respond to sound or light, but he was prepared to probe it with both. He looked about the room, and announced that the experiment would begin in five minutes. Chuck Singer, the laser physicist, was the designated operations controller. He queried each work station in the circumference around the sphere through his console and confirmed the readiness of all systems. "We are 100 percent online with all systems, Dr. Tamura. The choir is tuned up."

"Thank you, Dr. Singer." Dr. Tamura turned to Betty Swanson who had been watching from the side of the platform. She was dressed in a full-length, colorfully beaded, soft moose-hide dress and moccasins. Her long black hair flowed over a beaded band around her forehead which carried the symbols of her people's history on the Tanana. Kenny knew what each symbol meant since Betty had taken the time to share the many stories that they represented with her children, and with her nieces and nephews. She was a storyteller, a position of great honor and responsibility in the world of the Salchaket Athabaskans. Only in her generation were the stories now being written down. To this time, their history had been carried only by word of mouth from mother to daughter. For this day, Dr. Tamura had asked Betty to tell the oldest story that she could clearly relate from her family's history.

Betty stepped up onto the platform and walked over to Dr. Tamura and Kenny. She had explained that the story would be acted in dance and song, with a musical background of singers which she had prerecorded for the sound system. Kenny and Tom were the actors, playing the role of mammoth hunters.

Dr. Wescott, the UAF Museum Director, had prepared part of the presentation from the museum archives. She had prepared a videotape from previously recorded ceremonies of the Tanana-basin Athabaskans, including several segments which Betty Swanson and her extended family had collaborated on. The videotape machine was programmed to download into an analog-to-digital converter, which Dr. Singer had interfaced with the laser and sound system. The result would be a holographic image of the videotape, complete with full surround sound, projected onto the platform. Betty, Kenny and Tom were to perform in the center of the holographic projection, and would appear to be inside the three-dimensional display on the platform. To enhance the laser projection, a slight mist of dry ice was arranged to cascade over the platform during the program.

Betty had prepared an outline of the presentation, which had been carefully time-programmed into the data stations around the perimeter of the presentation platform. The time sequence had been initiated at Dr. Tamura's direction, and would start in sixty seconds. "Hold," Dr. Singer announced. "We are at the programmed initiation start hold point. All stations report in." One by one, each of the data stations around the perimeter signaled to Chuck Singer that they were online and ready. Ben Smith checked his radiation monitoring system again and reported a nominal condition. Only background geological emitters were being detected on the instruments, and at normal levels.

"Secure eye protection," Dr. Singer called out, and everyone donned laser-protective goggles. Betty, Kenny, and Tom had specially fitted lenses with elastic bands so they could move about freely without worrying about adjusting them. Betty saw the room darken slightly and take on a greenish hue through the lenses. She looked up across the room and saw her husband watching from a distance. Carl smiled at her in the same admiring way she remembered when he first saw her as a young woman performing one of her family's ceremonial dances at a community potlatch in Fairbanks. She had caught his eye at that moment, and had smiled at him as she whirled about gracefully to the rhythmic beat of the skin drums, swaying clusters of falcon feathers in the air over her head. Carl had immediately fallen completely in awe of this elegant young woman, and never let go. She returned his smile now as she had done then.

Kenny watched as Tom walked to the edge of the platform to the case with the small orb. Tom adjusted his goggles slightly, and reached into the case to pick up the spinning orb which continued to pulse in the triad-pause cadence, perfectly in unison with the larger orb. Kenny looked past Tom at Shanna. She was supervising the time-monitoring equipment, and looked up as Tom lifted the small orb and its luminescent green light began pulsing throughout the room. Then she saw Kenny watching her. She smiled and silently mouthed, "Don't fall down," and smiled broadly. Kenny fought back a chuckle and gave her a small thumbs up sign. Tom turned toward them both with the orb levitating slightly above his outstretched palms.

"All ready," Chuck Singer announced. "On your signal, Dr. Tamura."

"Thank you, Dr. Singer. Resume the countdown, now." Dr. Tamura had been watching the exchange between Betty and Carl Swanson, and somehow knew the energy of their relationship was a factor in this experiment. He didn't know why, or how it could be translated into some physical manifestation in the behavior of the orbs, but he felt oddly at peace with the premise that an aura of love between two people would provide the basis for the next level of understanding of this interesting phenomenon. He also had observed a similar aura grow between Kenny and Shanna. The effect of their relationship on the smaller orb's behavior had also been clearly documented. "Very analytical," George Tamura thought to himself. "Very analytical indeed. How very beautiful." He looked up as a digital time clock ticked down 0:59, 0:58 ....

Tom Peters was still "holding" the small orb in his outstretched palms. Actually, his hands were little more than a reference platform for the levitating, spinning sphere. He gently placed the small orb on an elevated platform to one side of the two-meter orb. The small sphere continued to spin, levitate and pulse in perfect time to the large orb.

When the countdown finished, the laser and sound show began. The dry ice mist was being evenly distributed throughout the stage by an overhead fan, and the red laser began sweeping a brush of light back and forth through the mist. Images appeared of a group of Athabaskan drummers sitting in a semicircle around the octagonal platform. In unison, the drummers commenced a rhythmic triad-and-pause cadence, precisely in sync with the pulsing of both orbs. The sound poured clearly from the quadraphonic speakers, and filled the aluminum geodesic with the ancient rhythm. Instantly, the larger orb shifted color from luminescent green to a slightly darker green, and the intensity of the pulsing grew. Tom and Kenny both noticed the smaller orb respond in precisely the same manner.

Betty Swanson began to dance, stepping in the triad-pause beat. She had two long curved sticks in front of her which she held up and swayed back and forth like the tusks of a mammoth. The drummers began to chant, now accompanied by a background of female voices. The music grew in volume as Betty stepped back and forth on the stage, swaying the wooden tusks. Kenny and Tom were stepping in place to the triad-and-pause beat of the drummers, left-right-left-pause. Betty now seemed to be almost in a trance. She swirled in a full circle and came about facing Kenny and Tom, the mammoth hunters. "Owooo!" she cried out loudly in as deep a voice as her small frame could muster.

The ghostly drummers cried back in unison, "OWOOO!!!" in a loud response. The hunters watched silently, stepping left-right-left-pause. Both orbs suddenly shifted color to a blue translucent hue. The pulsing deepened and the smaller orb began to rise slightly off its waist-high platform. She thrashed back and forth defiantly as the two hunters continued to pace slowly toward her, still stepping in the triad-pause beat. Each had a willow bow, with gut strings. Still stomping they drew imaginary arrows and set them in the bows to fire.

The mammoth bellowed again, immediately answered by the drummers and female chorus. "OOWWOOO!!!" The hunters continued to march, stomping harder on the wooden platform, now raising the bows up in front while drawing the invisible arrows in unison. The mammoth stomped and thrashed harder, and bellowed again as loudly as she could. Immediately, the chorus cried back, but this time accompanied by a thundering four-octave harmonic chord from the two-meter orb and a simultaneous three-octave higher chord from the smaller sphere.

At the booming under and overtones from the orbs, Dr. Tamura felt a tingle run quickly down his spine. He glanced at the time monitors as the ones closest to the large orb began to slow down perceptibly, now losing a few tenths of a second every three or four seconds near the center of the stage. Shanna looked up to see if he had noticed. He nodded to her and returned his attention to the platform. The mammoth was stomping in place facing the two hunters head on. The hunters stomped loudly in place with arrows drawn fully and aimed at the mammoth's neck. "OOWWOOO!" The mammoth literally screamed out.

"OOWWOOO!" the chanters roared back as their images vibrated in the tremor of a five-octave under- and four-octave overtone from the two orbs. The orbs were now deep blue in color and pulsing so intensely the laser light appeared to almost fade with the three on-beats of the triad-pause rhythm.

Then the hunters fired. The mammoth tusks whipped sharply

into the air in response. She cried out but in a muffled, strangled sound, "Ooowwffff."

The response from the chorus was almost querying, "OOOWWFFF??" The orbs responded at precisely the same time in diminished three- and two-octave tones, with a slight upward twist at the end of the chord. Again the hunters drew arrows and fired, still stepping solidly in the triad-pause beat. The mammoth thrashed upward again, then dropped to one knee. "Oowwff," she cried almost quietly.

"Oowwff," the chanters responded in almost hushed voices. The orbs emitted a chord again with a precise decrease in volume exactly in time with the holographic chorus.

Betty now dropped to both knees and rolled over on her side gently laying down the long curved tusks. The mammoth lay still. The hunters still stepping in rhythm to a now subdued beat set down their bows. The drums thumped and the chanters hummed quietly in the background. The deep blue of the orbs softened now, and a gentle harmonic chord accented that of the holographic chorus. Kenny and Tom turned to the small sphere, still stepping in unison, and gathered it between their hands. Lifting, but not touching the fluorescent blue, pulsing sphere, they moved toward the fallen mammoth. They kneeled near the mammoth's slumped frame, moving their shoulders in the triad-pause rhythm as they set the orb near the mammoth's heart.

Betty's arm formed a cradle in which the small sphere now levitated near her. The hunters rose and stepped back in rhythm as the drumming and chanting continued quietly. Then ever so gracefully, Betty rose, cupping the orb with the skill of an Olympic rhythmic gymnast, rolling the sphere over her arm and raising it above her as she stood up. Holding the orb high in her right hand she twirled about and murmured, "Oowwoomm."

"Oowwoomm!" the chorus sang back. The spirit of the mammoth had risen.

Betty twirled under the small sphere which hovered precisely in place over her hand, eyes closed. "OOWWOOMM'" she called out again, but more loudly.

"OOWWOOMM!" the chorus sang back accented by a deep melodic chord from the larger orb. The small orb began to emit a swirl of violet light, first upward, then descending like a waterfall over the sphere and surrounding Betty. She turned about slowly stepping in the triad-pause beat in her soft moccasins, now completely surrounded by a violet curtain of light which pulsed with the same rhythm. Then she stopped. The drummers stopped and the chanting stopped. She opened her eyes, looking up through the cascading violet waterfall spiraling about her, and raised her other arm under the orb. She looked deeply into the small orb and smiled.

Betty felt a warm sensation, like an early winter williwaw, the warm wind. She could hear voices murmuring and laughing from the sphere. Looking very far into the depth of the violet light, she smiled and uttered a single word: "Greetings." The small orb pulsed once and a wave of warmth flooded over her extended arms and face. She heard the voices say greetings to her, but in fluent Athabaskan. She looked up in surprise and pulled her hands down to her mouth. The small sphere stayed suspended in the air above her.

Slowly the violet shower of light began to fade. Betty was still looking up at the small orb, but now began to back away, sensing something was changing. She moved back by Kenny and Tom, near the opposite edge of the platform, and watched the small sphere begin to increase the intensity of its spinning. Both orbs had ceased the triad-pause rhythm, and were now pulsing in a deep blue light in a gentle, even cadence, accompanied by a low harmonic tone. The small orb was spinning at a very high speed, pulsing in harmony with the larger orb, and emitting an increasingly high-pitched tone. The velocity increased exponentially as the orb seemed to shrink in size. Still faster, the tiny orb was now only half of its original size and a very deep blue in color. Within seconds it was spinning so fast that the air around it began to swirl in a small cyclone. The high-pitched tone transcended out of audible range, and the now very tiny orb spun so fast that it was nearly invisible.

Then, spinning at an extreme rate, the tiny orb began to descend diagonally toward the larger orb. Within seconds, it reached the edge of the two-meter orb and passed directly into it and disappeared. When the small orb was gone, the larger sphere stopped spinning, turned black and became silent. Dr. Tamura approached the platform. He stepped up on the wooden octagon, and walked toward Betty, Kenny, and

Tom. Together they approached the large sphere and looked at it closely.

It was not just black, but appeared to be an area of complete absence of color. More accurately, Dr. Tamura thought, of a complete absence of matter or energy. Betty reached out and touched the surface, followed by Dr. Tamura, Kenny, and Tom. It felt warm and smooth to the touch, and seemed to elicit a tingling sensation on their fingertips. Betty gasped suddenly, "Look!"

Even as the others turned to see what had surprised Betty, they saw the area of the sphere under their own hands begin to glow like a translucent, three-dimensional screen. Dr. Tamura looked closely at the image in the screen and recognized a sequence of small characters. Peering closely, he recognized them as oriental. The characters formed and reformed before his eyes until something familiar appeared. Suddenly he touched the surface of the orb with his index finger. "Look. I think it says greetings, but in Japanese."

Kenny and Tom looked at Dr. Tamura, both of them smiling. He looked up at them inquisitively. "Ours is in English," Kenny said.

"Greetings." Betty laughed and said, "Mine is in a sort of badly translated English version of Athabaskan. In the background, though, there is a picture of a wild tea leaf. That is the old symbol of greetings in our culture."

Dr. Tamura stood back and turned to the assembled group of scientists and observers. "I believe we have just made contact."

CHAPTER 6

Response

Early Winter, A.D. 1975

D r. Tamura sat quietly in his office in the Geophysical Institute. He turned off the overhead fluorescent lights, leaving only his desk lamp on to work by. This was a mid-morning ritual which he had established for this time of the year. His office faced south, and the early December sun rose in a long, low arc over the Alaska Range, casting amber light into the office at odd angles which changed slightly each day. Fairbanks was losing five minutes of sunlight per day now as the Winter Solstice approached. The Tanana Valley was enshrouded in brilliant white snow, which reflected even the faintest of the oblique rays of sunlight.

He could see the bright crown of the sun just clearing the sharp peak of Mt. Deborah near Black Rapids Glacier. Closing his eyes he imagined the sun was the glowing orb that cast its light on him and his colleagues just a few months ago. "Greetings," it had said. "Greetings." He opened his eyes and saw that in the past five minutes the sun had shifted slightly to the west, but was still only halfway above the horizon.

"And greetings to you, whoever you are," George Tamura said out loud. The sound of his own voice lifted him out of his half-dreamlike trance. He leaned back in his chair and tapped his mechanical pencil on the arm rest.

The small orb had levitated out of Betty Swanson's hands

and had drifted into the two-meter orb just before the larger one shifted to a mirror-black color and ceased its pulsing tones and color displays. Had the small orb merged with the large one? Was it transported somewhere? There was no end to the questions this event raised. The entire staff had pored over tapes and data for weeks trying to understand what happened in the "chorus experiment." What they knew as fact only made what they didn't know all the more agonizingly mysterious.

They knew the area in the vicinity of both orbs exhibited some sort of a time anomaly, in effect a slowing of time which was inversely proportional to the radius from the surface of the orb. The time anomaly was only exhibited when the orbs were active, but the intensity of the anomaly peaked at a value which appeared to be mathematically constant. Only a certain amount of time displacement occurred at maximum intensity of orb activity, peaking at the same level every time.

George Tamura looked at the sun again. The bright sphere was now completely above the distant mountain peaks, having taken nearly ten minutes to do so, and shifting several degrees west along the horizon in the process. He watched the sun, squinting at the direct light even though the triple glass panes of the Elvey Building's windows were slightly mirrored just for this effect. His pencil stopped tapping. At two hundred thousand kilometers per second, the light of the sun had taken 8.3 minutes to reach the earth. The sun had been clear of the west side of Mt. Deborah's Peak even as he saw it just rising above the east side. It had taken so long for the light to reach him that he was watching it in the past. He also knew that relativistic physics predicted a time anomaly due to deflection of the space-time continuum in the vicinity of any sufficiently massive object, such as a star. The sun was such an object, as he recalled the experiments conducted on shifting of starlight during a solar eclipse in a precise validation of Einstein's predictions.

The orbs were not such massive objects, though. Indeed, the small orb could be carried freely about by a single person, although weighing it had proved difficult since it tended to levitate when touched. To complicate matters more, it levitated better when Betty Swanson or her family members touched it than when other people did. They had ultimately determined its weight in the old-fashioned way, by displacement of water.

The orb displaced very close to one kilogram of water, hardly enough to shift the space-time continuum.

The large orb's mass they still did not know. It remained in the same location where they had found it, and would not move. They had discovered a smooth 2.5-meter-diameter channel of rock leading away from it as the glacier had been carved away. Tom Peters had been the one to postulate that what the channel represented was tectonic plate shifting. The crust of the earth had moved, not the orb. The protective field around the orb had simply removed the rock as it approached the orb. The line of travel showed the orb had started above the surface, most likely in the glacier, and was now slowly channeling its way into the rock.

The travel time from when it had first touched the rock and begun carving its perfectly round trench was estimated to be around twenty-five thousand years. That was based on known rates of tectonic plate movement in the Alaska Range of about two centimeters per year, and the length of the trench to its present point, about 500 meters. The research team tried to estimate how long the orb had been above ground prior to that. Based on the angle of the glacier's advance down the valley, the orb could have traveled several kilometers at least, which would add as much as another one hundred thousand years to its travel time. No similar round channel in the rock wall on the opposite side of the glacier had been found, so the current estimated range was between 25,000 and 125,000 years since the orb had appeared? George Tamura began tapping his mechanical pencil again. "Appeared? From where, or from when?" he thought to himself.

Suddenly the phone rang, startling him out of his reverie. As he reached for the speaker button, someone knocked on the door. "Come in," he announced, and picked up the handset instead.

"Dr. Tamura!" he heard simultaneously from the phone and from Shanna McLane who had just burst through the door.

"Whoa, wait a second," he told Chuck Singer over the phone while holding up his hand to Shanna. "Shanna just came in."

"Put her on the speaker with you. We have the same information for you," Dr. Singer said. Dr. Tamura tapped the hold key and set the receiver back in its cradle. Shanna was excitedly hopping from one foot to the other as he tapped the "speaker" key.

"Okay, what's up?"

Both Shanna and Chuck Singer began speaking at the same time, then stopped. Dr. Tamura sat back, somewhat amused by this. "Try again, Chuck. You go first." Shanna nodded and scurried over to a bookshelf looking for something. She found a large atlas, and pulled it down on top of multiple stacks of papers on Dr. Tamura's credenza. He watched with consternation as she dropped the huge book on top of his neat stacks of documents and began frantically flipping pages.

"Dr. Tamura," Chuck spoke. "I just received a call from a colleague of mine working in South America. Dr. Sergio Chambelán, with the Instituto de Los Planetarios in Buenos Aires, Argentina contacted me this morning. An international geophysical team working in the southern Andes near Santa Cruz, Argentina just found another small orb!"

"Here," Shanna pointed at the atlas, "at the upper end of Lago Argentino. Lake Argentino." Dr. Tamura was up out of his chair and scanning the map where Shanna was pointing.

"It thawed out of a receding glacier," Chuck said. "Glaciar Perito Moreno, which enters the Western end of Lago Argentino. Shanna was in my office when the call came in. She can show you the location on a map. I am waiting for another call from Dr. Chambelán. I'll be up to your office as soon as I hear from him again. He is getting more information from the field team as we speak. Shanna will fill you in with what we know so far. I have to hang up now in case he calls."

"We've got it now, Chuck." Shanna spoke loudly for the speaker phone to pick up just as Chuck Singer clicked off. Dr. Tamura stood quietly now, looking at the map, then at Shanna who was virtually beaming.

"Very interesting, Shanna. And what do we know so far?"

"The geophysical team was measuring the glacier's rate of receding, doing some survey work. It is summer there, late spring actually. The survey team was taking astronomical position readings to groundtruth the terrestrial survey at night, and saw a light in the glacier. They photographed it, marked the location and went to investigate the next morning. They traveled by boat since the glacier terminates directly in the lake, and found the point of observation on the southern edge of the glacier against the side of a rock wall. They found the orb on a ledge of rock recently exposed by the receding glacier."

"And the status of the orb?"

"Resting on the rock and glowing with a luminescent green light. They picked it up and it pulsed and began to levitate. It startled them, as we well could imagine, and they dropped it. It settled to the ground when they pulled their hands back. The orb was still completely intact from the fall, and sat there pulsing slightly with the same green light. One of the surveyors, a geologist, picked it up again and let it levitate in his hands. It began to emit tones, which increased to the extent that some glacial calving began to occur, a little too close for comfort. They wrapped the orb in a blanket and took it back to their camp when the calving of the glacier calmed down."

"Where is it now?"

"That is what we are waiting to hear," Shanna answered just as the phone rang. Dr. Tamura punched the flashing line button to activate the speaker.

"Tamura, here."

"Dr. Tamura, it's Chuck again. Sergio just called. The survey crew took the orb back to their camp on the southern edge of the lake. They were examining it in the early evening, watching it glow and levitate, when they saw an aurora australis, the southern lights, of unusual intensity. They said they saw the light from the aurora reflecting in the glacier. The aurora faded, but the light inside the glacier did not. A bright red glow continued inside the ice, not far from where they found the small orb. They marked the precise location of the light. Some of the survey crew believe it is a sign from God."

"Perhaps it is," George Tamura spoke quietly. "Dr. Singer, please check on the status at Black Rapids now and meet us in the conference room in thirty minutes. Shanna, let's pull the project management committee together." She was already out of the room before he reached the phone to shut off the speaker.

"At approximately 14:30 hours, the two-meter orb at the Black Rapids site became active again." Chuck Singer spoke with excitement in his voice, calling out the facts with precision, but with decided enthusiasm. "The first sign was a shift from the mirror black to a slight green color. Here is a video image transmitted from the site, recorded just forty-five minutes ago."

The video screen image showed the interior of the aluminum dome. The large black orb sat silently in the center of the wooden octagonal platform, under the watchful monitoring of an array of instruments and cameras patiently waiting for a sign of any change in status. The video image zoomed forward suddenly and the black orb filled the twenty-nine inch screen. From deep inside the orb, a wispy swirl of green light began to spiral up. The phosphorescent green glow looked like an aurora, but from the top rather than underneath. The intensity grew and the color deepened. In the center of the swirl, a red glow began and became more distinct. Green light now filled the orb, and the red spot in the center began to pulse. The green became even more luminescent and the spiral of color began to swirl counterclockwise with increasing energy. The orb had begun to spin. For nearly ten minutes the red glow in the center pulsed and swirled, then it faded out. It was luminescent green again, and spinning in place with a steady pulsing rhythm which was an echo of the pulse of the red center glow only moments before.

"I have asked Dr. Chambelán to set up a video link to the field crew at Lago Argentino if possible. He advised me that would be difficult, but could be done with the assistance of a U.S. military communications satellite in polar orbit if we could arrange that." Chuck Singer looked up at Dr. Tamura who nodded and picked up the phone on the table in front of him. He dialed a single four digit number and waited for several seconds.

"Colonel Wells. George Tamura here. We have a significant development occurring in the project and require your assistance." He paused for a moment, then spoke again. "Thank you sir. We will see you shortly." Dr. Tamura looked up at Chuck Singer, "No problem. What else do we need?"

"I recommend we start planning for a field team to go to Argentina. I also think it would be useful for Sergio Chambelán to come here first for a few days so we can brief him on our findings. Since the preliminary announcement of our discovery at Black Rapids a few weeks ago, we have been receiving up to a dozen requests per day from scientific research teams and institutes around the world. Sergio's institute had already inquired, then they discovered their orb near Santa Cruz. He has tentatively assembled a project team, but is hampered by a lack of funds to do very much. Maybe we can expand our project funding to assist them."

Dr. Tamura nodded again, this time jotting down some notes. "We should be able to do that. This is the breakthrough we have been hoping for." The phone on the conference table rang, and Dr. Tamura picked up the receiver. "Yes. Thank you. Please have the Colonel join us in the conference room right away."

Moonlit night cast long shadows across the glaciated landscape as Sergio Chambelán peered out of the window of the Boeing 727. This was the first time he had seen Alaska, and the late evening moonlight was putting on a wonderful show as the Alaska Airlines jet slipped quietly over the top of the Harding Ice Field. Bright snowy peaks of the Chugach mountains filled the scene. Then he saw the lights in the sky. First, just a dim band of green, more like a curtain, stretching across the northeastern sky. Sergio cupped his hands around his face to block out several bright reading lights near his seat. The auroral energy was building, and shimmering waves of light rippled through the bright curtain of green. A sharp red line began to glow on the bottom edge of the green curtain of light. It flickered rapidly as the waves pulsed through the starlit night.

Then he saw the Denali massif. Mt. Aconcagua and numerous other mountains of his native Andes were taller, but this giant granite mass stood cold and huge in the moonlight, climbing nearly seven kilometers vertically from the valley over which it towered. The light of the aurora reflected off of the double peaks of McKinley as he felt the three steady engines of the jet begin to throttle back for the approach to Anchorage. He leaned back in his seat, and looked over at his assistant, Laura Manesto, who sat next to him. She was sleeping fitfully after the nearly two days of travel from Buenos Aires. An announcement from the flight attendant that they were preparing to land awoke her.

"Los luzes del norde alli, circa de Montana McKinley," Sergio spoke quietly. She leaned forward to look, but the bright lights of the interior of the jet had been lit to allow the flight attendants to ready the cabin for landing. She brushed back her hair

and responded in English, partly to practice, and partly to remind herself of where they were.

"How bright are they?"

"Much brighter than our aurora australis, and very dynamic.
The primary green band reached virtually across the entire sky,
and waves of green and red light rippled through it like a flag
waving in the wind." Laura smiled. All Latin men were a bit
poetic. It seemed to come with the territory.

"So here we are in Alaska. I have no idea what to expect.
Dog teams and igloos, perhaps?"

"I don't think so, Laura. My friend Chuck Singer sent me
several photos of the campus in Fairbanks. It is a small but
scenic college, and it appears quite modern." Sergio stopped
speaking as the 727 touched one wheel on the runway and
then the other two. The thrust reversers snapped into position
and the jet roared loudly for a few seconds. Its forward inertia
dissipated quickly as a few gallons of kerosene atomized and
burned in the turbines, but exhausted forward rather than to
the rear of the engines. The jet taxied toward the Anchorage
terminal, then came to rest near one of the jetways with Alaska
Airlines printed boldly on the side. The flight from Seattle had
taken nearly four hours, and both Sergio and Laura seized the
opportunity to get off the plane to stretch their legs a bit before
the final forty-five minute hop in the same jet to Fairbanks.

Laura took the window seat on the flight to Fairbanks so
she could see the aurora. The light show was no disappoint-
ment, nor was the granite massif of Denali. She was still partly
lost in the dreamy trance of watching "los luzes del norde"
when the end of the jetway in Fairbanks opened up into the
brightly lit terminal.

"*Buenas noches, mi Amigo!*" Chuck Singer shouted out and
held his arms open. "*Como estas?*"

"I am fine, my good friend," Sergio answered as the two
men hugged like brothers. "Please, allow me to introduce my
assistant, Laura Manesto. She is a physicist at our institute."

"*Mucho gusto en conocerle,*" Chuck said as he embraced her
lightly and gave her a small kiss on the cheek. She was a striking
brunette, tall, thin and very Argentine, Chuck thought. He did so
enjoy the customs of his Latin friends, particularly how they em-

braced, touched and kissed openly. Unlike the standoffishness of so many cultures, including the North-Americans.

"You speak Spanish very well," Laura offered. "I would imagine that it is not so common to find people who use Spanish regularly here." Chuck was equally impressed with her command of English.

"Thank you," he smiled. *"Muy amable. Bienvenidos."* Sergio laughed and patted his friend on the shoulder.

"Very good, Charles. Very good."

"Well, please. Let us get your luggage and I will take you to your hotel," Chuck said. "We have much to show you, and much to talk about."

"Yes, my friend, we are very eager to see what you have uncovered here. The small orb we discovered is a most extraordinary object, we have come to learn. I am particularly interested to see how it compares to yours. Also, Chuck, I have just learned by phone during our layover in Seattle that the survey team at Lago Argentino is now tunnelling into Glaciar Perito Moreno, and are within about 100 meters of the source of the light inside the glacier." Sergio enjoyed watching the intense interest on his friend's face. He and Chuck Singer had spent nearly two years together in graduate programs at the University of Michigan. Sergio had helped him learn Spanish, and Chuck assisted Sergio with his English. Even today, they would lapse into dialogue with Chuck struggling through his Spanish verb conjugations, and Sergio responding in thickly accented English.

Laura was somewhat amused by this, but lapsed back into her dreamlike vision of the aurora out the window of the jet as they carried their luggage out to Chuck's Chevy Suburban. The dark Alaska sky swallowed up the bright lights of the airport as they drove off to town in the heavy vehicle.

Shanna McLane and Laura Manesto immediately hit it off. They were about the same age, and quickly discovered they had similar interests in mathematics and physics, although they were from quite literally opposite ends of the earth. Shanna was showing Laura some of the time anomaly data from both the large and small orb, while Chuck Singer and Dr. Tamura struck up a conversation with Sergio about the behavior of the Argentine orb. Kenny Swanson arrived with Tom Peters and Ben Smith a few minutes later. Chuck had graciously arranged for a pot of very strong coffee and milk to be served, Argentine-style, during their meeting. Introductions were followed by demitasses of coffee. Shanna hooked Kenny's arm and shuffled him over to meet Laura.

"This is Kenny. He and his cousin Tom are the ones who discovered the orbs at Black Rapids Glacier. Kenny's mother is the Athabaskan woman whom the orb responded so intensely to."

Laura smiled and immediately got lost in Kenny's misty blue eyes. How striking she thought, those intense blue eyes, but with that black hair similar to that of the indigenous people in the Andes. "I am honored to meet you, Kenny," Laura said, still gazing into Kenny's eyes. "This is a very nice laboratory you have here."

"Thanks," Kenny responded a little uneasily at first. "The project has been well funded from the outset, and we have been able to obtain just about anything we need." He broke the stare first, smiling a bit and then looking away. He was a bit unnerved by her intense stare. Suddenly, Laura realized that she was making Kenny nervous. She began to pick up where she had left off with Shanna, who was tapping away steadily on the computer keyboard, accessing more data for Laura to see.

Kenny headed back over to the conference table to refill his little cup with that wonderfully strong coffee. He looked up at Tom as he sipped his coffee, and Tom quickly poked a thumb up as he slurped his and nodded emphatically. A new Tanana Valley camping tradition was in the process of being born.

Dr. Tamura motioned for Kenny to join them, and called over to Shanna and Laura as well. "People, we have a lot to show our colleagues from Argentina, so we must organize the effort to maximize the available time. First, however, I would like to open the forum to Dr. Chambelán to bring us up to date on developments with his project underway at Lago Argentino." George Tamura pronounced the name perfectly, replacing the 'g' in Argentino with a solid 'h' sound so that it sounded like Arhenteeno. Sergio Chambelán was impressed.

"Thank you, Dr. Tamura. And please allow me to extend the sincere appreciation of the Instituto de Los Planetarios and of the República de Argentina for your generous assistance with our project. As you know, we are continuing to tunnel into the

Perito Moreno Glacier and expect to reach the source of the light within a few days. Based on your experience, we are anticipating that we will find an analog to the two-meter orb you discovered here in Alaska. We are using the insights gained from your work to define our approach to the object and to select the instrumentation we will examine it with. At this time, we know the small orb appears to exhibit very similar properties to the one here, before it disappeared into the larger sphere. In fact, we hope to compare our data with yours from the small orb to see if it is, as it is beginning to appear to be, an exact duplicate." Sergio Chambelán paused for a moment, then added, "It has even been postulated that it is, in fact, the same orb, but has somehow reemerged in our country. We are open to suggestions on how we can prove that theory."

Dr. Tamura looked straight at Kenny, then at Tom. Kenny and Tom looked at each other, then back at Dr. Tamura, both nodding almost imperceptibly. "The orbs at Black Rapids seemed to respond more to certain individuals, particularly members on the maternal side of Kenny and Tom's family. Although it may appear to be somewhat subjective, I would suggest we have Kenny, and perhaps his mother, examine your orb to see if it ..." he paused for a moment, "... recognizes them." Sergio Chambelán's eyebrows rose with that one.

"Do you think the orb has some sort of recognition capability, Dr. Tamura? If so, it would imply an extraordinarily high level of intelligence, I would think."

"Yes, Dr. Chambelán. That is precisely what we believe, or at least strongly postulate at this time based on what we know. Perhaps when you see the videos of our experiments in communicating with these orbs, that will help to elucidate our reasoning. It might be helpful to let Kenny explain in more direct terms."

Kenny picked up the cue and stated as clearly as possible the feelings and images he experienced when he held the orb or was otherwise in its presence. Tom Peters added his experience in the ice tunnel with the two-meter orb when it changed rhythm. "Probably the oddest thing Tom and I both experienced was what sounded like voices. Not just a few, but thousands of voices at times, like in a stadium during a sporting event or a concert," Kenny explained. "The feeling was so strong I am certain that if your orb exhibits the same property, then Tom or I should readily detect it. Dr. Tamura," Kenny said, "it will likely have to be Tom or me. I don't think my mother will want to travel that far, particularly with my younger sisters in school."

"Hmm, yes. That would present a bit of a problem," Dr. Tamura said. "Unless we can bring the small orb here for her to examine. For now, though, I believe Kenny and/or Tom could do such an experiment quite acceptably." Dr. Tamura turned back to Sergio. "Is there anything else you would like to add before you begin reviewing our data?"

Dr. Chambelán thought for a moment, then added, "Just for the sake of curiosity, Dr. Tamura, what do you believe these orbs are, and what is their purpose?"

George Tamura had spent most of the past year wrestling with precisely that question. "My theory? They are some sort of a communications link to some distant place, or some distant time. Right now, we are just beginning to learn how to dial up the operator. We hope to figure out how to do that without accidentally ringing up some sort of a 911 number. The orbs exhibit tremendous power in their near-steady state. We have seen glimpses of what can happen when they get a bit more intensively stimulated. The bottom line is that I believe there is some very high order of intelligence at work here. We are like prehistoric cavemen who just discovered a modern telephone, and don't have much of a clue what to do with it."

"Thank you for your observations, Dr. Tamura. Miss Manesto and I are very much looking forward to seeing what you have done thus far."

The afternoon twilight was now fading outside the tinted windows of the Elvey Building, although Sergio Chambelán hardly noticed. He was completely intent on Ben Smith's discussion on his radiation monitoring at the Black Rapids site.

"The orbs were never observed to emit alpha, beta, or gamma radiation at levels detectable above the background geologic source intensity. The only anomalous energy we have been able to measure is a slight increase in x-ray output." Ben paused when he noticed Laura Manesto and Shanna McLane look up at him at the same time from a pile of data they were pointing at and discussing. "Something, ladies?" he inquired.

Shanna and Laura looked at each other in a querying fashion and began discussing something about emissions from the event horizon of a gravitational anomaly. By now, the pause in Ben Smith's presentation and the curious display of some sort of awareness between these two very attractive and very intelligent young women had caught the attention of the entire room. Dr. Tamura had been talking with Kenny and Tom about an experiment to test the Argentine orb, and noticed the shift in the focus of the room. He walked over to the conference table and stood next to Dr. Chambelán.

Laura was tapping one finger on the table and circling her other hand around above it. Shanna was nodding, at first just a bit, then a bit more. Laura's hand gestures increased in intensity as she spoke, which made for a very pretty scene since she had very lovely long fingers and delicate arms. Tom and Kenny walked over to join the scene, and both were studying, or rather enjoying the hand gestures. Chuck Singer noticed Kenny's and Tom's interest and smiled. Latin people spoke as much with their hands as with their voices. When a pretty set of Latin hands was speaking this intensely, it was quite attractive.

Dr. Tamura started to speak, but stopped when the two women simultaneously scooted back their chairs and paced briskly to a nearby chalkboard. Laura began drawing a circle with arrows and tangential lines. Shanna stood back and studied the drawing as Laura explained something about a "Chandreskahar Limit," then quickly chalked several lightning bolt figures emanating from near the center of the figure. Her hand with the chalk now swirled gracefully about in a downward spiral, then repeated the gesture several times. Shanna picked up a piece of chalk and drew two circles, joined by a funnel-shaped tube. Then she began writing a complex equation over the top of the tube, paused, and thought for a moment. Dr. Tamura again started to speak, but stopped when Shanna's chalk began noisily tracing on the board.

"What if we apply a smaller mass constant at the core, perhaps with some very heavy material which has a density exceeding anything on the current periodic table of the elements. A "super-element" with a mass of, of …" Shanna tapped the point of the chalk on the board, "… say 200 atomic units."

"It would be incredibly unstable," Laura said. "It would have a half-life in the micro- or nanosecond range."

"Yes," Shanna said excitedly. "You bet it would. If it was in this room it would flash out of existence so quickly we would never even be able to see it. But we would see energy emissions, perhaps lower mass particles probably consisting of both matter and antimatter." Laura was standing with her arms crossed looking first at Shanna, then at the chalkboard. The rest of the room sat back and just watched. Then Dr. Tamura started to nod as he saw Shanna begin to smile.

"But not inside the event horizon," he muttered softly to himself, but just loudly enough for Shanna to hear.

"Yes!" Shanna nearly shouted. "Exactly!" Shanna was smiling at Dr. Tamura, then for the first time noticed the assembled collection of observers surrounding them and watching intently. Laura finally picked up on it, too, and actually blushed very slightly, Tom Peters noticed. Kenny was enjoying this immensely for all the wrong reasons. He had only a spec of a clue what his amazingly enthusiastic red-haired, green-eyed young friend was going on about, but the display of energy and grace between Shanna and Laura was, well, sort of stimulating. Tom caught Kenny's vibes and nudged him with his elbow lightly.

"Pay attention, Swanson. This is science."

Kenny grinned and muttered back, "And how."

Shanna was now writing again on the chalkboard, creating a second line below the first equation, but this time with numerical values replacing several of the mathematical symbols. "Look, Laura, if we collapse our super-element inside the event horizon where time slows down, the element stabilizes. Only the most energetic emissions result. Some gamma radiation perhaps, but more likely x-rays."

Shanna looked up at Ben Smith, who was just starting to catch up with the theoretical drift. He nodded to Shanna, then asked, "How much energy emission are we talking about here?"

Shanna looked up at her equation again, then tapped the chalk at the number describing the value of the mass of the super-element. "It is a function of the amount of this," she paused, "and of the input of mass/energy into the gravitational anomaly on the input end." She tapped the chalk at one end of the funnel. "Let's say this end is the black hole." Her chalk moved to the other end of the funnel. "And this is a 'white hole', an emitter. The x-rays are actually an artifact of the very slow decay of our super-element in the slow time field of the black hole."

"How would you stabilize such a system?" Chuck Singer asked.

"Good question, Dr. Singer. It would take some sort of a powerful containment field, perhaps something like the torus-shaped magnetic field designs being tested for fusion reactors in Switzerland and Stanford. The power required would certainly be a function of the mass of the black hole." Shanna paused, again studying her second line of calculations. "If the black hole was very small, microscopic in size let's say, then the energy field to contain it could be relatively small, too. By relatively small, I mean something that could be no larger than this building, perhaps, assuming a suitably powerful energy source could be tapped from somewhere."

"Maybe a large fusion or fission reactor?" Ben Smith offered.

"Possibly," Laura spoke again. "But it would have to be a pretty substantial reactor. Other possibilities could be a maser beam, microwave, not light, directed from a nearby star, or a captive black hole. A collapsed companion star in a binary system with a relatively stable orbit would work. But how would you tap the energy out of it?"

"That is why they can do this, and we cannot. Yet," Shanna added with emphasis. "That is a technology question. Compared to who or whatever has figured this out, we are technologically prehistoric. Our physics is just barely able to begin to guess what the structure of this system might be, let alone sufficient to decipher how to build one."

Dr. Tamura spoke up. "A very interesting theory. It appears that a fair amount of our data and observations might fit your model. Very good work, Shanna and Laura. Quite creative. Can we take Dr. Smith's x-ray emission intensity readings and back-calculate some ranges for the mass of the object creating the black hole, assuming the orbs are the white hole end of the funnel?"

"Yes, but with no shortage of assumptions," Shanna said. "Also, we have another interesting feature to the behavior of the orbs which puts another twist on this theory. The flow of information or energy, or whatever is the device of communication here, is two-way." She paused again and looked up at Kenny. "At least two-way. If our discoverers are hearing hundreds or thousands of voices, it may be much more than bidirectional. This implies that each end is both an emitter and a receiver."

"Like a telephone?" Sergio Chambelán asked.

"Yes, Dr. Chambelán. Or perhaps like the computer network being discussed that would be developed between campuses and research centers where data can be sent quickly between mainframes, in almost real time."

"There must be some very advanced technology at work here," Chuck Singer added. "Look at all the heat generated by our IBM 360 and data corruption through the transmission lines. What we have here is a communications device which remains cool, and presumably accurate in its transmission quality, probably across interstellar distances."

"Exactly", Dr. Tamura added. "But technology does not stand still. The IBM mainframes are very fast, particularly compared to the older, larger machines. Project the technology line forward and you could imagine data processing speeds in a few decades at megahertz speeds in computers no larger than a hand calculator. Add to that the experiments with fiber-optic cables and data corruption rates fall by orders of magnitude. I think Shanna said it most accurately. We are, in fact, technologically primitive."

"But we are awakening," Sergio Chambelán stated. "And the interstellar phone just rang."

The tall blond man with the misty blue eyes pointed to the sky. The belt of Orion, the hunter, shone brightly in the moonless black night. A soft trace of green aurora arced gently through the star field of the Milky Way galaxy. His long, slender finger moved across the belt, then down the sword, and paused at the middle star. He smiled, then cupped his hands in the shape of an upside down bowl. His fingers slowly straightened and formed two flat, sloping edges with straight sides formed by his hands.

Kanak nodded in understanding. He spoke to Sheenak the word for home. She smiled and snuggled close to him under the warm, heavy blanket of short-faced bear hide. A slight breeze stirred the fire and a swirl of glowing sparks climbed swiftly into the cool night air, flickering and dissipating as quickly as they formed. Kanak studied the bright object in the fair-skinned man's hands. It was a beautiful shimmering orb, glowing in a soft green luminescent light like the aurora. The man held the object in his hands, which were straight in front of him now, palms up. The orb began to spin slowly and rose up from the upturned hands like a bird hovering in the updraft along a mountain slope.

Kanak felt like he was dreaming. Sheenak stirred and freed her right arm from under the bear hide, and reached forward to touch the spinning orb. As her fingers approached it the object began to emit a low, beautiful tone. Her fingers caressed the orb and the tone deepened with a second harmonic, then a third. Kanak pulled her shoulder back cautiously with his arm reaching around her. She nudged him slightly and smiled, then reached forward with both hands to touch the spinning orb. As the blond man now pulled his hands back to his lap, Sheenak saw the orb begin to change color. The soft, luminescent green began to change to a blue color. A point of red light began to form and swirl in the center of the orb as the blue color intensified and the tones deepened further. The blond man smiled as Sheenak pursed her lips and hummed in harmony with the tone. Then she looked up in surprise, momentarily pulling her hands away. The orb fell nearly to the ground but the blond man reached forward and caught it.

Sheenak snuggled back under the hide next to her mate. She pulled the hide close around her and uttered the word for *voices* into Kanak's ear. The blond man set the orb on the ground near them. The tone dissipated and the color returned to the soft green hue. Kanak and Sheenak watched as the blond man rose from his cross-legged sitting position near the fire. Kanak had heard the voices, too. Among them he heard his father.

The Bell 206 Jet Ranger bounced slightly in a down draft, and Kenny's head bumped the window. The padding of his parka hood softened the thump, but he awoke from his dream. He looked out the Plexiglas window and saw the long sloping valley of the Delta River leading up to the mountains of the Alaska Range. Shanna stirred next to him, and awoke too. She stretched and sat up. She had been leaning on him, something Kenny found to be quite pleasant. He smiled at her and said, "Good morning."

"And good morning to you, Mr. Swanson. I was dreaming about the small orb. A blond man was showing it to me, and I was with you under a heavy blanket, like a bear skin or something. There was a fire and the stars were bright and clear. I dreamed that I touched the orb and it sang to me."

"I heard it, too," he said. "There were voices. I believe we had the same dream." They looked at each other curiously, trying to understand how they could share the same dream. "Your name was different, though. It was ..."

"Sheenak," she interrupted him. "And you were ..."

"Kanak?" he posed.

"Yes," she said. "How odd."

The smooth whine of the turbines changed pitch as the sleek helicopter banked to the right to land. The Black Rapids camp was blanketed in snow before them. Kenny pointed out of the left window. A long line of yellow side-boom Caterpillar tractors puffed and steamed as an insulating machine wrapped a coil of material around the 48-inch-diameter steel pipe which would be the Trans-Alaska Pipeline. Work crews scurried about, while welding sparks flashed brightly on steel beams between vertical support pipes frozen into the hard ground. The nearly kilometer-long assembly of workers, pipeline, and equipment arced up the side of the Richardson Highway toward Isabel Pass. Sergio Chambelán was in the passenger's seat next to the pilot, and was taking in the view from the bubble. Laura Manesto was watching out the left side of the chopper next to Shanna. She was enjoying the scenery immensely, and was wondering to herself what all those rough-and-tumble Alaskan men building that pipeline were like. She sat back and smiled. This was a pretty neat place for a young woman to find herself in for a while.

Dr. Tamura addressed the group of researchers assembled in the mess hall. "The Argentine crew has reached the source of the light in Glaciar Perito Moreno." He enunciated the name in precisely correct Castilian Spanish, once again impressing Sergio Chambelán. "I would like Dr. Chambelán to explain what they have discovered."

"Thank you Dr. Tamura. Yesterday, the tunneling crew reached a cavern in the glacier and found a two-meter diameter orb, virtually identical to the one here. Using the military communications satellite data link we were able to determine that the rate of spin, and the frequency of pulsing is precisely matching that of the large orb here. The colors appear to be identical as well. At this time there is no tone emanating from either object, but both appear to be active. The small orb is in a field lab in the geological survey camp near the glacier, and is in a case which is a duplicate of the one you used here to transport your small orb in. I would be happy to answer any questions about this."

"Dr. Chambelán, what is the status of the structure you are building around the two-meter orb, now?" Tom Peters asked.

"That is moving forward nicely. The aluminum dome is being installed in the cavern, and the tunnel has already been completely reinforced with corrugated metal sections. We hope to be finished within a few days. At this time a half-shell exists over the top of the orb so we can conduct an initial experiment in reasonable safety."

Dr. Tamura looked out over the room. "If there are no more questions, we can proceed with the first passive comparison experiment. In about forty-five minutes the polar orbiting com satellite will be in range to provide a video link from Argentina to here. A video monitor to view their orb has been set up in the chamber near our orb for this. A second monitor has been installed near the orb in Argentina which will have a view of our orb. The data link will last about twelve to fourteen minutes, then will be lost as the satellite's orbital path swings around the South Pole."

"Our experiment will simply be to have two people, one here and one in Argentina, touch the two-meter orbs at the same time, and to observe the response. This is more a test of our ability to simultaneously probe the two orbs while monitoring both from nearly opposite poles of the planet. Precise timing has been arranged by setting two atomic clocks, one at each location, which will cue the events. This is necessary because there will be a few seconds delay in the video transmission. If everybody is ready, we need to move to the chamber now to get ready for the experiment."

"Ten, nine, eight, seven, six ..."

"Cinco, quatro, tres, dos, uno ... "

"Now!"

"Abora mismo!"

Kenny reached forward and placed his hand on the smooth surface of the orb. At precisely the same time, his counterpart, an Argentine geologist who had introduced himself over the video monitor as Juan Tomas did the same. They watched each other in the video monitors and waited for a few seconds.

Then both orbs pulsed, emitting a vivid green light, almost explosively like a camera flash. Both Kenny and Juan jumped back and broke contact with their respective orbs. Dr. Tamura quickly announced for Kenny and Juan to step back. "Hold, everybody. Let's see what happens. Kenny, how are you doing?"

"I'm fine, I think. Just a little surprised at the intensity of the reaction. I think Juan was, too." Kenny peered at the monitor which showed the half dome in Argentina lit up with the turquoise light of the glacier ice. The dozen or so researchers who had been monitoring their orb were all crouching down behind crates and equipment, peering up at the orb like soldiers in trenches in some old war movie. Juan had rather quickly joined them when the green light flashed. They had been startled by the display from the orb, as had their counterparts in Alaska. A whole lot of pulses were racing on two continents right now.

Kenny noticed the orb begin to change slightly in color, to a deeper green. Then part of the green surface began to clear to the mirror black shade they had seen when the orb went silent. Dr. Tamura saw the orb in Argentina doing the same thing. He glanced at the time clock and noted that they had only about five or six minutes of video link left. "Kenny and Juan, please approach the orbs and observe the black mirrored surface area closely," Dr. Tamura requested.

Kenny stepped up to the platform again and walked directly to the orb and peered into the circular black region which had formed in one-third of its top hemisphere. Juan Tomas took a little longer to approach his orb, moving rather hesitantly forward, while keeping an eye on Kenny in the video monitor. The Argentine orb was half imbedded in rock, or, more precisely, levitating in a circular hollow in the rock. Thus a platform was not needed like in Alaska. Juan finally reached the orb.

"We have only about three or four minutes of video linkage left." Dr. Tamura said. Do either of you see anything?"

"No," they responded at the same time.

"Then reach forward and touch the black surface again, precisely at 18:30:00 GMT," Dr. Tamura requested. The clocks had been set to Greenwich Mean Time since the six-hour time zone difference between Alaska and Argentina added an unneeded dimension of confusion to the experiment. "Hold your hands in place for only one second, then pull back. Ready, countdown, five, four, three, two, one, now!"

Both Kenny and Juan touched their orbs at precisely the same time, paused one second and pulled back. Both orbs pulsed slightly with a muted green flash, then the mirrored black region began to swirl with violet light. An image of a hand formed, palm facing up at Kenny, and an identical palm facing up at Juan. The hand was like a human hand, only much smoother, and the fingers were very long and thin. Kenny felt a tingle in his spine as he looked closely at the image. It was the hand in his dream. He glanced up at Shanna who could see the image as well in video monitors around the room. Her hand rose to her mouth, almost touching her lips as the same realization struck her. It was also the hand she remembered in her dream. Their dream.

It was the hand that had presented Kanak/Kenny and Sheenak/Shanna with the orb. It was the hand of the person who had shown them how to make it levitate, how to sing to it and how to make it glow.

Kenny reached forward to touch the image of the hand. Dr. Tamura watched quietly. Kenny's fingertips touched the fingertips in the image. Juan took the cue and did the same a second later. Kenny reached forward now with his left hand and touched the surface of the mirrored area with both hands. Slowly, he reached into the orb with both hands, gently grasping the image of the long slender hand and touching. He thought he could feel something, not like solid matter, but like a fuzzy static electric field shaped like the hand. It was like touching a fleece glove, he thought.

Juan had pulled his hand back and stepped away from the orb, partly because the video image from Alaska had begun to flicker and fade. Kenny now felt the fuzzy, static electric hand touch his hands. He held his hands perfectly still as the hand in the orb caressed his lightly. Then the image pulled back into the sphere, and returned to a palm up position, like the universal sign of hailing. Kenny withdrew his left hand, then turned his right palm to face the image in the mirrored black area. He pulled his hand back just until it was on the surface, which he felt become smooth again. He watched as the image faded slowly, and the violet color swirled deep into the center of the orb. Then the black mirrored surface vanished until only the cool, green light and gentle spinning motion of the orb remained. Kenny looked up to see the last image of Juan Tomas fade in a hail of static as the satellite link was lost.

He turned to Dr. Tamura, who was standing next to Shanna, and said, "I think we just shook hands with the operator. I think also that Shanna and I have done this before."

Dr. Tamura looked at Kenny curiously, then at Shanna. She looked up at him, still almost in a dreamlike trance, and nodded affirmatively. "I heard voices, too," she said quietly.

CHAPTER 7
The Question
Spring, A.D. 1976

The longer daylight in the spring always raised spirits. Shanna was no exception. She found she could think more clearly and creatively as the sun seemed to energize her mind. The confusing anomalies in her equations and calculations had seemed to almost solve themselves over the past several days. It had to be the light, she thought, although it might very well have something to do with the sparkle of the diamond in the engagement ring on her left hand.

She held her hand up in a sunbeam, and the colors of the rainbow glistened in her eye. She turned her palm outward facing the sun, and felt the warmth on her hand. Yup, it had to be the increasing daylight, she chuckled to herself. No other reason she knew of.

George Tamra paced back and forth in front of a large diagram on the wall of the conference room. He, too, had noticed the light, and contemplated the increasing angles of the sunbeams entering the room through the tinted glass windows. He paused on occasion to tap his ever-present mechanical pencil on a chair, table top, or when a particularly strong intuition bubbled to the surface, on the diagram itself.

"Here ..." he thought to himself, tapping the pencil on the end of the funnel near a cluster of equations, "... and here, at precisely the same time." He stopped and smiled. "Time? Whose time, or what time? Maybe not any measurable time at all. Time distorts at the terminus of the funnel, and maybe-no, probably-inside the funnel, or tunnel, or whatever it is, as well. And most certainly at the other end."

George Tamura turned and looked five meters down the

wall at the other end of the diagram, toward the origin of the funnel. "Who are you?" his mind beckoned. "Who are you?" he spoke out loud this time, half startling himself.

"Maybe we should ask?" a soft voice spoke from across the room near the door which was open. The new voice jolted him out of his reverie.

"Betty! You startled me. How good to see you. Please, please come in." Betty Swanson had been watching Dr. Tamura for a few minutes, but she knew the question even before he spoke it. She smiled broadly, and entered the room with her nearly silent walk which always surprised George Tamura by its almost primitive grace. Her people had walked the game trails and silty banks of the Tanana River, virtually isolated from the rest of emerging humanity, for thousands of years. Yet her walk could be that of a princess in an English castle.

"Maybe we should ask, George," she repeated. Betty was the only person on the project that routinely called him by his first name. George Tamura was not a particularly formal person, or so he thought. But everyone associated with the project always addressed him formally, a habit that he made no attempt to modify. He was one of those gifted organizers, a natural leader. You could assemble any random group of a hundred or more people under any circumstance, and within an hour, they would be looking to George Tamura for leadership. And he would provide it, ever so naturally. He gave little thought to this, and only passively recognized his own talent in this capacity. That considerable talent had been recognized by highly placed people in the Federal Government, however. So when the project began, his selection as the principal investigator had quickly emerged from none other than the White House itself. There was not even an alternate choice. He was it. He was called. And he led the project team with consideration, vision, and strength.

He was actually honored to have Betty call him George. He was not quite certain why, but it had something to do with the orb, and with her role in her culture. She was the matriarch of the chosen family lineage, and carried her responsibility with care and love. Love for her family, for her elders and, particularly, for her children. She guarded her people's traditions with tenacity and shared the stories and songs of their history with

142

precision. No European or Japanese royalty could claim more importance to their culture, or represent their people with more grace and sincerity than Betty Swanson.

And, for whatever reason, "they" had chosen her family. She seemed to be able to communicate with them at a level of understanding that he had only begun to grasp through the rigid analytical processes of his own mind. It seemed that at critical moments in the project she simply knew what to do. No, she felt what to do. Or dreamed it. Betty Swanson was one of the few people on the project George Tamura felt like bowing to in the subtle Japanese tradition of his parents. But they had become Americanized when they arrived in California at relatively early ages, so he only bowed when he was in Japan, in deference to the customs of that land. The feeling that he should bow to Betty, though, was instinctive. It was the Japanese custom of respect. Even as his conscious self chose not to, he knew that the urge was pure.

"Maybe we should ask, George," she repeated again, approaching him across the brightly lit room. He finally broke out of his contemplative reverie and acknowledged her statement.

"Do you think they will tell us?" he asked. "Could it be that simple?"

"I can't imagine that it would hurt to try. They are friendly, if not a bit curious themselves. Perhaps they have a question for us, too, and are only politely waiting for us to begin the conversation." Betty paused and studied his reaction. The mechanical pencil was tapping evenly on the back of one of the chairs around the large conference table. The tapping pace picked up, then stopped.

"Is this something you feel we should do, Betty?"

"Yes," she said without hesitation. "Ever since Kenny and Shanna explained their dream of the scene around the campfire with the strange visitor, I have been thinking about what it means. George, they shared a dream. In my tradition, that is an omen of great power and importance. Kenny and Shanna were visited by those on the other end, and the message was one of peace and offering. They are waiting for us to speak to them."

"It certainly seems like a reasonable thing to do, Betty. You seem to be very certain about this."

"I am more than certain," she spoke evenly, then paused.

She turned toward the window and studied the sunlight for a moment. The soft amber glow flooded across the room like an ethereal hand caressing the furniture. She looked back up at him. "When I was a young girl, younger than Kenny is now, I had the same dream, only I was the woman in the dream. I felt the man who was with me was my husband, but I did not know him yet. The blond visitor was exactly the same in my dream as in Kenny's and Shanna's. George, I never shared this with Kenny or Shanna before they had their dream. I have never shared it with anyone outside my family until now. I have been expecting this event nearly all my life, not knowing why, but with certainty that it would occur."

George Tamura stood in complete silence, again totally amazed by this person. "Why do you think the second orb appeared in Argentina?" she asked.

"Hmm," he started, and turned to look up at the diagram. "Here, at our end," he pointed with his mechanical pencil, "the funnel has a second pathway." The drawing showed two funnels, one straight ahead, marked BLACK RAPIDS, and the second, extending downward at an angle, marked GLACIAR PERITO MORENO. "We found no significant tunneling at the Argentine site, even though the orb was half buried in bedrock. That means it is recent, unlike the one here in Alaska, which has carved out a channel in the rock as the continental plates shifted over millennia. We presume that the second orb was ..." He paused to select his words carefully, "... created, only after we discovered the Alaska orb. It was sort of random chance that it was discovered, but they both certainly responded to being accessed simultaneously."

"You haven't answered my question, George." She peered at him like only a mother could. He felt like an elementary school student trying to explain a homework lesson to his mom. "Why do you think the second orb appeared?"

"My guess, Betty? It was a test of our technology, and of the extent of our civilization's range on the earth." He was beyond facts, now, a somewhat uncomfortable realm for George Tamura, Ph.D. But he proceeded in earnest, now revealing his feelings and imaginings to Betty Swanson as he sometimes found himself unwilling to do with the science staff on the project. "I think that they wanted to know how quickly we would find a second orb a great distance away, and whether or not we had the technology to simultaneously access both orbs in a coordinated manner. We did that, and they responded. That is my theory, Betty. It was some sort of a test."

"That would seem to make sense," she said. "Perhaps when Kenny reached into the orb here and touched the image of the hand, that was the reward for passing the test. It was a higher level of communication than before." She looked at him thoughtfully for a moment, then added, "I think they are ready for a question, now. The quality and substance of the question might be the next test." She smiled.

George Tamura nodded. The project team had wrestled with the data from the "simultaneous contact experiment" as they had referred to it for several months. The conclusions and theories were all pretty much speculative, but the math had advanced somewhat. Shanna and Laura had created the working model with the black hole/white hole funnel. The appearance of the second orb had modified the physics and math significantly, actually producing some intriguing solutions to the gravity equations. The orbs seemed to be somehow connected to the gravitational center of the planet, being precisely equidistant from the center. One mathematical solution resulted when a gravitational anomaly was present at the center of the earth. The theoretical anomaly was essentially a black hole sufficiently large to slightly modify the mass of the planet, but so small that the material collapsing into it, i.e., the earth itself, jammed up around the event horizon and did not disappear into it like it would into a stellar-sized black hole. From that model, Shanna had derived a working equation for a series of microscopic white holes that were linked to the black hole at the center. One of the scientists described it as a connected node, like a telephone switchboard.

"Betty, would you be so kind as to be the presenter of our question?"

"I would be happy to if you think that is most appropriate. What would you like to know? Who they are?"

"Exactly," he said. "I don't know how to pose the question, though. Both orbs have reverted to the mirror-black resting state, and will somehow have to be reawakened. We have tried again to access them simultaneously on several occasions, but they have not responded. Do you have any ideas?"

"Just an intuition. Have you been trying to signal them with anything besides touching their surfaces?"

"Yes. We have tried sequencing tones and light from laser probes, simultaneously timed to contact both orbs. We have even tried individually, but so far they have remained silent. It is like they have been switched off." He crossed his arms and shrugged slightly. "Our theory of what makes them tick seems to be getting clearer, but it seems we don't know how to get their attention. What is your intuition, Betty?"

"They communicated with Kenny and Shanna in a dream, and with me many years ago in the same dream. I think that the three of us need to contact them back."

"What do we need to do?"

She smiled and her clear, brown eyes sparkled. "Let's invite them to our campfire. The last time we did, they came in person."

Tom and Kenny spent an afternoon together in the Goldstream Valley behind the UAF campus, gathering firewood. They had carefully selected dried willow and birch hardwoods which would fuel a long-lasting, warm fire. White spruce kindling and birch bark had also been mustered to start the fire. The wood was packed in cardboard boxes in the bed of Tom's pickup truck, then delivered to the Alaska Helicopters' hangar on the east ramp of the airport for transport to Black Rapids. Even though there was still too much late winter snow at the site to allow decent firewood gathering, the ice bridge across the Delta River from the Richardson highway would not allow safe passage.

In their camping tradition, only one match would be used. Tom, who had originated the idea while he and Kenny were on a moose hunt one fall, referred to it as "Tom Peter's world-famous one-match fires." On the rare occasion that it took more than one match, Tom would proudly announce that the first, albeit gloriously brief, one-match fire would now, with no small amount of fanfare including the clinking of beer cans, be augmented by a second one-match fire conveniently located in the same fire pit. The secret was birch bark.

The Alaska mainland was heavily forested with white paper birch, a particularly handsome tree which actually grew in a variety of shades. Many of the birch trees in the Tanana Valley were a brilliant white, though. The outer layer of bark slowly dried and peeled off from the live layers underneath, protected from rain by the tree's thick foliage. This was pure fire-starting material. The dried bark curled up at the ends, providing additional surface area for the tinder with its high fuel content. A single spark would usually ignite a fast-burning, hot flame, which could quickly be augmented with a small handful of spruce twigs to build a serious fire.

Kenny had cleared out the fire pit on the small hill near their first camp at Black Rapids. Spruce rounds and birch logs were neatly arrayed around the pit for seating. Several thick pieces of partially burned birch logs ringed the fire, to protect the starting fire from the wind, and then to contain it. The heavy side logs also provided support for green alder or birch poles to hold a grill if the fire was to be used for cooking. Ultimately, when the side logs burned through, they became long-duration fuel for the fire as new side logs were rolled into place.

Tom had long wondered how his ancestors had ever gotten along without chainsaws. He could whip up a classy fire pit with all of the appropriate timber accouterments including side logs, poles and seats with only a few minutes of effort using his reliable, German-built Stihl. Perhaps his ancestors had more time on their hands, though. Not a bad trade-off at all, he thought as he deposited the last cardboard box of carefully selected fire wood in the area Kenny had cleared the snow from. Tom began to assemble the starting tinder and twigs for the fire.

Kenny paused to look over their handiwork. Everything was ready at the fire pit now, but technicians were bustling around busily in the bright late afternoon sunlight. An assemblage of monitoring equipment, consisting of cameras, microphones and various electromagnetic sensors was being set up around the fire pit. That equipment was sheltered under boxes or other makeshift covers to protect them from the weather, which was actually quite agreeable at the moment. Long cables connected the monitoring equipment to the data acquisition consoles in the ATCO trailer a hundred meters away. The data consoles were already connected by cables to the monitoring equipment in the geodesic dome inside the glacier.

The video displays in the ATCO trailer revealed the two-meter orb sitting silently, mirror-black in color, and at the same cool temperature as the observation area inside the dome. The thermal monitor graph was more or less a flat line, rising very slightly in a smooth bump in the late afternoon, and falling slowly at night and the early morning as the temperatures inside the glacier fluctuated a few degrees Celsius in response to the more dramatic swings outside. The thermal trace was about the only line moving. Every one of the fifty or so other sensors, including spectrographs, microwave monitors, radiation counters and so on revealed not even the slightest fluctuations in their readings.

The original transient satellite link to the orb at Glaciar Perito Moreno in Argentina had been augmented by a second link to a high powered communications relay satellite in a stable geosynchronous orbit twenty-seven thousand kilometers above Ecuador. The large, commercial com satellite was new, and had a direct line of sight to Buenos Aires, where a microwave link to the Argentine glacier had been set up. A microwave link from Black Rapids had been established to Fairbanks, which was also in the line of sight with the satellite.

Laura Manesto glanced at the video monitor in the lab at the Instituto de Los Planetarios in Buenos Aires. *"Sergio, mire. Están Tom y Kenny en Alaska."* Dr. Chambelán looked up from his work and walked over to the video monitor. Tom was carefully placing a teepee of spruce twigs over several curled pieces of birch bark, after which he leaned back, studied his handiwork and began breaking apart small birch branches to place around the twigs. Laura was amused at the precision with which Tom was assembling the firewood. She was further amused at the fact that Tom and Kenny did not seem to be aware that the video link was live, and that they were on transcontinental "Candid Camera."

"Es un hombre muy guapo, no?" Sergio Chambelán asked, watching his bright-eyed young assistant study the Alaskan on the monitor.

"Yes, a very handsome man, indeed," she responded in perfect English. "I don't think they know the video is on."

Kenny was standing to the side of the fire pit, looking thoughtfully up the slopes of the clear white mountain peaks behind the glacier. He glanced sideways at Tom's emerging masterpiece. "Nice work, cousin. That should actually be a one-match 'one-match fire' this time, unlike the one you built last fall when we were caribou hunting."

Tom was bent over the fire pit fiddling with the curled bark inside the teepee of twigs. He glanced over at Kenny and straightened up on his knees, sitting back on his heels. "Hey critic. That was a windy hilltop, in the rain, in the dark, and without the magic ingredient," Tom protested.

"There was plenty of birch bark!"

"Beer," Tom said flatly.

"Oh. That magic ingredient."

"Yeah. The situation was a bit challenging. Besides, it was precisely at midnight since you chose to shoot that caribou practically in the dark, and the first match was on Saturday, while the other first match was on Sunday, a few minutes after midnight."

"Hmmm," Kenny grunted. "Pretty weak, but marginally passable. No excuses here, though. Everyone from Alaska to Argentina is going to be watching, and your reputation is on the line."

"Hey, check this out," Tom said sweeping his hand over the top of the neatly arrayed unlit fire. "A first-class project, if I do say so myself. I would love to see the flame from this baby twinkling in Laura Manesto's eyes."

Two continents away, Laura Manesto blushed and put her head in her hands. Sergio Chambelán laughed out loud and slapped his leg.

"That you would, I'm certain, cousin," Kenny added. "That you would. A very pretty woman she is, and smart, too. When Laura and Shanna get together to talk physics, I'm pretty much left to just watching and having fantasies."

This was too much for Laura. She looked back at Dr. Chambelán and pursed her lips, nodding a bit. "I don't believe this," she said. "I just don't believe this."

"Hey, you are the one playing … what's his name on American TV… Señor Funt. You know 'Candid Camera'," Sergio joked.

Laura picked up the phone near the video monitor and dialed up the long-distance country code for *Los Estados Unidos*, the United States, then the area code and number for Shanna's lab at the Geophysical Institute in Fairbanks.

"Hello, Shanna McLane," a friendly voice answered.

"Are you watching TV today?" Laura asked without introducing herself.

"Hi Laura! What's up? TV? Why? What channel?"

"Try Black Rapids, channel six. We are the topic of a purportedly clandestine discussion between two young Athabaskan men building a fire." Before Laura finished the sentence, Shanna had the video link on. "Just listen and learn. *Adios, mi amiga.*" Laura hung up.

"I … good-bye?" Shanna looked at the phone, then at the video monitor. She reached over and turned up the sound as she set the receiver down on its cradle.

"Hey, watch out, cousin Kenny. You are almost a married man."

"I didn't say who I was having fantasies about, Tom. It's just easier to contemplate the corporeal structures supporting those bright intellects than to bemoan the fleeting substance of their esoteric dissertation."

"Smartly, stated, Mr. Swanson. Quite smartly stated," Tom bowed slightly to Kenny. "I would still like to see the fire twinkle in Laura's eyes," he added.

Kenny raised one eyebrow toward Tom. "I think some kind of fire is twinkling in somebody's eyes already. Pray tell, how many matches were consumed trying to ignite that one?"

Shanna sat back in her chair, totally amused by this. "Get it right, boys," she said out loud to herself. We're recording this for future use." She glanced over to see that the recording light was blinking silently on the video tape deck.

"Only one, I think," Tom said after a contemplative pause. "At least for this man's flame. She ignited my tinder from the first spark."

Laura was now leaning back in her chair, one arm across her waist, cradling the elbow of her other arm which supported the hand under her chin. She was rocking slightly, half-amused, and half something else. Something between flattered and curious.

"Enough of this prate. We have serious chores to attend, Mr. Peters," Kenny announced. "The late afternoon chill is upon us and I am led to believe that fresh coffee has been prepared in the mess tent along with a repast of some consideration. Shall we be away, good sir?"

"Aye, with haste," Tom laughed as he placed a small piece of military surplus canvas over the top of several poles spanning the side logs on the fire pit to protect his creation. It would now wait until the following evening when the experiment would begin. Tom stood up and followed Kenny out of the field of view of the video monitors in Buenos Aires and Fairbanks.

Shanna hung up her phone for the second time and smiled.

The mess tent was filled with the aroma of strong coffee and fried chicken Tom and Kenny noticed immediately after they stepped inside.

"Hey, Kenny, a message." Kenny looked up at the cook who was pointing at the corkboard on the wall. A small, folded chicken-grease-stained piece of paper with Kenny's name on it was pinned up. He pulled it down and read the message out loud.

"Nice fire pit, fellas. We particularly liked the view from the back as Tom was leaning over the kindling." It was signed, "Shanna and Laura".

"Oops," Tom said chuckling. "Do you recall if we did anything lascivious or otherwise disparaging?" Kenny stuffed the note in his shirt pocket and started pouring himself a cup of coffee. Tom went on, "Man, it's one thing having Big Brother watching, but this is embarrassing."

"You won't have to work very hard breaking the ice with Señorita Laura, Mr. Peters. I think you just had a fairly serious assist from our global telecommunications network."

"So what was the menu for the Last Supper?" Tom asked. "Coffee and fried chicken?"

Carl Swanson opened the large cardboard box and lifted out the brown fur. The grizzly bear hide had been professionally tanned, so the skin was supple and lined with a velveteen material. Unlike a trophy hide, the head was not attached. The head was still standing marble-white from weathering on the corner stake of Grizzly One mining claim where Carl and the bear had struggled many years ago. His right hand did the heavy lifting, his bear-claw-scarred left hand pushing the flaps of the box back.

"It looks pretty good after all this time in storage," he said to Betty. "A bit musty, but we can air it out tonight."

She reached over and brushed the fur with her hand, then brushed her husband's hair, letting her hand pause against his cheek. "It is a good blanket, but it brings back difficult memories, no?"

Carl Swanson usually took a reasonably pragmatic approach

to such matters. It was one of the many things Betty loved about him. "At least I get memories. Old Griz, here, gets his skin in a box and his skull on a post. I'll take the memories."

Betty leaned forward and hugged him around the neck. "The blanket is perfect. Kenny and Shanna will put it to good use tomorrow night."

The sky was clear. Not just free of clouds, but free of dust since the glacial silt was still wetted down under melting snow. Constellations burned hard in the night, with stars steady, not twinkling. A slight glow from the rising moon edged up in the east behind the stark white peak of Mt. Silvertip. The evening breeze was cool, but not cold. At least not yet. Fading twilight in the northwest would linger for another hour or so. It was time to start the fire.

Tom Peters lit a box match with the fingernail on his thumb, cowboy-style. Laura was impressed, watching from half a world away. He touched the flaming match head to the birch bark tinder and it lit instantly, crackling in the night air. The tongue of flame rose quickly into the spruce twigs and flame shot straight up. The twigs burned brightly, casting warm shadows around the fire pit. Betty Swanson sat on a spruce stump seat next to Kenny and Shanna. Tom sat back, studied the rapidly growing fire and handed Kenny the diamond willow poker stick. "A classic one-match job."

"Nice work, my constructively pyromaniac cousin," Kenny said. He turned the poker stick over in his hand and examined it. Every fire pit needed at least one well-engineered poker stick. It should be of hard, green wood, with some sort of a handle. The section of diamond willow pole Tom had selected sported a neat, slightly curved handle, a bit like a cane. The tip was charred and pointed, and it was long enough that you could sit more than a meter away and reach the far side to encourage branches and logs into the fire.

Flames leapt higher as surrounding birch branches and split white spruce ignited. Several larger pieces of old burned-through side logs began to heat up and smoke as the fire reached out to them. Tom stood up now and watched as the center of the twig teepee disappeared and the neatly stacked birch branches around it began to fall into the center of the fire. Kenny added a few more sections of spruce and birch wood and the fire roared on evenly as the night darkened. "Good luck, family," Tom said. "Say hi for me."

Betty smiled at her nephew, "Thanks for the nice fire, Tommy. Stay warm."

"Thanks Tom," Shanna added.

Kenny raised the poker in a salute. "One match! Master of the Dark Night you are, good cousin."

Tom faded into the blackness outside of the ring of light from the fire, as a programmable video camera began to scan the scene. In microseconds, the image was translated electronically into a laser projector inside the aluminum dome. The sharp blue and red lights of the lasers quickly swept back and forth, spraying the images from the fire pit outside the glacier into a fog of dry ice surrounding the orb at Black Rapids. An identical scene traced out in Glaciar Perito Moreno in Argentina. Both domes were totally darkened except for the laser lights and dry ice mist.

Light from the fire flickered inside the domes, reaching the hands of Juan Tomas in the Argentine glacier. He was holding the small orb and watching it closely. It was mirror-black, like both of the larger orbs. Then a swirl of violet light began to rise inside the small orb. It began to tingle in his hand, and start to spin. The array of monitors on two continents recorded the same swirl of violet light as it appeared simultaneously in the larger orbs.

Kenny probed the fire with the hardened diamond willow poker stick, and a river of sparks spiraled upward into the Alaska night. Shanna and Kenny sat in the crook of a large birch log in front of the fire. The large, tan grizzly bear skin provided a comfortable seat and a warm wrap to ward off the night chill on their backs. Betty watched Kenny work the fire, and pulled a soft caribou hide around her shoulders.

"Look," she said pointing up to the southeast. "The aurora is beginning."

Shanna and Kenny turned to watch as long wispy fingers of green light began to appear in a row across the sky above the moon. At first, the lights were just a few streaks painted against the black of the night, punctuated with bright stars of the constellation Cassiopeia and the swarm of stars in the Pleides Cluster. The aurora began to build.

Dr. Tamura had studied many auroras in the same way that most Alaskans did, standing quietly in the chill of the night in awe of the incredible beauty and energy created by the collision of massive streams of charged particles with the upper atmosphere above the arctic. His analytical side churned with theories and data assimilation as he studied the flow of light down the magnetic lines of force arcing smoothly into the North Pole over northern Canada. His artistic side marveled at the color and motion, but complete lack of sound from this gigantic cosmic collision. He had listened hard for the hissing or static electric crackling that so many claimed they could hear during particularly intense activity. He had never heard it himself, and carried a small shred of doubt that it was any more than wishful exaggeration by overly enthusiastic aurora fans. Until now.

The broad green fingers widened at the top and grew into a curtain, spilling light in a cosmic waterfall which now reached nearly a third of the way across the sky. A surge of red signaling a very high energy level began to weave through the green strands of light near the bottom of the curtain. The red glow sharpened, gathered energy, then erupted in an explosion of motion, rippling across half the sky like a giant wave crashing against a darkened beach. A second red wave followed quickly along the bottom of the green curtain which now pulsed and began to curl into spirals and wisps. Then a third followed, and the night sky became full with a concert of red and green light.

Dr. Tamura pulled his parka hood back so he had a clear vision of the sky, then he heard the hissing. He turned his head away from the fire, which was about ten meters away. He looked quickly about to see if there were any electronic or mechanical sensors within his immediate range of hearing and found none. He cupped his ears and stared hard into the night as the reflection of the surging aurora flickered on the white peaks of the Alaska Range. He watched to see if some nearby willow branches were moving. There was not even a breeze. Just a subtle hiss like the background static from a radio telescope.

Betty saw him cupping his hands over his ears and smiled. "It speaks to us tonight," she said softly in his direction. He turned back toward the fire and put his hands back inside the large warm pockets of his parka.

"Yes. I've never heard it before. It sounds like static electricity." He noticed several others observing the aurora nodding their heads in agreement. The aurora continued to boil across the sky in red and green waves of intense light.

Sharp lines of a half moon rose over the eastern mountain peaks, casting even more light on the earth. The fire burned steadily as more embers rose into the night air. Shanna reached for Kenny's hand under the fur, as he sat back after tossing a few small rounds of birch on the fire. She held her hand between her eyes and the fire to watch the aurora, and squeezed his hand as a particularly active wave curled rapidly across the sky. The red glow from the aurora reflected off the peaks and glacier. Then inside the glacier, a point of violet light began to emerge.

"We have activity in all three orbs," Chuck Singer announced. His clear voice projected from speakers mounted outside the ATCO unit where he watched over the array of monitors and communications links between Alaska and Argentina. "Violet light, some tone and spinning is being exhibited in all three," he said, "and levitation of the small orb in Argentina. They have an aurora Australis of considerable magnitude lighting up their sky, too."

A video monitor flickered under an awning set up just outside the circle of monitors and sensors surrounding the fire. Dr. Tamura watched as a camera zoomed in on Juan Tomas who was inside the geodesic dome in Glaciar Perito Moreno. The small orb was spinning energetically and was fully levitated above his outstretched palms. Then, it began to move away. Juan pulled his hands back like a falconer who had just released his raptor. The small orb was spinning energetically, glowing with violet light punctuated with red like a small aurora. It levitated quickly across the room heading directly for the two-meter orb inside the Argentine glacier, then disappeared inside the larger orb. The larger orb pulsed with light and emitted a deep harmonic tone, then settled quickly into a steady pulsing rhythm of gentle harmonic tones and violet light.

An instant later the small orb, or an exact duplicate, emerged from the two-meter orb inside Black Rapids Glacier. Both of the larger orbs were spinning and pulsing in precise rhythm and harmonic tones with each other. The small orb levitated and pulsed with light and tone in exactly the same rhythm. After it emerged inside Black Rapids Glacier, the small orb floated down the access tunnel in a straight line right past several of the technicians who watched with amazement. It drifted along at about the speed of a fast walk, moving through the tunnel and casting a violet light onto the ice as it passed. Several of the technicians had now begun to walk along behind and under it, carrying various instruments and sensors to study it.

Chuck Singer had announced its arrival, and was giving brief updates on its position. "At the tunnel adit, now, speed constant, activity constant, direction change toward the fire."

Kenny probed the fire again with the willow poker stick. A large swirl of embers rose into the sky. He looked up at the glacier which was visible from the small hill upon which he and Tom had sited the fire pit. He saw the small orb emerge from the adit, and turn toward them. Shanna and Betty were watching, too.

The orb drifted through the night directly toward them, pulsing with light and a melodic chord which sounded like it could have been from an electronic organ. It flew straight across toward the small hill where Kenny, Shanna and Betty waited. It did not follow the changing elevation of the terrain, but levitated forward in a straight line. At the fast walking pace of about one meter per second, the orb took nearly six minutes to arrive. As it reached the outer perimeter of the fire pit observation equipment a sequence of three shooting stars lit up the night.

All three fell in precise motion, starting from the top of the sky directly above them, then plunging downward toward the southeast through a green curtain of the aurora. The first shooting star, which lasted perhaps three or four seconds, disappeared as it reached the second star of the sword sheath of the constellation Orion. Then the third shooting star vanished in exactly the same spot, followed a moment later by the third. Kenny and Shanna both saw the shooting stars and recognized that they had disappeared where they had seen the blond man pointing in their dream.

The small orb arrived at the fire pit and stopped, levitating two meters above the ground across the fire from Kenny and Shanna. A smooth harmonic chord played as it pulsed with violet and red light. Betty rose from the spruce stump she had been sitting on and walked toward the orb. Holding the caribou skin close around her, she reached up with her right hand and held her palm open underneath the orb. It settled down gently onto her hand, and the rate of spinning slowed. The colors muted and the tone quieted, but remained steady and clear. She turned toward the fire, looking across at Kenny and Shanna. The orb was levitating and spinning just above her hand. She stepped carefully around the fire and returned to the small circle of stumps where she had been sitting near the fire.

Betty had now positioned the orb to the side of the fire, near her, but also facing Kenny and Shanna who watched from under the grizzly bear hide. She pulled her hand back inside the caribou skin, and stepped back away from the orb. It remained in place, levitating, spinning and emitting the pleasant harmonic chord.

"Welcome," Betty announced to the orb. Then she sat down, watching.

The orb pulsed once and added an octave above and below the first chord. The sound pulsed and echoed smoothly in the night air. Then the tone returned to the original chord. From deep inside the orb a swirl of light began to form, like a reflection of the energetic aurora overhead. The swirl of light was a deep violet color, spiraling upward out of the orb and began to cascade over the orb like a waterfall of light touching the ground below, but not splashing. The light intensified, filling an area around and below the levitating orb in a circular curtain. Then it rose one meter as the shower of violet light spilled upward and arced downward to the ground. The fire pit glowed with purple and reddish hues from the orb which was now flowing with light like a water fountain.

Suddenly, several traces of bright white lights in arches began to emerge from the orb, flowing along the lines of the cascading violet stream like phosphorescent plankton in the wake of a boat on a dark night. The white lights flowed out of the orb now in increasing intensity, swirling around inside the fountain of violet light. The swirl of bright white points of light began to trace out a pattern inside the violet fountain, and soon the image of a man began to appear.

Within a minute, the image cleared and stabilized. It was the blond man with the intense, clear eyes, which were deep violet in color. As the image came into focus, the color of his eyes changed to a misty blue. Then, the man reached slowly up and grasped the spinning orb over his head. Suddenly, the cascade of violet light stopped and the blond man stood glowing in the night, holding the orb in his left hand, and looking straight ahead at Betty, who sat calmly on the spruce stump only a few meters away.

Dr. Tamura watched with great curiosity and awe. The man was exactly as Betty had described him, and as Kenny and Shanna had, too. Then George Tamura saw the blond man bow toward Betty. It was ever so slight, but clearly distinct. George Tamura gasped, then caught himself. He felt his eyes fill with salty water at this gesture of respect from the alien visitor for this slight, but elegant Athabaskan woman. Betty rose, pulling the supple caribou skin around her shoulders and smiled. "Welcome back," she said.

The visitor smiled, and reached inside his smooth, tan coat. He produced what appeared to be a small twig at first, and handed it to Betty. She laughed pleasantly when she took it, with her musical voice. "Thank you," she said. "You are very kind to remember." She twisted the small plant in her hand for a moment and turned to Kenny and Shanna. Kenny immediately recognized the twig of Indian tea, the Athabaskan symbol of welcome and peace, and whispered into Shanna's ear. She smiled and squeezed his hand under the bear hide.

Betty turned back to the visitor, who now spoke. "Thank you for inviting me back to your fire, Betty. It is a lovely evening with a beautiful aurora." He turned slightly to look up at the sky, then back to Betty. "It speaks to me, too," he added.

"I would like you to meet my son, Kenny and his fiancée Shanna," she spoke. The visitor turned toward them and smiled. Kenny reached out from under the bear hide with his right hand. The visitor leaned forward and shook Kenny's hand, then Shanna's, who had followed suit.

"I am very pleased to meet you," Kenny said. "I believe we may have shaken hands once before."

"Yes," the visitor said. "We have. And we have visited before, as well," he said to both Shanna and Kenny as the image of their simultaneous dream clarified in their minds. The visitor smiled and turned back to Betty. "You have a question for me, I believe. What may I share with you?"

Betty glanced back at Dr. Tamura who remained standing

just out of the circle of light from the fire. She motioned for the visitor to sit. "First," he said, "you have another guest who would, perhaps like to join us?" The visitor turned to Dr. Tamura and smiled warmly. Dr. Tamura came forward into the circle of flickering light from the fire, stood before the visitor and bowed.

"Kon ban wa," he said to the visitor in his best Japanese.

"Good evening, to you too, Tamura-san," the visitor said as he also bowed slightly to Dr. Tamura. He offered his hand to Dr. Tamura, who noted that the visitor's hand was warm to the touch as he shook it. Then they all sat down.

Betty spoke first. "We would like to know who you are." She paused and waited.

"My name is very long, and difficult to pronounce in any of your languages," he said. "But you may call me Erryl." He spelled it for clarity. "In my culture, our family name describes the unique sequence of our genetic heritage. Erryl is the equivalent of a sequence of bases in what you call DNA that describes my personal uniqueness, as it makes me distinct from my parents."

Dr. Tamura caught an inflection in his answer and asked, "How many parents do you have, Erryl?"

"One hundred and sixty eight. But only twelve who actually raised me."

"You are from one of the stars in the middle of the sword sheath of Orion, aren't you?" Kenny asked. "Yes," Erryl answered. "That is where my home is."

"How do the orbs work?" Dr. Tamura asked. Erryl paused, then spoke to Dr. Tamura, "Your theory is very close to correct, Dr. Tamura. The orbs are gravitational nodes connected by superstrings which perforate the space-time continuum."

"How do you control them, Erryl. And please, call me George." Kenny and Shanna both looked up. That was the first time they had ever heard Dr. Tamura say that.

"George, we are able to control them and move them about in any sufficiently stable gravitational field. Your mathematics does not yet allow you to understand how we do that. I must apologize, but I am not able to provide you with any information which will advance your understanding. Please know that you are on the right path, however, and you will likely know someday." Erryl paused, anticipating the next question, and spoke again.

"As you have postulated, the orbs provide a means to communicate instantly across interstellar distances. They also allow the level of visual and corporeal interaction that I represent now. This knowledge and resource is both valuable and potentially hazardous. Some civilizations do not interact well with others as you might imagine. We have a code of nonintervention which requires that a civilization develop the mathematics and related scientific knowledge to master the orbs independently. It has been discovered that the length of time to do that, and the advanced degree of cooperation and exchange that is needed within a civilization tend to allow only certain civilizations to access it. Those that are too aggressive, predatory, or reclusive cannot put this knowledge to good use, and may harm themselves or others. For that reason, we have developed a series of contact levels which define the readiness of a civilization to safely use the system."

"Can you explain the levels?" Dr. Tamura asked.

"Level One was your civilization's first physical contacts with the orbs which had been placed in your planet's gravitational field. Betty's and Kenny's ancestors were the first to do that, and they carry the genetic heritage of this planet's first Level One contact. Often, a Level One contact is broken, and then reestablished as the civilization matures. Your second Level One contact was when Kenny discovered the small orb here. The fact that he was a lineage carrier of the genetic marker for the first contact was a clear sign that your civilization was apparently stable over millennia."

"Your first Level Two contact was when we established a second node on your planet, and you demonstrated the ability to find it and contact both simultaneously. To do that, your civilization has to have global reach, and a sufficient level of cooperation to allow a simultaneous contact to occur. Also, it implies a certain technological level, either with some form of communication over the surface of your planet, through the use of satellites or other means which allow for relatively minimal time delay. We measured the length of the delay in your simultaneous contact experiment to determine the state of your science."

"My visit tonight is a Level Three contact." Erryl paused again and looked at Betty. "A Level Three contact requires that an observer, which is what I am, initiate part of the contact. Betty and I, and Kenny and Shanna and I have met in their dreams. My hope was to meet the person who was the carrier of the first Level One contact with your civilization. You should know that it is quite rare that a direct lineage between Level One contacts survives for as much as 10 thousand years as Betty's and Kenny's family have. Betty, you are actually quite famous in this part of the galaxy."

Betty Swanson blushed. "Clean living, I think," she said. Suddenly, the whole group began to laugh.

"It is, indeed a great honor for me, Betty," Erryl finally said after a moment. "But I must leave now."

"How many civilizations are there?" Dr. Tamura asked quickly, trying to gain more knowledge before Erryl left.

"Many, George. Many more than you could possibly believe. Life is opportunistic and tenacious. You will find life forms in places that will completely rewrite your understanding of biology and chemistry. Sentient life is similarly opportunistic and tenacious. You have discovered only one of several forms which likely exist in your own solar system. Explore with care, with understanding and with love. Life is precious. Sentient life is even more so. But it is everywhere."

"I must go." Erryl stood as his image flickered slightly. Several heavy rounds of birch burned slowly and evenly in the fire pit, and the night was becoming quite cool. The aurora had finally settled down, and had faded under the bright glow of the half moon. "Thank you for welcoming me to your fire. I believe I will see you again some day."

Erryl turned to Dr. Tamura, and extended his hand which George accepted. "I know you have many questions, George. That is your strength. Never stop asking. Never give up trying to find the answers," Dr. Tamura started to ask something, but Erryl interrupted. "You want to know how you will achieve a Level Four contact. I can not tell you, but when you do, you will recognize it."

Erryl shook hands with Kenny and Shanna, and then turned toward Betty. He bowed again and she stepped forward and gave him a hug.

"Thank you Erryl. Say hello to my ancestors, please."

"I will, Betty. And they send their greetings to you." Dr. Tamura felt a chill race down his spine.

Erryl vanished. The orb lay quietly on the spruce round where he had been sitting. It was mirror-black and silent, but on its surface Betty could see the stars of the constellation Orion, with the belt and sword sheath stars clearly visible. The cool night air swirled the fire as the birch logs in the center glowed with orange-red embers.

CHAPTER 8

Level Four
Late Winter, A.D. 1998

The Arctic Cat Panther buzzed noisily over the hardpan snow on the Tanana River. Kenny turned back to see if the smaller 340 Jag was following. He held his left thumb up and Shanna Swanson responded in kind, gunning her engine to catch up. She did wish Kenny would slow down a bit, even though she knew he was just trying to impress Erryn, who was racing alongside his father on his fast Polaris 550. A second blue Polaris 550 burst through a snowdrift on the left, shot through the air and landed hard just behind Erryn's.

For a seventeen-year old girl, Beth could stay up with the best of the boys. Her mechanical skills on snowmobiles were legendary, which helped to ease the taunting she took on occasion when she ended up with grease stains in her long red hair. Although only sixteen, Erryn was proud of his sister, and was known to defend her grease-stained hair when she was not looking, even if it involved explaining the facts of life to her classmates, who were seniors.

The four snowmobiles buzzed loudly, spitting up rooster tails of snow when they rushed through drifts deposited by the wind from the last snowstorm which had wound its way up the Tanana Valley. They rounded a broad bend in the river, passing a row of tree branches which had been stuck in the snow to mark a dog team trail merging onto the river from the low hills to the north. Beth had taken the lead, followed closely by Erryn. Kenny had sensed Shanna's unwillingness to run quite so fast and had fallen back a bit to let her catch up. They rode side by side and simultaneously saw Beth's brake light come on. Beth raised her hand in a motion to stop as Erryn skidded to a stop next to her.

Kenny and Shanna saw the two children's brake lights go off as they approached from behind, which indicated they had shut off their machines. They slowly pulled up alongside, squeezing the brake levers, then tapping the kill switches. All four machines were silent now, parked on a snow-covered cut bank of the river about two meters above the ice level. About a hundred yards ahead, two fourteen-dog teams were mushing down the river, having just entered along the branch-marked trail.

"Gee!" shouted the lead driver, a man, followed by a female voice calling out the same command a moment later from the second team. The lead dogs from both teams arced smartly to the right on a well-worn path, slipping along the hard snow smoothly and quietly in the bright sunlit day. Kenny had taught Erryn and Beth the unwritten courtesy of the trails that gave dog teams the right-of-way. To that, Beth had added the additional courtesy of shutting off her machine which she had seen her mother and father do to let the dog team drivers pass in silence without the idling growl of the snowmobile engines to disturb their peace and reverie. The silence of the trail, broken only by the soft padding of the dogs' feet and the occasional swoosh of the sled's runners biting into the hard snow or ice, was one of the qualities of dog sledding that had made the ancient sport so popular again.

The Swanson family watched the two large teams and their dedicated drivers slip quietly down the Tanana veering toward a large rock outcropping on the right which defined the upper bend of the river at that point. A great silence filled the chilly air as they watched what was likely a husband-and-wife team work their dogs. "Distance runners," Kenny said. "Probably Quest teams," referring to the more than one-thousand-mile Yukon Quest race which ran between Fairbanks and Whitehorse, Yukon Territory. No long- or short-time Fairbanksan ever tired of watching the strength and quiet elegance of dog teams.

When the teams reached the next bend in the river, they

veered to the right on a small slough channel where the trail to Nenana was marked. Kenny pulled his starter cord and the 440 Panther jumped to life immediately. He waited to ensure that all four machines would start, particularly the older 340 Jag which Shanna rode and which was a bit of a cold starter. Three pulls on the starter cord were necessary for the Jag to come alive, then all four machines headed off single file toward the left bend of the river, away from the dog teams.

The Swansons entered the mouth of the Salchaket Slough where it merged with the Tanana from the south. The four snowmobiles buzzed down the fifty-yard-wide slough channel lined by tall white spruce and cottonwood trees, picking up the pace now as fresh snowdrifts presented an opportunity to play a bit. The two Polaris machines driven by Erryn and Beth punched through high drifts on either side of the main trail in the center of the slough channel where Shanna conservatively stayed. Beth's machine surged upward and went completely airborne for a second, then plunged down into a fresh blanket of snow, almost disappearing. A second later, the powerful 550-cc engine roared back out of the soft snow, driving the track sufficiently fast to literally come up on step like a boat. A rooster tail of snow shot out behind the machine as Beth regained the high ground on top of the snowdrift.

Erryn howled with delight, his voice ricocheting off the spruce trees above the roar of his machine as he surpassed Beth's performance by launching straight up a cut bank and remaining airborne for a full second and a half before plopping hard into a deep drift on the far side of the bank. His machine also surged out of its soft snowdrift and quickly rose on step, now zigzagging back and forth along the edge of the slough channel around an oxbow bend. Kenny punched ahead of the entourage, watching carefully from the main channel for signs of slush or mist which would signal hazardous open water or overflows. The trail appeared fine on this late February morning, having been recently hardened by a week-long stretch of minus-forty-degree weather. Kenny's people had not survived for nearly twelve millennia in the Tanana Valley by being careless, however, so he continued his watch at point.

About two kilometers up the winding Salchaket slough, a trail appeared to the right leaving the slough channel and disappearing into the spruce and willows. Kenny took the trail, slowing down to weave around the trees. His family followed single file again, with Shanna taking up the rear. About 100 meters ahead, the trail emerged onto a broad shallow muskeg over one kilometer across and perhaps seven kilometers long. The four snowmobiles lined up side by side at the edge of the trees facing the open field. Kenny hit his kill switch first, then the other three followed suit.

The silence of the huge Tanana Valley filled the air. Clusters of cattails protruded above the snow as far as the eye could see, and several beaver mounds were frozen solid into the winter landscape on the far side of the muskeg lake. Off the river, the trees were no longer the tall, slender white spruce, but were dense clusters of short, scraggly black spruce and tamarack that appeared as skeletons without their needles, which had turned yellow and fallen off in the autumn. Thick stands of willows laced in and out of the black spruce and tamarack stands around the edge of the lake. Clumps of handsome birch rose incongruously above the taiga scene, signaling "high" ground. Their crisp white bark and black twigs stood sharply against the bright, robin's egg blue sky. To the south, peaks of the Alaska Range stood in watchful silence.

"Look, there!" Erryn pointed across the muskeg lake at several moose grazing in a stand of willows. A large cow and two yearling calves which, without antlers at this time of the year, one could barely tell from a distance if they were male or female. A larger moose suddenly stepped forward from the willows and ran straight at the two yearlings, which separated from the cow and ran off a slight distance and turned, watching warily. The larger moose was obviously a bull, evident from his thick neck and beard, and already budding antlers.

"What an attitude!" exclaimed Shanna. "Not much of a socialite, is he?"

"Chasing the teenagers out of the nest before the next batch is born in the spring, it appears," Kenny observed. "Beth, Erryn, take note."

Piercing stares from two sets of young eyes.

Kenny was chuckling at his bit of humor, ignoring the kids at first, then beginning to feel the ice melt on the tracks of his snowmobile from their glare. He glanced to the side and smiled at his two young charges, then turned grinning toward Shanna on his left.

Very icy stare.

"Oops!"

"Big oops," Shanna added.

"What say we do some exploring," Kenny offered hopefully, tugging haphazardly at his starter cord.

"What say we bury Dad and leave him here, instead!" Erryn shouted. On cue, Erryn and Beth leaped off their machines and tackled Kenny off the Panther, which had not started in time. Kenny, laughing so hard that he couldn't even fight back, found himself lying flat on his back with a teenager kneeling on each arm. Shanna straddled his waist, looking very Alaskan style sleek and sexy in her black and green Arctic Cat snowmobile jump suit. She sat down on his stomach which was heaving with laughter. He could hardly breathe, and sputtered helplessly as his family debated his sentence.

"No, please," Kenny gasped.

"So, tell me about the 'next crop' in the spring," Shanna inquired, holding a double handful of very cold dry snow above his head which was exposed after his snowmobile helmet had rolled off in the scuffle. "Something I should know about?"

"No, please ..." he sputtered, laughing. She allowed a tiny bit of the snow to fall lightly onto his face. "I'll get frostbite, then you'll have to look at an ugly face!" Several more flakes fell to his lips and nose.

"So what's new?" she inquired.

"Uncle!"

"What? We can't hear you, Dad." Beth was giggling.

"Uncle!!" Kenny shouted so loudly, the bull moose across the lake lifted his head and looked in their direction. Uncle was the official surrender declaration which, when called out by any member of the Swanson family signaled the end to a tickling event or some such. It was an agreed-on safe harbor, ending the torture in whatever form it might be occurring, but did so as unconditional surrender. Recently, it had proven to be as useful for Dad as it had been for the kids when they were smaller.

Shanna dumped snow to the side of his helmet, and engaged a sturdy high five first from Beth, then from Erryn. "Good work, kids. That certainly puts a lot of old bull in its place." All three jumped up and freed Kenny, who rolled over, still laughing.

"Uncle," he said once again.

Shanna looked up at the picture on her desk. The camera had been set on a timer, and had snapped a perfect shot of the four of them standing beside the snowmobiles, helmets in hand and smiling. In all her youth, she'd never dreamed that she would end up here in the wilderness of the Tanana Valley, married to a gentle, handsome half-Athabaskan man who loved to spend his weekends romping in the snow with her and their two fine children. How the orbs had so wonderfully changed her life, she thought.

The first green twilight was emerging from the southeast behind the mountains of the Alaska Range. It was 8:30 in the morning, and she was beginning to feel a sense of optimism with the return of the light. She thought of herself as an Alaskan now. In fact, it was hard to imagine being anything else. It was a gift that this strange and beautiful place quietly shrouded its children with, be they young or old. You become part of this land, of its changing light, dancing auroras, verdant summers and of the ever-present wilderness waiting patiently only moments from your front door to explore, even as the land becomes part of you.

Shanna tapped the keyboard when prompted by the flashing cursor on the screen, breaking her reverie for a moment. The Silicon Graphics workstation sent a command through the wide area network, the "WAN," to the Silicon Graphics "Onyx-2 Infinite Reality XL" supercomputer which functioned as the WAN server. The "SGI" then signaled back to the heart of the system, located in the Butrovich Building near her office in the Elvey Building on the West Ridge of the UAF campus. The SGI message bypassed "Denali," the huge Cray Y-MP M98 vector supercomputer and went directly to "Yukon," the even more powerful Cray T3E-900, a massively parallel-processed supercomputer with ninety processing elements, each with 256 megabytes of memory churning along at 450 megahertz. UAF benefited from a very powerful and well-placed Senate delegation. The UAF supercomputing center was now among the most powerful in the world.

Here on the edge of the Alaska wilderness, Shanna Swanson, Ph.D., physicist, was creating a new reality. The quest to access Level Four had been in progress for over twenty years, but for the first time, major parts of the theory could now be tested. Shanna had continued to collaborate with Laura Manesto on their model for the power source of the orbs.

Laura was in Buenos Aires, still working at the Instituto de Los Planetarios with Sergio Chambelán who, like Dr. Tamura, was now approaching retirement. Dr. Chambelán had encouraged Laura to proceed with her concept of a stable, super-massive element, particularly after the possibility of its existence was conceptually confirmed by his peers in Argentina. Using the resources of the Low Energy Physics Research Department at the University of Buenos Aires, the super massive element concept had been extensively debated and examined. It would have to be an element beyond atomic number 108, perhaps as high as 118, the Argentine physicists had concluded. The length of stability for this element in our universe would be measured in microseconds, albeit an eternity by subatomic physics standards. The breakthrough had been modeling the creation of the element in a collapsed gravitational field, essentially a black hole. The stability of the element expanded significantly, since the time constant was distorted, along with gravity.

Then, at Dr. Tamura's suggestion, they postulated what would happen if a theoretical element 118 or higher was merged with an antimatter element of the same mass. The mathematical derivation suggested that a stable energy field of incredible power resulted at the moment, or micro-moment actually, of matter/antimatter collision. The element and anti-element, in a surprisingly small quantity, could rip open the fabric of the space-time continuum. Amazingly, it appeared that the rip might actually be stable at selected energy levels. Furthermore, the energy levels appeared to be a nonlinear function of the mass, or size, of the two pieces of matter and antimatter.

The trick was to calculate the result of a collision between matter and antimatter element 118 at various increments, increasing the mass a few atoms at a time. Then, each collision would have to be recalculated for a gravitational field of varying strength. By ratcheting up the field strength incrementally, each collision could then be checked for relative stability, in terms of time, space and energy levels. Shanna had a hunch, but no proof yet, that the stable energy levels would somehow manifest themselves in harmonics, like octaves on a music scale.

She was beginning to wonder if human physicists would have to figure out how to manipulate multidimensional harmonics in order to access the orb communication system. She had heard the music of the orbs, though, both in real life twenty years before, and more recently in her dreams. Her sixth sense told her this was important.

"Hi Laura. How's Tom? Did he go fishing last weekend like he had planned, or did you guys just snuggle up next to your swimming pool with some of that delightful Mendozan red wine?" Shanna paused, then finished the Email message. "I have started run Alpha One. The processing speed is amazing. We should be able to calculate twenty to thirty billion iterations per hour. At this rate, we will be through the element 118 tests in only three months. The data will be out in real time, or nearly so. If we get lucky, we bracket the stable reaction field. If not, we jump to element 119 in late May and start run Alpha Two." She tapped the send button, and leaned back in her comfortable swivel chair. The SGI workstation delivered the Email message to the Internet and the transfer to Argentina was complete before she removed her hand from the palm rest on the keyboard.

"Yukon" hummed along, happily crunching nearly 80 billion calculations of the complex model every second. The data were translated into a visual three-dimensional image of a funnel on Shanna's screen. The funnel was fuzzy. As a region of stability began to appear, the image would become sharper. Then, it would collapse, only to start again. Shanna studied the image for several minutes. Perhaps an algorithm with a feedback loop from the graphics interface could speed things up. No sense calculating every possible iteration if a stable image started to form. It would be more productive to change the input parameters for mass if a stable field strength started to emerge.

And, she thought, if we could manipulate the field strength, we might be able to actually control the event horizon diameter. And then, maybe, the white hole at the other end, wherever it emerged could be somehow controlled, too. Wherever that was.

Tom watched the night sky fill with stars as the last light of the evening faded in the west. The fact that the sun peaked in the north from latitudes south of the equator still struck him as odd. Orion, or Tres Marias as the three belt stars of the constellation were called here in Argentina, rose upside down in the northeastern sky. That constellation, more than any other, grounded his perspective that he was in the southern hemisphere. From his childhood home in Nenana, Orion rose in the southeastern sky, with the stars of the sword sheath pointing south, below the hunter's belt. To those who lived in the north, Orion was a hunter, a warrior. To those who lived in the south, Orion was three incarnations of the Virgin Mary, a gentle spirit.

Tom thought of last fall's moose hunt in the Tanana Valley with Kenny. Orion was still a hunter to the Athabaskan men. He turned around and leaned over backwards until he was nearly falling over, then picked out the stars of Orion in the sky. From this awkward vantage point, Orion again looked normal, at least his idea of normal. The fact that he was bent over backward further confirmed that he was standing on the bottom of the sphere which was earth.

"Daddy, what are you doing?" Christina Peters de Manesto asked in perfect English.

"Ugh!" Tom grunted as he fell over backward onto the grass. He lay there quietly, then tilted his head back scanning for Orion again, but the view was blocked by the fence and shrubs along the back side of their yard.

Christina giggled. At seventeen, she still had a lovely, childish giggle that sounded like the voice of an eight-year old. Tom could close his eyes when she did that and still see the flowing black hair and lovely brown eyes of his child-daughter as she rubbed noses with him, Eskimo-style. She loved the traditions of her Alaska Native father, and even more so, she loved those of her grandmother, Betty. "Are you okay?" she asked as she plopped down beside him and put her hand on his head.

"I'm fine, sweetie. Just trying to get the stars straight. Orion keeps rising upside down here." He smiled at her. "Remember how Tres Marias rose in the southeast when we were in Alaska? I was just falling all over myself trying to turn Tres Marias into Orion again."

She giggled in that charming voice again. He reached over and put his arm around her and she snuggled into his armpit, laying her head on his chest. He stroked her soft, black hair. "I sure love you, little lady."

She purred like a cat and stretched out on the neatly trimmed lawn. From the backyard of their suburban Buenos Aires home, the sky was dark. A few kilometers away, the ever-present lights of the city dimmed the sky from night viewing. Tom and Laura had chosen this comfortable suburban home away from the city partly for that reason.

They had planted trees around the perimeter of the yard and encouraged small birds with hanging birdhouses. A small, but productive garden and greenhouse in one corner of the quarter-hectare yard kept the family in fresh vegetables most of the year. Next to the swimming pool was a covered patio with a barbecue grill and an empenada oven made of real adobe. Tom constructed the oven himself, building the interior frame of wood, then bricks, then mud which dried in the sun. The first several fires finally burned out the wood frame, and a strong, well-insulated igloo-shaped oven remained. With glowing hot coals inside, Tom could place his hand on the outside of the oven without getting burned.

Laura had taught Christina how to make empenadas in her family's traditional style, with meat, cheese, eggs, and olives. The small meat pies were baked precisely four minutes in the oven, and served hot with cold, fresh vino blanco, white wine. Tom really liked this tradition, and had proudly served hot empenadas to Kenny and Shanna when they visited. Those had been made with a twist, however. The meat was moose. Not bad at all. And particularly good with the Mendozan Chardonnay which was so light that it took a moment for the crisp flavor to check in on your tongue. Tom truly loved the Argentine cuisine, and his beautiful Argentine wife and Argentine-Athabaskan daughter.

"Tienes sueño?"

Tom and Christina sat up as Laura approached. "Nope, we don't have tired," Tom answered laughing. "Just admiring the night sky."

"Bueno," Laura answered back, "pero, ahora, tenemos empenadas y vino blanco." She smiled, raising and then lowering her eyebrows twice as she kneeled and presented a tray of piping hot empenadas in one hand and two glasses of white wine in the other.

"Ah, muchisimo gracias, mi esposa bonita," Tom allowed in perfect Argentine Spanish. Laura was truly his "wife beautiful" and he was sufficiently grateful to acknowledge the wonderful empenadas in her native language.

"You are most welcome, my handsome husband," she said in perfect English.

Christina laughed at the antics of her parents, then upped the ante. "Das is gut. Ich habe zehr hunger," she announced in pretty good German. They all laughed and headed to the patio for dinner. After a taste of the empenadas, they all had much hunger.

Yukon crunched more calculations, even though it was 2:08 in the morning. The processors worked happily all night, without complaining, asking for a raise, or taking a day off. All they wanted was raw data, a little air conditioning, and someplace to dump the results. The funnel twisted and warped slightly on Shanna's computer screen, presenting a slightly crisper image than just a few moments before. The monitor proudly displayed the sharpening image of the funnel to the unlit, unoccupied office. Then the image started to fade again.

But Shanna had imbedded her algorithm in the system. The clarity of the image triggered a subroutine activated by the algorithm. It told Yukon that it liked what it saw, and to vary the steady march of repetitive calculations from every possible iteration to one of a targeted scan of this version. Yukon paused for approximately twelve microseconds, reloaded the data that had created the sharp image of the funnel, and another twenty-eight microseconds later, began varying gravitational fields for the precise mass of element and anti-element 118 that, when smashed together in the calculations, had created some sort of a stable energy field.

Yukon had calculated the access code to a cross-dimensional communications link. It had found an area code to one of the stars in the belt of Orion and logged it into the 190 gigabyte disk storage array hardwired to the Cray T3E. It would have just kept on going, but Shanna's subroutine told it to start encoding the local phone directory for that interstellar area code. No human knew this yet. In a total time lapse of sixty microseconds from the initial discovery, Yukon was back on the path, punching data sets at 79.2 gigaflops. The image on Shanna's computer monitor sharpened, twisted in a long arc, and a second funnel began to open on the other end.

The air conditioning in the Arctic Region Supercomputing Center increased slightly to compensate for the additional heat generated by Yukon and the disk array.

Shanna turned in her sleep and began to dream.

The fire seemed unusually bright. Patterns of light flickered across the branches of the tall white spruce trees. A large white paper birch with a straight, thick trunk glowed like a marble column against the dark sky. Shanna reached under the bearskin and found Kenny's hand, squeezed it lightly and snuggled up a bit closer to him. The night was not really cold, and the fire was casting out a steady heat as the birch logs were slowly consumed by the flames. It was really more for comfort. Kenny responded by squeezing her hand back, his blue eyes sparkling in the firelight.

Still, it seemed so very bright. She leaned her head on Kenny's shoulder and glanced across the fire pit. Certainly, that made more sense, she thought as she finally realized why the fire seemed to be so reflective. Actually, it felt like she had known all along, but the truth had been residing in the back of her consciousness and had finally come forward to be seen. Erryl's bright, white suit was reflecting the light, magnifying its effect almost like a halo.

A halo, she thought. How pleasant. But he was not an angel, just an observer. No, the halo effect was simply reflected light.

Betty smiled at the two young women. Beth's red hair seemed so natural in the firelight, so much like her mother's. And Christina's black hair reminded Betty of her own Athabaskan heritage. She felt blessed to have such a wonderful family. But these two were something very special. They had her power of intuition. Betty knew that from the time they were both only three years old.

Beth had crawled up on her lap, hugged her tightly as only a child can, and asked Betty why the stars were so far apart. Betty had looked at her granddaughter in surprise. This tiny three-year old had just wandered in from playing in Grandma's yard and had somehow fathomed that stars were not just points of light in a dark tapestry which we called the night sky. This child had felt the depth and multidimensionality of the universe. And only three years old!

Her nephew, Tom, had brought his family to Alaska, and had been visiting that night. Christina was playing with little Erryn, who was laughing and rolling around on the carpet as Christina tickled him. He had rolled over and over, trying-but not too hard-to get away from her fingers which probed at his ribs. Then, as he rolled toward the fireplace, his head flipped around suddenly toward the long, flat reddish-brown stone mantle. The stone was Shaw Creek rock, a handsome granite quite popular with Fairbanksans for building fireplaces. Erryn's tiny head was going straight for the square edge of the rock, toward certain injury.

Betty had been watching and started to call out as Erryn quickly approached danger. But in an instant, Christina's hand was between Erryn's head and the rock. There had clearly not been sufficient time to think, only to act. Her hand cradled his head for a moment, then she pulled him to her and hugged him to calm him down. Erryn relaxed in her arms as she stroked his uninjured head. Then Christina looked up at Betty, who watched in amazement at the quick, adult-like behavior. "Está bien, Gramma. Está bien."

Betty realized that even as Christina was comforting Erryn, she was now comforting her, too. Remarkable, these two beautiful girls. Extraordinary, actually.

Betty watched Beth and Christina by the fire pit. She was happy she could finally introduce them to Erryl. She was proud of the girls and knew that Erryl would be pleased to meet the next generation of her family. Beth and Christina had both adopted Betty's love for the family traditions and her strong sense of history. She had told them the entire story of Kenny's and Tom's discovery of the orbs, of the glaciers in Alaska and Argentina, and of the observer. And tonight, they could meet him and begin to understand the wonderful mystery he had brought to all of their lives.

Shanna and Kenny watched from the far side of the fire, and next to them sat Laura and Tom. Both couples were shrouded in bear skins. Kenny and Tom each had a poker stick to tend the fire, which they skillfully managed together. Kenny would roll a log up with his poker stick, and hold it in place while

Tom maneuvered a new log under it. The poker sticks then pulled back together in slow motion, were laid on the ground simultaneously, and the now freed hands returned to their wives' shoulders. Like a dance, Betty thought.

All eyes were on Erryl now, who was facing Beth and Christina. The girls sat on a flat log, Erryl facing them with his back to the night. He held out both hands, like a statue of Buddha, palms upright and elbows bent down. In each hand a tiny light started to glow, then swirl and increase in intensity. The lights were green at first, spinning slowly and forming into small spheres. From inside the two spheres, the lights began to change to a blue color. The spin rate increased, and the lights began to form solid surfaces. Betty recognized the small orbs which were forming in Erryl's hands. She felt a comfortable familiarity with them, and realized her hands were cupped in her lap, facing upward as if holding an orb.

Then she felt a tingle in her spine, and almost imperceptibly gasped in surprise. Beth and Christina's hands were precisely mirroring Betty's. But they were not watching her. And they seemed to be unaware that they were cradling some invisible sphere in their hands. Betty raised her hands slowly a few inches in front of her, and saw Beth and Christina do the same. There was no delay, though. All three women were performing exactly the same hand motions, but only Betty was doing so consciously. It was like they were connected, somehow.

Erryl's suit glowed in the reflected light of the orbs, even more now than from the fire. Then a low, pleasant harmonic tone began emitting from both orbs in Erryl's outstretched hands in a stereo effect. The tone deepened and a second, matched set of harmonics began. The color shifted to violet and the rate of spinning increased. Both orbs were now levitating several centimeters above Erryl's upturned palms, spinning rapidly and glowing in a phosphorescent violet color. Three full octaves of precisely matched harmonic tones emanated from the small, spinning orbs.

Beth and Christina both had their hands cupped upward in front of them. They glanced at their hands simultaneously, both finally realizing that they were holding their hands up in front of them. A flash of red and black hair danced across their shoulders as they both turned to look toward Betty. Betty

176

smiled, nodded to them and relaxed her hands to her lap. She nodded toward Erryl, and both girls looked back at him, their hands still upturned.

A birch log in the fire popped loudly, and a swirl of embers rose into the night sky. An aurora was flickering overhead, far above the dark outline of the spruce trees. Nobody seemed to notice.

Erryl stood up slowly, hands still outstretched with the spinning orbs levitating above them. The rich harmonics of the multi-octave tone filled the dense forest. Beth and Christina rose together, then stepped slightly apart, and spread their arms apart to each side, emulating Erryl. Betty felt a slight chill. It was a motion from an Athabaskan dance she had taught to Beth and Christina. In the dance, the women would twirl around now, arms outstretched and hair swirling around their heads. It was a very attractive dance, designed to catch the eyes of young men. The women all knew that. It was their secret.

But Beth and Christina did not spin around. They stood facing Erryl, palms outstretched and elbows bent. Erryl smiled and began to curl his fingers into the palms of his hands. The orbs began to shrink in size as his fingers slowly rolled into his palms. The intensity of the light dimmed, and the orbs grew smaller. But the harmonic tone remained, full and strong in the night. The tone, which was in even octave steps, grew louder, and began to form a warmly resonant chord. There were now two distinct tones, each a full chord. Then each chord split into two more, and filled the night with a sound like the start of a symphonic concert, when the instruments begin playing a single chord to tune up.

Four distinct chords, each with multiple octaves resonated through the dark forest. Erryl's hands closed gently into a fist, and the two orbs vanished. Instantly, a point of intense violet light appeared in each of Beth's and Christina's still upturned palms. The light grew in intensity as four spinning orbs appeared, glowing and pulsing with violet light. The four harmonic chords deepened and intensified as the four new orbs formed and levitated above the girls' upturned palms. Their long hair stood straight out, filled with static electricity. Their eyes sparkled, reflecting the spinning orbs. The two girls looked at each other in surprise and gasped, mouths open wide in amazement.

Erryl smiled at Betty, then suddenly vanished. The fire snapped again, and another swirl of embers rose into the sky.

The second funnel grew in size and clarity on the monitor. The two funnels were connected by a long, thin tube, but they just hung in space, slowly twisting around like they were looking for something. Yukon hummed along processing at slightly faster than the normal 79.2 gigaflops-billion floating operations per second-it was rated at. Perhaps it was the heat generated by the ninety processors. Or perhaps it was like a car running downhill, with the transmission disengaged, freewheeling and running faster as gravity pulled it along. Yukon was on a roll.

The second funnel was now as sharp and clear as the first, but then slowly started to fade a bit, getting fuzzy around the edges. Shanna's algorithm kicked in again, commanding the Cray T3E to go back and rerun the previous clear image version of the calculation, at that mass and gravitational field strength, but to now begin varying the time constant slightly. The pause this time was nearly eighteen microseconds. Yukon reloaded the appropriate data and ninety-four microseconds later was again churning out 79.2 gigaflops of computations.

Green light from the monitor flickered on the walls of the empty office. The double-funnel image reappeared, sharp and clear. The funnels slowed their twisting motion slightly, then came to a complete halt. The connecting tube undulated, but the funnels held rigidly in space. A tiny point of light began to form at the end of each funnel, which grew in intensity, and began to form two small green spinning orbs.

The computation rate rose to 79.6 gigaflops. Yukon was on a roll again.

The red numbers on Betty's alarm clock scrolled forward to 2:12 A.M. as she dreamed of a campfire …

"Buenos dias, Christina," Laura said to her daughter.

"Good morning, Mom," she answered without realizing she was speaking in English. It was 8:12 A.M. in Buenos Aires, and nearly time for school. The sun was bright and cheerful. Leaves had not started to turn color yet, even though autumn had arrived south of the equator.

"Mom, remember the man you told me about? The observer, I think you called him? I dreamed about him last night, and about the orbs. We were at a campfire with Uncle Kenny and Aunt Shanna, Great-Aunt Betty, Beth, and you and Dad. There was light and sound. It was beautiful, but strange. What do you think it means?"

Laura Manesto felt a chill in the air. "I think we should call Shanna, sweetie."

Christina looked up from her breakfast. "Why, Mom?."

"Because I had the same dream."

George Tamura still rose early, and was frequently the first one in the Geophysical Institute. He dipped the tea bag up and down in his cup of hot water as he walked down the quiet hallway. His office was at the end, in the southwest corner where he had a magnificent view of the Alaska Range. As he walked by Shanna's office, he stopped and turned around. The tea bag was suspended toward the top of the water level in the cup. Slowly, the tea bag settled into the cup, and he turned toward the closed door. A familiar green pulsing light was visible under the door from inside the room.

Dr. Tamura tried the door knob and confirmed that it was locked. He glanced at his watch and knew that Shanna would not be there for another hour at least. He reached into his pocket and pulled out a master key, inserted it into the lock and turned the knob, all with one hand. The cup of hot tea was still in the other.

As he opened the door, a flood of green light filled the room. Shanna's monitor was active and was displaying a double funnel. One end, the black hole side, had the familiar image of a small spinning orb in the center of the funnel. The other end, the white hole was twisted around facing out of the monitor like the end of a trumpet. A second orb was visible, spinning in the center of that funnel. But it was not in the monitor.

The second orb was levitating in front of the computer screen, pulsing with green light and spinning in a steady motion. A subtle harmonic tone hummed from the orb. Dr. Tamura gasped, and nearly dropped his cup of tea. Watching the spinning orb carefully, he walked slowly into the room and crossed over to Shanna's desk where he set down the cup of tea and picked up her phone. He dialed her home number, and waited for her phone to ring. "Welcome back my friend," he said to the orb. "We have been waiting a long time."

Shanna answered as he finished his sentence, "Hello? A long time? Dr. Tamura, is that you."

"Good morning, Dr. Swanson." He glanced at her monitor and noted the time clock and a message. Shanna still got a bit tingly when he called her Dr. Swanson. Most of the time he just called her Shanna. When it was very important, or very official, he called her Dr. Swanson.

"I took the liberty of checking your office this morning. I hope you don't mind."

"No, Dr. Tamura. That's fine. What's up?"

"You will be pleased to know that your calculation was completed at 2:18 A.M. Yukon terminated the run at that time, apparently having found a successful solution." He studied the spinning orb. "Shanna, we have a visitor. The small orb is back, levitating in front of your monitor."

"Oh, my. I'll be right there." Shanna hung up the phone and turned to Beth. "Come with me, honey. You can tell me about the rest of your dream on the way to my office. You're going to skip school today, because we have an important visitor." She walked over to her daughter and gave her a very big hug.

CHAPTER 9

The Messengers
Spring, A.D. 1998

T
he Tanana River resumed its normal silty color with the onset of spring thaw. Ice moved out as the water level rose, the large rafts bumping together as they slowly drifted downstream. Chunks of ice and mass of slush would randomly dam up on a sand bar or behind some sweepers, half-buried trees, which had washed into the river. The water level would back up until the blockage over-flowed and broke away, moving the ice and debris further down-stream to the next blockage.

Occasionally, a village or fish camp would be caught in the temporary flood, and cabins, fish wheels and other structures would be damaged or lost. It was part of the rhythm of this wild river with no artificial dams. It could be dangerous at times, so it caused one to be careful and thoughtful. The cold, silty water was very unforgiving if you fell in, or foolish enough to build on an eroding cut bank. You learned to watch the river, and to build on high ground where it was not going to flood you out. For those who learned from it and discovered how to harvest its bounty of fish and wildlife, it was a source of life.

For 12,000 years, it had been so for the Athabaskans. Betty shared this knowledge with her family. It was important that she had another generation to pass the traditions and history of her people on to. She was pleased that so many of her children grandchildren, nieces and nephews were interested in her stories. In this modern age, it was unusual that with so many distractions, they really seemed eager to learn. Betty tended to underestimate the character and life that her strong personality brought to this process. She just marveled that her stories would live on in her heirs.

In each generation there were at least one or two who were particularly adept at giving life to the stories of their ancestors. At times, in the not too distant past, someone with such insight might be called a shaman. The power of words was very strong, and some believed that the right words could heal. But Betty was just a storyteller who carefully preserved the heritage of her people. That her stories brought her family closer together was a gift which she gladly shared with the next generation. This day, she had selected Beth and Christina as the ones who would receive this priceless gift.

"Look Grandma, the ice dam down the river is breaking!" Beth pointed to the southwest from the hillside where Kenny and Shanna had built their home.

Betty looked up and smiled. "Yes, Beth, spring is definitely here." She turned to Christina who was walking over from the barbecue pit where Kenny and Tom were laughing, drinking beers with Carl Swanson, and stoking the fire. "Look Christina. See what the river is doing now."

"Wow!" Christina practically shouted out. The Tanana had been backing up for several hours, reaching nearly two miles to the edge of Chena Ridge where the Swansons' house was nestled high on the birch- and aspen-forested slopes. At Christina's loud exclamation, everyone turned to look. The silty water of the river started to move as the ice dam failed, then burst. The high water had risen far enough to flood several homes built right on the edge of the river down in the creek valley below the ridge. Now, the flooding would dissipate in only a few moments as the river forged downstream, shoving the mass of ice and slush ahead to the next blockage, or all the way to the Yukon River and finally the Bering Sea if no more blockages occurred.

"This is magnificent," Christina said. "Does this happen every year?"

"No, but fairly often," Betty replied. She put her arms around Beth and Christina who stood on each side of her.

Soon, three generations of Swansons and Peterses were gathered around watching the river, and enjoying the vista of the Alaska Range in the distance across the broad expanse of the Tanana Valley. The bright spring sun was high in the west.

"To breakup!" Carl toasted, raising his Alaskan Amber beer high in the direction of the breaking ice dam.

"Hear, hear!!" A chorus of approval ensued, accompanied by clinking of bottles and glasses.

Betty hugged the two girls a bit tighter for a moment. "Remember this moment," she spoke softly just to Beth and Christina. Then she turned and looked back up the hill toward the handsome white-spruce log home her son and daughter-in-law had built, and waved. Dr. Tamura had just arrived for the barbecue, and Chuck Singer was with him. "Hello, George and Chuck. Welcome to our spring breakup celebration."

"Thank you Betty," George said. "Look who I found at the airport." Chuck waved at Betty, but was already busy shaking hands and greeting his coworkers on the now reinvigorated project. It had been nearly a year since the last project meeting had taken place in Fairbanks. That one had led to Shanna's experiment with the supercomputing center, and that had started a new series of events when her calculations had somehow triggered a reemergence of an orb.

Dr. Tamura paused and admired the Tanana. The silty waters were swirling and gaining speed as the river disgorged the temporary lake. "Magnificent. Truly amazing. And how are you, Beth and Christina?" he asked the two young women on either side of Betty.

"Just fine, Dr. Tamura." Beth answered.

"Muy bien, el Doctoro Tamura," Christina added in lovely Argentine Castillano. He smiled at the three women.

"Well, we have much to talk about," Betty said. "But first, let's have dinner and catch up a bit with Chuck."

The project team had assembled in the conference room of the Elvey Building. Dr. Tamura had invited Shanna to present first. A video monitor was replaying the final thirty minutes of the calculation sequence that had led up to the reemergence of the orb.

"Here was the second realignment of the computational sequence," she noted, addressing the group and tapping her finger on the edge of the monitor. "The T3E paused and ... right here." She clicked the pause button as the double-funnel image was just beginning to form. "The algorithm redirected the processing sequence and this is what happened next."

The funnel started to lose its clarity, then the image suddenly sharpened and a second funnel emerged. Shanna tapped the play button and the image continued. "At this point, the second funnel, a white hole or emerging end of the sequence, begins to form. Notice how it twists around in a random manner, then ... here." She tapped the pause button again. The white end had suddenly turned and was pointed directly out of the screen. "At this moment, the second event was occurring. Betty will explain."

The group of nearly thirty researchers and observers turned to listen as Betty Swanson described the dream sequence that each of five members of her family had shared. "As I have explained before, a simultaneous dream is a powerful omen in Athabaskan culture. When two people share a dream, it usually portends something very important in the lives of those involved. This is the first time I know of, however, that this many people shared a dream. What is truly extraordinary is that it involved five women, connected not just by blood lines, but all in the same family, and on two continents separated by very great distances. This event is unprecedented in the known history of our people." She paused to let that sink in.

"The precision with which each person independently recalled the events of the dream is also extraordinary. In our best estimation, all five of us had the dream at precisely the same moment. That moment corresponds to the emergence of the second funnel on the video monitor that you see here." Betty walked around the table at the center of the room and stood directly behind Beth and Christina. "Several particularly intriguing events occurred in the dream sequence when Erryl, the observer, apparently transferred two orbs each to Beth and Christina.

"First, the sound from the orbs continued undiminished even as the orbs in his hands vanished. Up to this time, the sound from the orbs has been linked to their presence. When the orbs are dim or quiet, the tones are silenced. This time the orbs disappeared, but the sound continued.

"This is also the first time we have seen two small orbs present at one time and in one place. Previously, we have seen two large orbs, in separate locations, and a small orb apparently move in and out of the large orbs in a manner suggesting it was being transported from Black Rapids Glacier to Perito Moreno Glacier in Argentina.

"Finally, when the two orbs in Erryl's hands disappeared, a total of four small orbs emerged, one in each of Beth's and Christina's hands. Also, the new orbs were immediately very active with a violet color, which has only occurred before after the orbs have been active for some time. Remember, all of this was happening in a dream, shared simultaneously by five people, and with amazingly precise detail." She paused for a moment.

"Betty," Dr. Tamura asked, "do you have any feeling as to what the significance of this event is?"

Betty was standing behind Beth and Christina now. She reached forward and placed a hand on one of each of the girls' shoulders. She smiled and looked a bit embarrassed. "Well, I only have a feeling, Dr. Tamura." She shrugged her shoulders very slightly.

"Go on, please."

"Well, I think Erryl has selected these two young ladies as his messengers," she hesitated for a moment, "very much like I have."

Dr. Tamura had already discussed this with Betty, at least the part about Erryl's selecting the girls for something. But this was new, and he sensed that this was very important, and very personal to her. "How so?" he asked quietly.

"I have asked Beth and Christina to be the storytellers for the next generation of our family. Bless their hearts, they have accepted." Beth and Christina both reached up and placed one hand on Betty's hands resting on their shoulders. They turned to look up at her. Her sparkling brown eyes filled with tears. She stopped for a moment, then added with a slight waver in her voice, "This is a very proud moment for me, and for my family." A small tear fell out of one eye, and coursed down her cheek. "Very proud ..." Her voice trailed off and she couldn't speak for a moment.

Dr. Tamura sat back in his chair and watched with great curiosity. Shanna and Laura had risen and walked around the table. Beth and Christina had also risen and now all five women were embracing. Half crying and half laughing, they tried to apologize to the group. No need. There wasn't a dry eye in the place.

On a lab bench across the room, the new orb was sitting in an open velvet case. The orb had remained active, spinning slowly and quietly at a very constant rate. The color was a pale, fluorescent green, indicating an idling state. As Betty finished speaking, all eyes were on her and now on the five women embracing. No one noticed as the orb pulsed several times, each time with a violet swirl of light forming and then fading. A video monitor recorded the event and accurately marked the time. The orb returned to its steady, idling green state a few seconds later as Dr. Tamura suggested that it was a good time for a coffee break.

Inside the aluminum dome near Black Rapids Glacier, the two-meter orb awoke. At exactly the same moment, half a world away, inside a similar aluminum dome near Glaciar Perito Moreno, the other two-meter orb awoke. Both had been idle for nearly twenty years. In that time the two glaciers had receded, exposing the two orbs and their protective enclosures. The orbs had been kept under tight scrutiny, guarded and continuously observed by numerous instruments and a few soldiers of the respective military forces of the US and Argentina.

A fluorescent green swirl of light formed inside each orb, then gravitated to the outer edges of the orbs as they started to slowly spin. The spin rate and color intensity precisely matched the small orb in the Elvey Building where Dr. Tamura had reassembled the project team to continue their analysis. A digital electronic message arrived at the Geophysical Institute in Fairbanks and simultaneously at the Instituto de Los Planetarios in Buenos Aires, alerting a central computer in each facility that an event had occurred.

Shanna continued her video presentation to the now reassembled group. "At 2:18 A.M., six minutes after we believe the dream sequences occurred in all five of us, the program halted. The prime algorithm identified a solution of high precision and clarity and told the T3E to stop. At that moment, this occurred." Shanna had paused the monitor again to complete her statement. She hit the play button, and the large video screen continued, showing the image as it had appeared on her computer screen.

The white funnel was pointed directly out of the screen. A small point of fluorescent green light formed in the center of the funnel and began rotating. The light intensified as the rate of rotation increased. It seemed to be coming forward, out of the funnel toward the viewer. The light swelled in brightness and diameter, soon filling the entire view of the funnel. A second light emerged from the black hole end of the image pointed to the left on the screen. The image of a small orb suddenly emerged out of the black hole end of the funnel, at the same time the large swirl of light vanished from the white hole end of the funnel facing out of the screen.

"At this moment, we postulate that the new orb actually appeared out of the image of the funnel and levitated into the room, right in front of the video monitor where Dr. Tamura found it the next morning. The image of the second orb, rotating in front of the black hole end of the funnel on the screen remained, and continues to pulse in precise sequence with the new orb." Shanna pointed to the orb in the velvet case across the room. "The facts are these," she continued.

"One. We now have a solution to the power source model. The super-heavy element and anti-element 118 collision, created and merged inside the singularity of a gravitational anomaly, a black hole, with a slightly modulating gravity field produces a stable system. The system appears to be a sort of tunnel or pipeline to another location and time. The length of the tunnel is unknown, but in the distorted time constant of the singularity of the black hole, the reaction, which would be measured in nanoseconds in a synchrotron, appears to be stable. The two ends of the tunnel, which appear as funnels seem to be able to be fixed at some location. The stability of the location is related, connected if you will, to a larger gravitational field such as the core of a planet. In short, the funnel is hanging in the gravitational equivalent of geosynchronous orbit some distance from the center of gravity of a planet or other large gravity source, a star perhaps.

"Two. The strength of the field can be modulated by tweaking the gravitational and time parameters. In effect, this means that we might be able to steer or control the movement of one end or the other. It is probable that this is how the system is directed to new locations. We don't have the exact solution yet, but it can be calculated. That could be the next experiment using the T3E.

"Three. The orbs seem to form at the focus or center of the funnel, held in orbit by the strength of the gravitational field inside the tunnel. This is analogous to a superconducting material levitating above a magnet. Changes in the size of an orb, in its color, tone and rate of spin can all be mathematically derived by varying the gravitational field strength parameters at the other end. We believe we can calculate this with the T3E. Again, another excellent experiment for the Cray.

"Four. We don't have so much as a clue how on God's green earth you do this mechanically. Everything we have so far is strictly computational. In short, we have a pretty functional theory on how this thing works. We just don't know how to build one." Shanna shrugged and stopped.

Dr. Tamura leaned forward and thanked Shanna for her presentation. "Questions, theories, comments?"

Chuck Singer tapped his fingers on the table for a moment, then asked, "Did the model calculate the x-ray field strengths?"

"Yes," Shanna answered. "The data are stored and are available if you would like to look at it. We have not done anything other than record and store the results. What are your thoughts, Dr. Singer?"

"I am curious how closely the model predicts the x-ray emission strengths we observed from the two-meter and smaller orbs we have previously examined. It might be a good confirmation of the model against what data we do have."

"Excellent idea," Dr. Tamura said. "Any other questions?" He paused for a moment, then went on. "Dr. Swanson, how do you think running the computer model caused an orb to actually appear in this case? I know we have talked about this, but I am curious if you have any fresh ideas."

Shanna had given this a great deal of thought, as had most of the rest of the project team as soon as they had heard about what happened. "Well, it is quite possible that our derivation of the model was sufficient to initiate a Level Four contact as Erryl predicted twenty years ago in our last contact with him at Black Rapids. We are still not sure exactly what Level Four is, but we do know that two events occurred. The first was the mathematical model solution. The second was a five-person shared dream. It may be that Level Four is one or the other of these, or both. Without knowing which one, or whether it was the combination that was the actual contact event, the response appeared to be a reemergence of the small orb. At this time that is what we know."

"We know something else now," Kenny said. He had just walked back into the conference room after a research assistant had signaled him that he had an important message. All heads turned as he spoke. "We know that as of about thirty minutes ago, both two-meter orbs became active again. Folks, we're back on-line."

Dr. Tamura clapped his hands. "Excellent! Excellent news." He stood up and addressed the project team. "We now have an opportunity to communicate with the observer, or observers, again. We need to set up an experiment to see if we can move to a higher level of contact." He turned to Betty. "I would be very pleased to hear your ideas on what our next communication should be, Betty."

She was sitting near Beth and Christina. "I think that is very simple Dr. Tamura. Erryl wants to talk to Beth and Christina. He has something to ask them to do." The two young women smiled at her as she spoke. They both had already known what she was going to say.

Chuck Singer rechecked the calibration subroutine on his video monitor, carefully watching the value for x-ray levels scroll up as the monitor counted the emission level for precisely ten seconds. The count stopped and the number remaining on his laptop computer matched within 0.01 percent the relative percent difference from the known value of the calibration standard. The instrument was ready. Then he slapped his neck. "Got him!"

"Good work, Dr. Singer. Only 150 billion left, at least in this creek valley," Tom chuckled. Spring had begun in the higher elevations of the northern foothills of the Alaska Range. Black Rapids Glacier had receded so far that spring actually came a week or so earlier to the field station than it did twenty years ago when the last contact experiment was run. As usual, the first wildlife to emerge from the deep freeze of winter was the ever-present Alaska mosquitoes-the Alaskan State Bird as some folks would say, with apologies to the willow ptarmigan.

"Yeah, but they are learning not to mess with physicists from Michigan."

"Good, Chuck, training and conditioning are critical. Just think, some tourist from Michigan who took a physics class during his college career will be a hit on the tour bus as the mosquitoes carefully leave him alone even as they suck the last drops of blood from the withering bodies of his fellow travelers."

"Yeah, and he'll never know why. Just another element of my legacy in Alaska. Do you think they might name a lake or mountain after me for this?"

"Not if you give any more blood to the one draining the top of your head right now." Tom pointed to the rather bloated mosquito on Chuck's forehead.

Slap!

"Oh, yuck. Medic!" Tom called out. Chuck just stared at the blood splattered on his hand and could only imagine the smear on his forehead. "I don't think I need a medic, Tom."

"Probably not, but the mosquito sure could use one. And I think the committee to name a geographical place after you for this was probably just disbanded. At least I wouldn't hold my breath waiting for a decision." Tom left the ATCO trailer, laughing. As he quickly opened and closed the door, another half dozen opportunistic and very hungry female mosquitoes entered and began their search for the blood of physicists from Michigan.

A sandy-haired graduate student from the Russian Far East was working at the console next to Chuck. He smiled and handed Chuck a box of Kleenex. "Spaseeba," Chuck drawled out.

"You are quite welcome, Dr. Singer."

"Beth, just do what seems natural. There is no script for this, at least none on our end," Betty said reassuringly. Beth's bright red hair was pulled back into a pony tail, but glistened in the pastel light inside the aluminum geodesic dome. The bright afternoon sun poured in through the skylights at the top of the dome, giving an impression of warmth to the otherwise metallic structure.

Betty stroked Beth's cheek, and smiled at Christina. "You will both do just fine. They have chosen you for what you are, and what you can do. Just watch, be aware of what is happening, and enjoy. This should be a wonderful experience for you." Neither of the seventeen-year old young women seemed completely sure of that, but they had complete faith in Betty. "Now let's try the dance one time for practice."

Christina moved two steps to the side of Beth, her long black hair flowing over her shoulders. Both girls were wearing soft caribou-skin dresses and moccasins, all of which were brightly studded with ornamental beads. Beth reached behind her head and untied the band from her pony tail, and tossed her head once. Her long red hair draped over her shoulders. Beth stepped back and the two girls looked at each other, then at Betty.

Dr. Tamura watched from the other side of the dome. The two-meter orb was spinning steadily and pulsing rhythmically with a green fluorescent glow. He was not the only one who was captivated by the sight of the three women in their traditional Athabaskan dresses. A dozen technicians bustling about checking instruments, paused and watched as Betty clapped her hands three times and Beth and Christina twirled around in perfect unison. Their arms were extended from their sides, palms up. Sixty-five other scientists and technicians paused and watched video monitors in ATCO trailers and wall tents throughout the compound.

Betty clapped her hands again three times and the girls reversed direction and spun around again, this time bending at the knees slightly in a dip, then rising again. Their long hair pinwheeled outward from the centrifugal force of the spin, quickly settling on their shoulders as they rose from the knee bend. The arms remained extended, with elbows slightly bent. Their eyes shone and both girls smiled at Betty. They were in perfect unison. At least twenty young male technicians were rapidly falling in love. Betty smiled back at Beth and Christina, knowing quite well that the womens' dance to secretly attract suitors was working perfectly.

She clapped her hands again twice and the girls stepped to the right and twirled again, arms still extended. One clap and they stepped back to the left, and twirled again. This time

Betty twirled in place. All three were in perfect unison. Four parents watched with complete pride. Dr. Tamura watched with great interest.

Betty clapped again to reverse the spin, and the two-meter orb pulsed twice as she clapped. Betty saw the orb pulse, and stopped. Beth and Christina spun to a halt, too, their hair following a second later. Betty looked over at Dr. Tamura and spoke softly and a bit apologetically, "I think this is going to work just fine, Dr. Tamura, but maybe we should wait until everyone is ready." The orb was back to the steady idling state again. Two pairs of lovely arms fell slowly to the sides of the two young women.

Dr. Tamura nodded at Betty, and looked over at Kenny and Shanna, then at Tom and Laura, who were all standing behind consoles around the perimeter of the orb. "Are we ready?" he asked Kenny.

Kenny raised one finger and spoke quietly into a tiny microphone on his headset. A second finger went up, then a third and finally a fourth. "All stations report in as calibrated and good to go. Dr. Singer is on his way over to the dome now."

Betty and the two girls were still standing and waiting. Betty turned and held her hands out. Beth and Christina each took one of her hands in theirs and they reassured each other with a gentle squeeze.

Shanna and Laura watched intently, but simultaneously kept an eye on their monitors. They had an experiment in progress, with both Yukon, the Cray T3E, and Denali, the Cray XMP, linked in a parallel-processing mode. They had worked for nearly three weeks preparing the data acquisition and computational model that they hoped would find a solution for at least one of the control functions of the orb. The processing power of the two supercomputers was enough to receive and sort the initial data, but not enough to process them in nearly real time. To do that, an Internet uplink to a low earth orbit (LEO) satellite array had been prepared, with downlinks to twenty-eight other supercomputing centers on four continents.

A fiberoptic cable had been placed between the field station and the UAF Arctic Region Supercomputing Center (ARSC) as the initial land link. Alyeska Pipeline Service Company had graciously allowed use of nearly 150 kilometers of their brand-new fiber optics communication system between the field station and Fairbanks for this. Raw data from a sensor array around the orb at Black Rapids would flow at nearly the speed of light into the ARSC, then Denali would split the data into twenty-nine packets, and compress them for efficient transfer.

Packet one would flow to Yukon. Packets two through twenty-nine would flow to Seattle, Berkeley, Austin, Salt Lake City, Chicago, Atlanta, Tokyo, Zurich, Stockholm, London, Paris, Moscow, Tel Aviv, Buenos Aires, and so on, with a delay of about one half of a second for the satellite transponder relay. The total massively parallel-processing power of the twenty-nine linked supercomputers made this the largest single computational experiment in history. The data would be reduced at a rate of nearly fifty terraflops, trillion floating point operations per second.

Each supercomputing center had reserved at least one processor for uplink back to the LEO satellite constellation. The satellites would relay the data back to ARSC and Denali would receive the reduced data, assemble the information and compute an instruction which would be relayed back to Black Rapids on the fiberoptic cable. Inside the geodesic dome, the fiberoptic cable was connected to a mini computer which controlled the operation of three lasers on precisely actuated stands with micromotors. Each laser could be pulsed in intervals as fine as 0.5 microseconds, and moved in any direction as precisely as one micron. They were arrayed around the perimeter of the large orb, one meter away. A tiny blue light emitted from each one, directed into the center of the orb. The object of all of this was really quite simple.

After reviewing Shanna's data, Laura discovered an ultraviolet light pulse occurred just before each change in the small orb levitating in front of Shanna's computer. That pulse, she surmised, was quite possibly the control signal for the orb. It was not visible to the human eye, but she felt it should be capable of carrying sufficient information to control the small orb. A goal of the experiment was to identify one of these control parameters and to return a signal back to the orb presumed to be present at the point of initiation, wherever that was. In other words, Laura proposed to send a signal to the Observers so they would know we had figured out at least one of the control functions of the intergalactic communications system. Betty, in her own inimitable way, had suggested that the Observers probably knew what Laura was up to anyway, but they were likely curious to see if she could actually do it.

The consoles were all green lights. The LEO satellite constellation coursed through the skies above the atmosphere, ready to accept transmissions. Denali hummed along quietly, nursing the end of the fiberoptic cable and waiting for data. The three tiny blue laser lights were on and pointing directly into the center of the two-meter orb, which spun steadily in its idling state.

Laura and Shanna both looked up again at their daughters and Betty. Motherhood and science were wrestling for attention. Betty looked over at Dr. Tamura, who turned to Chuck Singer and Kenny. Chuck raised his hand and curled his thumb and forefinger in the okay sign. Dr. Tamura turned to Betty, "We're ready now. Good luck."

CHAPTER 10

Host

Late Spring, A.D. 1998

The late afternoon sunlight entered the dome from a low northwestern angle, reflecting off the inside of the aluminum structure. Betty, Beth, and Christina had moved to the center of the dome, about three meters directly in front of the orb. The two girls took their positions two paces apart and facing Betty who had her back to the orb. On Betty's nod, a sound system arrayed around the dance area near the orb began to play an Athabaskan chant, accompanied by fiddle and guitar music. The Athabaskans had become quite proficient with these very Western instruments when first introduced to them during the gold rush at the turn of the last century.

The music was accented by the beat of skin drums, and had a decidedly merry air to it. At the proper moment, in time with the music, Betty clapped her hands three times and the two girls began their dance, twirling around in place with arms rising from their sides, palms up. A flurry of red and black hair spun outward with the centrifugal force of their spin. Betty clapped three times again, still facing the two pretty young dancers. They reversed direction and twirled again, this time with the slight dip and rise which caused their hair to quickly flow back over their shoulders as they rose from the dip. This attractive step was accompanied by two very bright smiles.

Dr. Tamura watched the dance with enjoyment and interest, but maintained a steady focus on the orb, which was still in its idling state, spinning steadily and glowing with a fluorescent green color. Two more claps and the girls stepped to the right and twirled again, arms extended and palms up. Another clap was followed by a step to the left, now with all three women twirling in unison. The bright music resonated off the inside of the dome. As Betty clapped twice to reverse the direction of the step, the large orb pulsed twice in perfect timing to her claps. All three stepped to the right and twirled again, a flurry of hair pinwheeling outward. The next clap from Betty, again to reverse direction, was accompanied by a strong pulse from the orb, this time with a distinctively blue hue, and a deep, two-octave tone in perfect harmony with the fiddle and guitar music.

Laura glanced at Shanna who was watching her monitor intently while trying to keep an eye on the dance and the heightened activity of the orb. Shanna felt the look from Laura who nodded at her monitor and pointed at a readout tracking the UV intensity. With each clap from Betty's hands, a tiny but distinctive ultraviolet surge only a microsecond before the clap preceded the next pulse. The change in the orb's color and tone followed a slight variation in the intensity and duration of the UV pulse. Shanna smiled at Laura and nodded in a mental "two thumbs up" routine as several billion bits of data raced down the fiberoptic cable to Denali, which split the packets, compressed the information and zipped it off to Yukon and the twenty-eight other supercomputers.

Three claps and a twirl in place, a lovely dip and rise, elbows bent, palms up, eyes shining. Several young male technicians in the ATCO units outside the dome watched with interest, not fully aware that their pulse rate was a bit higher now. The accompanying three pulses from the orb were now in a blue-green color range with tones spanning four octaves. The UV sensors arrayed around the orb precisely measured the frequency and time shift just preceding the latest change in the orb's dynamics. Again, a burst of data raced through the fiberoptic cable to Denali. The fast Cray XMP split, compressed and launched the latest twenty-nine data packets off to Yukon and twenty-eight satellite transponders. Six of the LEO satellites had moved out of range on their orbital paths, but six more had arrived, replacing them without a microsecond's interruption in transmission.

196

Three more claps and the three women reversed direction, spinning, dipping and rising delicately to the merry music. The orb was now part of the orchestra, pulsing color and deep harmonic tones in perfect timing to Betty's lead and in perfect harmony with the Athabaskan suitor's dance.

In Tel Aviv, data packet number seven had been split by 180 Silicon Graphics, Inc., processors arrayed in particularly novel fashion. The Israeli technicians had selected gold wires for all the interconnections between the processors. The data moved slightly faster in the highly efficient conductance of gold, they claimed. It did. "Samson" deciphered the precise UV fluctuation which yielded a 0.99997 correlation coefficient to the shift from green to blue in the orb. Instantly, the solution was returned to the relay processor and transmitted to a LEO satellite just over Egypt. The message was transferred through a transponder aimed at a very large Hughes relay satellite in geosynchronous orbit off the east coast of Africa. The large satellite was on battery power, fully recharged several hours earlier from the nearly forty-meter-long solar panels which were now in earth's shadow. The information was relayed eastward around the equator through two more identical geosynchronous earth orbit (GEO) satellites, orbiting twenty-seven thousand kilometers in space at exactly the spin rate of the planet. From the ground, they appeared to be motionless in the sky.

Two claps and two colorful harmonic pulses, and the three women stepped lightly to the right and twirled. Beth's red hair shimmered in the reflected sunlight of the dome.

A Hughes-built GEO satellite just south of Hawaii received Samson's data just after "Fujiyama's." The Nippon Electric Corporation had endowed the Tokyo-based supercomputer with gallium arsenide chips, as Cray did, but with a larger data gate. Rather than funnel the electrons through a bottle neck, they opened the data flow like the flood gates of a dam. The patented part was the sorting system, actually a software function, which could catch a sea of data and handle it without spilling a drop. Fujiyama had calculated a 0.99993 correlation coefficient for the time sequence which altered the UV transmission preceding a change in pulse frequency in the orb.

The dancers were one-fourth of the way around in the latest twirl to the right.

"Rainier," Microsoft Corporation's generous gift to the University of Washington, had calculated a 0.99999 correlation coefficient for the UV frequency preceding the emergence of a three- to four-harmonic tonal shift. The higher correlation coefficient was possible, in part, due to the closer geographic location to the experiment in Alaska, allowing a much tinier fraction of the data to be corrupted by transmission relay. It was also due, the UW researches would argue, to innovative superconducting chips built into a new advanced processing array. The friction loss through the superconducting ceramic chips was virtually zero. Several of the somewhat nerdish UW technicians liked to impress pretty undergraduates with the interesting superconducting property of antigravity. They would spin one of the chips in mid air inside a vacuum flask above a superconducting field, encouraging the coeds to look just a little more closely ...

The twirl was now half complete.

Denali had received a total of forty-four solutions with a correlation coefficient of 0.99990 or higher. Yukon had contributed two, one of which linked a particular UV wavelength to a virtually simultaneous, but very subtle change in x-ray emissions. Denali identified that solution as a prime control parameter, and quickly matched the findings of Samson, Fujiyama and Rainier that would create a change in tone from three to four octaves, in color from blue-green to blue, and would time the pulse rate to an event, such as the next clap of Betty's hands.

The twirl was three fourths complete, and the three womens' hair was spinning straight out from their heads, pleasantly framing their faces ...

Within thirty microseconds, Denali had assembled a control algorithm. A specific UV wavelength and duration of pulse, directed at a precise angle into the two-meter orb was relayed up the fiberoptic cable to Black Rapids, and fed to a PLC, a process logic controller, controlling the three UV lasers pointed into the orb. The PLC commanded the micromotors on the multi-axis control stands holding the lasers to shift several micrometers, and downloaded the pulse wavelength and duration setting. A timing actuator in the PLC was linked to a video camera across the room. The zoom lens on the video camera automatically focused in on Betty's hands.

The twirl was complete and Betty raised her hands to clap

one time, which would bring the dancers back to the left. As her hands clapped together sharply, the orb pulsed, shifted from blue-green to dark blue and a four-harmonic tone played loudly and clearly in the room.

At precisely the moment that Betty's hands began to clap together, the three tiny lasers pulsed three carefully modulated beams of light into the orb, at an angle slightly off center. That was intentional, since the gravity anomaly in the center of the orb would bend the light and forward it to the center of another orb.

A half galaxy away, another orb pulsed. The blue-green color shifted to deep blue, and a three-octave harmonic tone started, then quickly expanded to four octaves. Erryl watched with great satisfaction and smiled. "Hello Betty," he dreamed.

Betty suddenly stopped spinning, her mouth opened in a wordless surprise. Beth and Christina stopped in midstep, nearly stumbling into her. Dr. Tamura looked up and saw Betty standing, holding her arms out and looking straight ahead as if she was in a trance. He reached over and quickly tapped Kenny on the shoulder. Kenny looked up and saw Dr. Tamura who waived his hand in a gentle chopping motion and silently mouthed the word "music." Kenny touched the screen of his monitor and the music quickly faded.

Shanna and Laura had grasped hands at their console the moment they realized the lasers had been commanded to send a signal into the orb. They looked up now at Betty, startled by the sudden cessation of music and motion. The orb was a deep late-evening blue color now, and continued to pulse in the three-three-two-one pattern of the dance, now unaccompanied by the dancers who were standing curiously facing the orb. Betty's arms dropped to her side and her mouth closed. She stepped back from the orb and was followed by Beth and Christina. The orb finally settled into a steady rhythmic pulse.

Shanna immediately disabled the laser PLC from sending any more commands into the orb, and looked over at Dr. Tamura. He stepped forward just inside the circle of monitors and instruments around the orb and raised his hand in a "wait" signal so everyone could see. The zoom lens on the camera trained on Betty retracted and focused on the orb.

Beth and Christina were standing to either side of Betty now, just inside the circle of monitors. Betty was smiling. She looked over at Dr. Tamura and nodded slightly. He relaxed his hand, and watched as she stepped forward one pace toward the orb. She held her arms out as if to receive somebody and said clearly, but gently, "Welcome."

The orb shifted to an intense violet color which filled the dome. A swirl of tiny bright lights formed inside the orb and quickly grew in intensity. They shone like white Christmas lights inside the violet backdrop of the orb. The swirl grew and formed a small sphere, which suddenly emerged from the orb and levitated toward Betty. She cupped her hands together and the tiny orb of sparkling lights levitated over to her hands and stopped, spinning just above her outstretched palms. Sparkles of light flew in every direction. And her hair began to stand out in a static electrical field. A fountain of light sparkles erupted upward and showered over her hands, raining down to the floor where they seemed to dissipate like the splashing of water in a pool.

The brightness of the sparkling lights dimmed the violet aura of the two-meter orb, and showered off her hands like a water-fall. The white lights began to form an outline of a small figure, about the size of a ten-year old child in front of Betty, under her hands. The flow of light from the small orb grew in intensity, and the orb suddenly vanished, replaced by a perpetual fountain of bright lights flowing up and over her hands and forming the figure in front of her. She pulled her hands down toward her, with palms facing outward.

Shanna and Laura noticed that Beth and Christina, standing a few meters away from Betty were, apparently subconsciously, emulating Betty's exact movements. The image inside the fountain of light began to form more clearly now. Betty watched with curiosity as the image became a small girl in a white full-length gown. She looked ever so much like an angel, Betty thought. Suddenly, somewhere deep inside her consciousness, Betty thought she heard Erryl speak again and say, "She is more than an angel, my friend. Much more."

The image became clearer now, with the lights diminishing somewhat. Two very pretty eyes looked up at Betty out of the flowing fountain of light. Then a small hand rose up out of the gown toward Betty. She reached forward and accepted a small twig of Indian tea from the child. The twig sparkled with light, but was firm to the touch. "Thank you," she said to the girl, and held her arms open.

A smile brighter than the shimmering lights lit up the child's face. She looked back over her shoulder into the two-meter orb for a moment, then turned and smiled even brighter than before. The child stepped forward and snuggled into Betty's arms, wrapping her tiny arms around Betty's waist. Betty hugged her gently, but the tiny arms clung to her tightly, like a child starved for love. But she seemed kind and beautiful, so gentle Betty thought.

"She is," Betty thought she heard Erryl say. "She has a gift for you and your family."

The little girl unwrapped her arms from Betty's waist and stepped back, still smiling. Betty saw a tiny clear teardrop slide down the girl's cheek. Then she reached into her white gown and produced a small tubelike object. The object appeared to be a silver pipe of sorts, with holes in the tube and tiny multi-colored lights on one end. The little girl had platinum blond hair and fluorescent green eyes. Her skin was fair and her fingers were very slender, much more so than those of a human child. Her eyes were very large for her head, a property which made the girl look very cute, but oddly very wise.

She touched several of the lights on the end of the small instrument, then raised the pipe up to her lips and began to sing into it. Her voice was very full and vibrant for such a small child, and the instrument amplified and added a field of harmonics several octaves above and below her voice. Her voice had a slight trill to it, perhaps accentuated by the instrument which she seemed to play very skillfully with her small fingers. The song was hauntingly beautiful, and reminded Betty of Irish music. It was sad and wonderful, and seemed to tell a story which was not quite clear, but which reached into one's heart, playing the emotions of the listener as skillfully as the child played the instrument. The clear, rich music filled the dome. An image of a story seemed to unfold with the harmonic reverberations. A story of great sadness and loss, but of great hope.

The music stopped. Betty found herself kneeling before the child, arms outstretched again. The girl eagerly stepped forward to her and hugged her neck like it would be the last time she would ever see Betty. Both the girl and Betty were crying now. Then, the girl stepped back, reached into her gown and produced a second instrument exactly like the first one. She presented one each to Beth and Christina, and warmly accepted a hug from each of them, too.

Then she turned to Betty again, pausing to look over her shoulder at the two-meter orb, then back at Betty. She raised her right hand and placed it on Betty's cheek, and Betty heard the words "thank you" in what seemed like a hundred languages, spoken by thousands of voices. Then the girl vanished.

The dome was silent. Betty remained kneeling, facing the orb. Then she grasped her arms about her and leaned forward, her head drooping. She was crying openly, almost as if she was in pain, like an empath who had felt a child die suddenly. Beth and Christina kneeled beside Betty. They were crying, too.

Dr. Tamura watched with curiosity. He had been moved by the music, but did not understand what great emotion was at work here.

Shanna and Laura stood up at their monitors, now, then walked over to embrace Betty and their daughters. For some reason, they were crying, too. Then the room filled with light again.

Another swirl of bright lights formed inside the orb, and grew until another small sphere formed and emerged. It levitated over toward Betty, stopped and began to cascade in a fountain of sparkling white lights. Within a few minutes, Erryl was standing beside Betty. He reached down to her and she accepted his hand. Slowly she rose, standing now and facing him. Beth and Christina stood to her side, and Shanna and Laura stood next to their daughters.

"Is she gone?" Betty asked, wiping a tear from her cheek.

"Yes," he answered simply. "Seeing you was her last request."

"Why me?"

"Remember, I told you before that you were quite famous in this part of the galaxy, Betty. That was a very sincere statement. Her people were part of an observation team which has studied your race since first contact. You and your daughters were the subjects of great interest in their culture."

"What happened, Erryl?"

"The same thing that, unfortunately, happens to many races and civilizations. Their home planet was lost in an astronomical collision with a very large, dark asteroid. In their case, the asteroid emerged perpendicular to the plane of the ecliptic where they routinely studied the planets, asteroids, moons, and comets within their solar system. The stray asteroid was apparently from another star system where it had shifted out of orbit in a near-collision with the moon of a large planet. It traveled across interstellar distances and arrived suddenly, directly from above one of the poles of their planet. They had very advanced astronomy, but were not looking in that direction until too late, and had barely a year to prepare for the collision."

Dr. Tamura had been listening quietly in the background, and now joined the conversation. "Did they attempt to divert it or break it up?" he asked.

Erryl turned to Dr. Tamura. "Greetings, Dr. Tamura." Erryl bowed slightly, which Dr. Tamura returned, a bit embarrassed that he had just jumped into a conversation with an alien he had not seen for twenty years, and had not properly greeted him. "It is good to see you again."

"Sorry, Erryl. Your very interesting story has caused me to overlook my courtesies." He bowed again to Erryl.

"Think nothing of it, please. To answer your question, yes. Most certainly they applied all available technology to first redirect, then disrupt the asteroid. They were partially successful, in that they split the object into three larger and numerous smaller pieces with a directed energy beam. They actually slowed it a bit, and were able to push two of the three large pieces around their planet. Unfortunately, one of the pieces hit one of two moons orbiting their planet. The collision was a nearly direct impact, shattering the moon and causing part of the mass of the moon to fall into the gravity well of the planet. The surface of the planet was rained upon by a shower of segments from the moon and pieces of the shattered asteroid."

"Did any of them survive, or escape?" Dr. Tamura asked.

"Fortunately, yes, but not many. Several thousand of their people were on planetary research stations elsewhere in their solar system. A few hundred thousand more were able to escape prior to the final collision. They were able to gather a significant amount of their genetic heritage, both of their race and their planet's biology, in the form of digitized genetic codes, seeds, eggs, and so forth. They successfully created a temporary home on one of the other planets in their solar system, but lost the only world which could serve as a home with a breathable atmosphere and sufficient water."

"What are their plans?" Dr. Tamura asked.

"They are recreating their home world. The shattered moon formed a debris ring around the planet, and the surface of their world was scorched from the heat of the collisions. Fragments continue to fall into the planet or are being swept up from the ring in collisions with the other moon. They are actively removing the ring of debris by attaching robotic propulsion systems to the larger objects and driving them together to reform the other moon, of which about two-thirds of the original mass remained in approximately the same orbit. They expect the process to take hundreds of years, but they are a very highly motivated civilization. They are survivors, and have great hope as you heard in their music."

"Is there anything we can do to help?" Betty asked.

Erryl looked at Betty and smiled. "You already have, my wonderful friend. Much more than you will ever know." She looked curiously at him. "The young girl who shared the song of her people with you was the daughter of a great leader of these people. She was the last of a long lineage of accomplished musicians with a rich cultural heritage, all of whom were female. The musical talent was passed only through the women of their race. Just prior to the tragedy with the asteroid, her mother wrote the song she played for you and taught it to her daughter. They knew that it would be the end of their world for many generations, but they believed they would some day return. That is the great tragedy and the hope which you felt in her music."

"Erryl, I sensed that she … " Betty stopped and couldn't speak. She couldn't say the word "died." "She is such a beautiful child."

"Betty," Erryl spoke softly, "she was gone a long time ago. Even before you were born." Betty looked curiously at him again. "I don't understand, Erryl. She was here and I hugged her. I felt her arms around me and her tears on my dress."

"Yes," Erryl said. "Perhaps Shanna and Laura can explain it to you in more understandable terms." Erryl looked at the two mathematicians and spoke to them now. "A time storage sequence was used in one of the gravitational nodes on their planet. They placed the image of the girl in the node just before the impact. This information was transferred to us and has been retained for several hundreds of your years in suspended time. Sufficient energy was input with the data for that term of storage, but there was only enough residual energy for one transfer event. At the moment of input when her image and her characteristics were stored, she was given the choice of where and when to transfer back out. She chose to share her music with Betty's family."

Betty cupped her hands over her mouth and her eyes watered.

Erryl turned to Beth and Christina. "Even more importantly, she chose the two of you to give her music to. This was what your dream was about when we contacted you earlier this year. We had to prepare you for the transfer event. The instruments she gave you encode the musical heritage of her race, and are, as I believe you are beginning to understand, accessible telepathically. She transferred that knowledge to you when she handed them to you. You now are sisters in time. It is a very great gift she has given you. Music, you will discover, is one of the great languages of the universe. It is diverse, it is everywhere. It is enjoyed by more civilizations than you could possibly imagine and in more forms than your ears can hear. Music is present in the physics of the movement of the planets, in the interactions of atoms and molecules, and as you know, in the sounds of your world. You can hear it in the wind, in the calls of animals, the rustle of leaves, in the voices of children. It is the harmonic vibration of matter and energy at all levels of consciousness. Skillfully applied, as you have just heard, it is a concert, a message."

"What was her name?" Betty asked.

"Her race did not use names." Erryl paused to let that sink in. "They were completely telepathic, and acknowledged each other by the equivalent of a mental nudge. Sort of like a cat rubbing up against your leg to let you know it likes you." Erryl seemed pleased that Betty appeared to be a bit less sad now.

"How did she know me if she was gone before I was born?"

"That is part of what Shanna and Laura are going to have to explain to you. Her time sequence was very different than yours. Your heritage was known by her race, and you were the carrier of the genetic endowment of your line when she transferred here. To her, your life scrolled before her like a fast story book. When she entered the time storage sequence, she did not know you yet. A few of her moments later, when she emerged, you were already well known to her."

Shanna spoke up. "Erryl, can we communicate with them, and can we communicate with you using the orbs?"

"You already have, Shanna. A pretty decent first attempt, too, I might say. Here, this should help a bit." He handed her a small, black, oblong device with colored lights and intricate patterns on the smooth surface. "It is an encoder, of sorts. You solved a first-order access code equation today with your experiment. Normally, we do not provide hard technology to civilizations just beginning to access the *Starlink*, which is what we call our network, but this is a gift from the civilization you befriended today. You will figure out fairly soon how it works, so I will leave that task to your enjoyment." He turned back to Dr. Tamura.

"I must go soon. I know you are curious about what level of contact has been made." George Tamura nodded affirmatively and listened intently.

"Technically, Level Four was your transmission back through *Starlink*. Our response to you would have been the confirmation of that level, such as by my visit. But, due to the circumstances you witnessed today, you were advanced to a Level Five contact immediately after achieving Level Four. Level Five is the transfer of music, specifically a musical instrument. Beth and Christina are the recipients, and your civilization this day is much richer for it. You will discover that these instruments will instantly open the access to *Starlink*. The encoder is sort of a directory, which will help you navigate the system. So you know, the first level of the encoder includes a link to me, and a link to the telepathic race who shared their music with you, today."

"Can you tell us about the significance of telepathic communications?" Dr. Tamura asked.

"It is," Erryl paused and studied his words carefully, "an even greater system than *Starlink*, which is a physical system. Some civilizations have a greater ability to utilize telepathy than others, but nearly all are able, with proper technological development and training, to use *Starlink*. The physics of telepathy is interesting. As you are aware, there are a number of known forces in the universe which are quantifiable. Of these, your science has described four, and seek to join them in a unified field theory. Consider the four primary forces you know of and their relative properties of strength of force and interactive distance. The strong nuclear force, which binds atoms together is the most powerful, but interacts over very tiny distances. The weak nuclear force, responsible for the decay of nuclei, and the electromagnetic force are much weaker, but have a greater relative distance over which they can interact. Finally, gravity. So weak it is almost undetectable by your technology, it reaches out and pulls objects together across intergalactic distances."

"Imagine a continuum of these trends. Imagine a force which is stronger than the strong nuclear force, but has an interaction distance which is even shorter in relative distance? What I describe here is encountered inside a gravitational anomaly such as the power source of the *Starlink* nodes."

"And perhaps ..." Erryl looked up at Betty, then Shanna, Laura, Beth and Christina, "... a force which is so weak that it is undetectable by the most advanced technology, but interacts instantly over virtually infinite distances. Such a force would be so diffuse that it might operate outside the present space-time continuum of our universe. It would be detectable, however, by some mechanism that is tuned in to receive it, as an object with mass feels the pull of gravity across the full span of the galaxy."

Dr. Tamura nodded, and thanked Erryl for the explanation as he began to grasp the full magnitude and significance of Erryl's description of the telepathic "force."

Erryl turned again to Betty. "There is one more thing you should know, Betty. My civilization was given the great honor of being the recipient of the transfer responsibilities for the telepathic race who sent the girl to you today. It is a high honor to be so completely trusted by an alien race, particularly one that is on the brink of cataclysmic extinction. It is, in the sequence of events, the equivalent of a Level Nine contact. It is the highest level my civilization knows of. It is called Host."

Erryl reached out and took Betty's hands. His eyes seemed to mist over slightly.

"Today, my gentle friend, you and your wonderful children have become Hosts to a civilization which is resurrecting itself.

They have chosen you and recommended this very great honor to the many thousands of civilizations who use *Starlink*. When the girl finished her musical message and you offered her your embrace, you imagined you heard many voices say thank you. Betty, those were representatives of all the civilizations of *Starlink*. Because of the great responsibility involved, the selection of a Host must be unanimous. As you opened your heart and embraced this lost child, you gave her message and her music a future beyond the terrible disaster that took her world away. What you heard was the telepathic equivalent of a mass vote. The affirmative answer does not translate as yes. It is thank you."

Betty smiled at Erryl, then reached out and gave him a hug. Then his image wavered slightly and began to fade. "Good-bye my friends. Thank you." His image vanished and the two-meter orb returned to the fluorescent green color of the idle state, pulsing in a steady rhythm.

Late evening twilight filled the aluminum dome with a soft warmth. Shanna looked at the encoder in her hand and admired the object. "Laura, I think we have work to do." She agreed with a nod, then looked over Shanna's shoulder at the two girls. Shanna noticed Laura's glance and turned to look, too.

Beth and Christina were showing the bright musical instruments they had been given by the telepathic girl to Betty. Beth put the instrument up to her mouth and blew into it like a flute. A clear, melodic tone filled the dome. Christina did likewise, and a perfect harmonic to Beth's note resulted. The music felt crisp and clear like the high mountain air of the glacial valley. Betty put her arms around the two girls and spoke softly to them. They both leaned over and embraced her, then kissed her on opposite cheeks. Then they left the dome.

Dr. Tamura had been observing with interest as he usually did. How strange and interesting the events of this day, he thought. That the warmth and embrace of this Athabaskan family could be of such great importance to another civilization struggling for its very survival was both astounding and wonderful to him. It made perfect sense, he thought. They were, indeed, great hosts.

CHAPTER 11

Epilogue
Early Fall - A.D. 2,000

The late afternoon light reflected brightly off sharp white peaks of the mountain ridges framing the long valley. Snow started even earlier this year than last, earlier than any one in the small group could remember since they had returned to this valley two generations ago. This was the time of the year the villagers gathered along the shores of the deep lakes which collected ice and snow melt from the newly forming glaciers in the mountains. The purpose of the gathering was to observe spawning fish returning to the streams at the head of the lakes.

Excellent habitat for the young of several species of fish was present in the clean gravel bottoms of meandering streams. Thick stands of brush protected the edges of the streams, and provided shelter. An occasional larger tree which had fallen across the stream here and there provided pools of water deep enough that the fry would be safe over winter even under an ice cover. Glaciers, and a giant ice field which had grown so rapidly in the last ten years were still a safe distance up the long valley. Heavy snows would likely continue to build the glaciers for several decades more, so there was some concern that the protected habitat so important to the fish, and thus to the villagers would be spared.

But today, the fish run was abundant. The larger species were healthy and fertile, with the females laying many thousands of eggs in the gravel as the males fertilized them with their milt. The carcasses of some of the first fish to arrive lay on the edge of the streams where they had become carrion for various birds and animals which feasted on the soft flesh of the dying fish. The cycle of life was evident here, and villagers watched with joy and wonder. It was a good fall. Life had returned to the valley, and, always tenacious, had found good habitat. The rhythm of nature was taking hold.

A celebration had begun around the evening fires of the camp on the edge of the lake. A few small log structures had been built years before, and various new structures were added each year. Most of the villagers simply camped in temporary dwellings, though, most of which were made of light, but rigid metal and plastic panels.

Evening twilight faded slowly at this high latitude, but eventually the dark of night settled in.

Light green wisps of the celestial lights could be seen building silently in the northwest. Wisps had begun to merge, forming a broad arc across the sky, bridging from the northwest to the eastern horizon where it disappeared over a mountain ridge. The villagers enjoyed these displays, particularly the high-energy ones which became very active and changed color. It almost seemed as if they had become more active as the weather had become cooler. Perhaps it was that the colors in the sky reflected brightly off the white peaks of the mountains and the clear ice of the glaciers. Most certainly, though, this display was building to be magnificent.

As the campfires cast swirls of glowing embers into the cooling night sky, the celestial lights seemed to mirror the fires, flickering now and glowing red and orange. Stars were bright and clear, glowing intensely in the velvet black of the night sky. Many of the villagers stood with their backs to the camp fires so they could clearly see the heavenly fires and awesome glory of the starlit sky. The air was thin at the higher altitudes, and it tended to lend a bit of giddiness to the mood. These were good times. The villagers were pleased to be alive and to witness the beauty of this place and of the celestial display.

Laughter reflected off the darkened trees in the forests surrounding the encampment as the elders shared the stories of their return to the valley. The children particularly loved the stories with music, which were played with instruments and song as much as they were told. The music rippled across the water of the lake, and could be heard far across the shore. Always the favorite, the musical story played as duet by two women on opposite sides of the encampment was saved till last, just before moon rise.

Excitement was building as more logs were tossed on the fire, and hot drinks to ward off the chill of the night were shared from pots steaming by the fire pits. The celestial lights flickered intensely now, rippling like a curtain fluttering in the breeze. The top of the streamers of light were green, the middle red, and the bottom edge a sharp, bright orange color.

One could almost feel the static electricity in the air, and at moments of quiet, almost hear it crackle.

A group of children giggled and huddled under a soft, warm blanket near a fire. A young man nearby turned and looked to the east, and saw the first twilight of the early moon beginning to reflect off the highest mountain peaks. He turned to the children and raised one long, slender finger to his lips in a motion requesting silence. Bright eyes saw the strong, handsome face of the young man, and saw him smile, then quieted with eager restlessness as only children do.

The music began.

A hollow, low tone floated through the night air from behind the children. The source of the tone was back at the edge of the forest, out of the light. The note was clear and strong in the cool night air. Small eyes grew larger and smiles emerged from faces framed by hands cupping ears to find the direction of the sound. A second, higher tone began from the opposite side of the encampment, one third octave above the first. The two notes played together now, steady at first, then with an elegant waver.

Then they stopped, the sound drifting across the surface of the lake for several seconds.

A moment passed as a vision of two young women walking in a forest with musical pipes filled the minds of the children. The two women in the vision, one with long flowing black hair, and one with bright red hair, emerged from the woods. It was evening and they were high on a hillside overlooking a wide, meandering, silty river. They paused there, admiring a great mountain in the distance which rose so high in the sky that the winds of the upper air swirled snow off the peak in a long funnel like a cold torch set against the clear, blue sky.

The women of the vision rested on a white log, and raised their musical pipes to play.

The music started again, piercing the night with a three-octave chord in stereo. The music was full, vibrant, and magical. The song was a story, and the two who played the story were in perfect unison, though separated on opposite sides of the encampment, each at the edge of the forest. Trees reflected the sound beautifully, with the harmonics reaching a focus precisely at the area where the children were assembled.

The same musical story unfolded from the two women in their vision.

Deep bass tones and trilling high notes interlaced, paused to let the sounds echo across the water, then started again. Mournful tones wailed through the trees, then reverberated toward the campsite. Images of courage and determination filled the young minds, but all the while a dark cloud of great loss loomed, accentuated by the warbling wail of the musical pipes. Small bodies shivered and small hands tugged the blankets more tightly around them as a deep, dark, multi-octave chord seemed to shake the ground. The celestial lights in the sky rippled with fire, as if shaken by the dark music and the quaking of the ground.

Then, suddenly, the music stopped.

The water in the lake rippled as the heavy chord floated across the water and vanished in the darkness. The strong young man reached for several small logs with fragments of dried branches, and tossed them into the fire.

A swirl of embers rose in the night.

The vision of the two women showed their eyes were filled with tears. Their heads were bowed as if in prayer, soft white hands clutching the silver pipes to their breasts as they paused. Then, as if with determination, they both stood, facing the great mountain. They raised the pipes and began to play once more.

The vision changed in the minds of the children as the music began again.

Clear, bold single notes flew through the night, twisting and curling like fine hair being braided by the hands of a loving mother. The music was hope. It was life. The vision erupted in a flurry of images in the minds of the children. A small child, very much like them, playing a musical story of hope and strength, even as her life ebbed into the blackness of a fading universe. The child's music was loud and clear, vibrant with determination, and filled with love. It was as if she played with such strength that her song would echo through millennia, ricocheting off planet after planet, until the dream, the hope, the wish that she prayed for her people would come true.

The embers glowed in the fire pit, hot and radiant against the cold, black night like the soul of the little girl in their shared vision. The pipes played clearly from the edge of the forest. They played the little girl's story, note for note, exactly as she played it in their vision. The children heard it with their ears, and felt it in their hearts. It was a song of life, of victory. The notes built to a crescendo, the bright tones of the pipes adding octaves and more notes as full chords resonated from the trees to the lake.

Then, the visions merged.

The little girl was playing with all her might, the two young women were playing exactly the same music in a duet so strongly that it reverberated off of the great mountain in the distance, and here, in this place, the same music played by two musicians ever so brilliantly in the clear mountain air to their ears. At that moment, a bright light streaked across the sky from the east. The early moon emerged from behind a sharply chiseled peak, and its brilliant light flooded the valley floor. Hope poured from the music like a fountain.

Small hearts fluttered with delight at the fullness of the moment.

The music quieted. In the vision, the two young women, black and red hair flowing in the soft breeze as leaves fluttered beside them, played an epilogue to the musical story. Their music was clear and warm now. It was the music of love. Love that would fill a small girl's heart with enough courage that she could finally cross the dark divide of life to afterlife. The vision of the small girl was now of long, flowing black hair on her face, which was pressed into a soft, tan hide worn by a woman with arms embracing the child. Arms hugging so tightly that the children under the blanket by the fire could feel the soft strength which flowed from the gentle woman to the young girl. A hand, tenderly caressing a small head as she clung to the soft tan hide with all the energy that her life could muster.

The music played smoothly across the forested lake now. Tears fell across the cheeks of many of the small children under the blanket. The little girl's love had been for them. Her love and her music was all that she had to give, her world having been torn away from her. So it was her love and her music that she gave to them, so carefully nurtured and carried for many years by the family of the woman with the soft hide dress.

By her granddaughters who played the young girl's music in the wilderness of a distant and beautiful planet, who would so carefully pass it on to their daughters, generation after generation, preserving that single moment of love and hope for these children gathered here, tonight, around this fire pit.

The night air filled with the soft, finishing tones of the musical story, wafting gently across the water of the lake and back to the ears of the children who were so filled with awe and hope now. The music played a final chord which could only be described as the sound of love. A simple, strong harmonic chord, played cleanly and steadily in the night.

At that moment, the later moon rose, casting a second, soft amber light across the valley.

The later moon was smaller than the early moon. It was darker, shrouded with volcanic clouds from its slowly cooling crust. Thus it reflected less light, but the light was warm, glowing, like the little girl's love. The bright light of the early moon, and the soft, amber light of the later moon blended and cast warmth and hope across the long valley. The white robes of the two women who had played the musical story could be seen clearly now for the first time by the children huddled around the fire. As they walked forward, nearing the fire, the children threw off the soft blanket and let it flutter to the ground. They ran, some skipping as children do when they are happy, to the two women, arms open and full of love.

Hugging, laughing, crying they swarmed about the two lovely young musicians, grateful for the beautiful story and for the wonderful performance.

The two women smiled at each other across the fire pit. Deep brown eyes under a head of hair as black as the night smiled at bright green eyes under a head of hair as red as the glowing embers of the fire. Their long, slender arms embraced as many of the children as they could reach, laughing, delicately holding their silver musical pipes.

The young man by the fire smiled at the two women.

"Thank you," he dreamed.

They smiled back, still hugging the swarm of children. Their images flickered in the night, and they vanished.